P9-CLQ-960

The Truth of the Matter

Also by Robb Forman Dew

Fiction

THE EVIDENCE AGAINST HER
FORTUNATE LIVES
THE TIME OF HER LIFE
DALE LOVES SOPHIE TO DEATH

Nonfiction

THE FAMILY HEART
A MEMOIR OF WHEN OUR SON CAME OUT
A SOUTHERN THANKSGIVING
RECIPES AND MUSINGS

The Truth of the Matter

A NOVEL

ROBB FORMAN DEW

Little, Brown and Company

NEW YORK   BOSTON

Copyright © 2005 by Robb Forman Dew

All rights reserved. No part of this book may be reproduced in any form
or by any electronic or mechanical means, including information storage
and retrieval systems, without permission in writing from the publisher,
except by a reviewer who may quote brief passages in a review.

Little, Brown and Company
Time Warner Book Group
1271 Avenue of the Americas, New York, NY 10020
Visit our Web site at www.twbookmark.com

First Edition: November 2005

The characters and events in this book are fictitious. Any similarity to real
persons, living or dead, is coincidental and not intended by the author.

"Disobedience," from *When We Were Very Young* by A. A. Milne, illustrations by E. H.
Shepard, copyright 1924 by E. P. Dutton, renewed 1952 by A. A. Milne. Used by permission
of Dutton Children's Books, A Division of Penguin Young Readers Group, A Member of
Penguin Group (USA) Inc., 345 Hudson Street, New York, NY 10014. All rights reserved.

Library of Congress Cataloging-in-Publication Data

Dew, Robb Forman.
    The truth of the matter : a novel / Robb Forman Dew.— 1st ed.
        p.   cm.
    ISBN 0-316-89004-9
  1. Widows — Fiction. 2. Traffic accident victims — Family relationships —
Fiction. 3. World War, 1939–1945 — Veterans — Fiction. 4. Parent and adult child —
Fiction. 5. Ohio — Fiction. I. Title.

PS3554.E9288T78 2005
813'.54 — dc22   2005500384I

10 9 8 7 6 5 4 3 2 I

Q-MART

Book Design by Robert G. Lowe

Printed in the United States of America

In memory of my father, Oliver Duane Forman,
and
Richard Brent Forman,
Evelyn Bernice Forman Stewart,
and
Stephen Burr Forman

And for Ralph Hylton Sims

Part One

Chapter One

AGNES SCOFIELD NEVER FORGOT, not over the course of her whole life, exactly how it felt to take flight. She remembered fleeing through a dark, entangled forest, emerging into a bright meadow, and lifting right off the ground straight up into the air. The memory was so clear to her that whenever it crossed her mind, she felt again that little clutch of initial euphoria and then the unexpected struggle of staying aloft. It had been nothing at all like the sensation she had expected. It was a more muscular, less buoyant experience than people imagined. With each rise and fall through the surprisingly dense atmosphere, there was the heavy drag of gravity.

In the third grade, when she was still Agnes Claytor, she had tried to explain this to her friend Edith, but Edith had only nodded; she was concentrating on the spill of jacks across the floor and how best to pick them up in groups of three. The only other person to whom she had confided her secret knowledge of flight was her husband, Warren Scofield, one summer evening when they were sitting out on the porch after supper. The children, including little Trudy Butler from next door, roamed the grounds of Scofields in the twilight, and although their voices could be heard, their words couldn't be discerned.

Small gray birds flitted and chittered in the rhododendrons, hydrangeas, and spreading yews that intermingled in a thick swath along the porch foundation, where they had been sparsely planted almost fifty years earlier but rarely pruned since then. The three large crows who inhabited the grounds of the Scofield houses and whose territory ranged over much of the acreage of Washburn, Ohio, circled the tall stand of Norway spruce, emitting bitter cries. Once again their hopes were dashed; once again the day had yielded nothing more than bleak disappointment.

Agnes sat quietly, watching them, and thinking that few people realized how grand they were, although she couldn't remember ever seeing a cheerful crow. Perhaps that explained their reputation: neither fierce, like hawks, nor robin-jolly, they failed to elicit human admiration and were loathed as nothing more than a nuisance. But they engaged Agnes's attention as she recognized the relief each bird experienced when finally it alighted at the very top of one of the spruces and settled there with a showy fluttering of wings, much shifting about, and loud crow mutterings as each balanced on its perch.

She told Warren that she remembered just how that felt, to attain certain footing on a branch, or, even more satisfying, she said, was the ease of a long, low glide into the meadow, where balance wasn't essential. She explained how it felt to rise and fall and catch a current of lifting air that allowed you to coast. "People don't imagine it at all the way it really is. It's more like riding a bicycle than, say, floating. Floating in water, I mean." Of course, she told him all this with a wry twist in her voice, tacitly acknowledging that such a thing never could have happened.

"You don't think you really did fly?" Warren said. "Even though you remember it so well after all this time? I think it was real. I think it was probably exactly like you remember it," he said pensively. "You can't know that it didn't happen. It's just other people who make you think it didn't."

"Oh, well . . . But, Warren . . . I haven't ever even told anyone but Edith —"

"No. What I mean is that if you were the only person in the world, then it would be true that you had once been able to fly."

"How do you mean? Like the tree falling in the forest? Whether it makes a sound if no one hears it?" Agnes asked. "But, anyway, if I was the only person in the world! I doubt if I'd even think about it much. If there was no one to compare myself to . . ."

"Well, that's right. That's what I'm saying. Say someone asked you flat out? If you had to swear to tell the truth — nothing but the truth — about whether or not you had ever been able to fly? You see what I mean?" Warren said. "What you know is that you flew. That's your actual experience. You only doubt it because no one else you know would believe it had happened. They'd put it down to a dream. Or an imagined memory. Don't you think so?" He wasn't really asking a question, he was trying to illustrate his point.

"I remember when I was about ten years old, I guess," he went on. "The first time I ever went with my father and Uncle Leo to see the new Corliss engine they'd just installed down at Scofields and Company. Even Uncle George was there. It was the first time we'd been allowed to visit the works. Robert and Lily came along, too. I'd heard my father and my uncles talk about that new engine. There was nothing else like it back then. Not in Ohio. Not anywhere west of the Mississippi. In fact, we manufactured the one at National Cash Register in Dayton," he said.

"But I hadn't ever seen one." He was no longer musing but briskly recounting the incident. "It was amazing to me. It was more astounding than I even had imagined. And the noise it made! All that power and the gleaming new metal. I realized all at once that I wasn't touching the floor. I was moving from one place to another, but I was floating. Well, no. I was taking steps, but not touching. . . . I was walking on air. Not very far, but I really did walk on air," he said, seeming to be surprised, himself, that it was so.

"You've heard people say they were 'literally walking on air'?" he asked her. "And everyone assumes they mean they were figuratively walking on air? That probably is what they mean most of the time. But there's got to be some reason that saying exists! People say, 'Oh, I was up in the air!' or 'I was over the moon,' or they even say, 'I was simply flying!'" Warren said.

"All those people who say that!" And he paused for a moment, considering it. "You know what? I think they forget that they know the feeling they're describing. Who can tell me that I didn't walk on air? Well, of course, I never said anything about it until just now. I don't know what Robert might have said, but I know Lily would've been annoyed. She wouldn't have believed me for a minute. Especially since she wasn't much interested in seeing that engine. But Uncle Leo was so pleased to show us. She wouldn't have wanted to disappoint her father."

Agnes knew immediately how Lily would have felt. She wouldn't have been annoyed because Warren had claimed to have walked on air; she would have felt left out. Since she had been the only girl of that threesome, she had told Agnes, she had always been on the verge of being ignored or left behind. "It turned me into a wily little tyrant," she had said to Agnes. "If I took charge — directed everything, made all the plans — they could hardly leave me out!"

Lily Scofield Butler was Warren's first cousin twice over: their mothers were sisters who had married the two older Scofield brothers. Lily and Warren had grown up next door to each other, and Robert Butler, who had completed their childhood threesome, had lived at the parsonage, just next to the Scofields compound on the Church Street side. Those three children had been born on exactly the same day: September fifteenth, 1888, and twenty-five years later, in 1913, Lily Scofield and Robert Butler were married. On this first warm evening of 1928, when everyone in Washburn had flung open their windows — when housewives had been able at last to hang their laundry outside in the fresh air instead of stringing it in rows among the pipes of their musty basements — all of the members of the Scofield family were in residence at Scofields, in Washburn, Ohio.

The three houses of the Scofields compound, just north of Monument Square, had been built in the 1880s for Leo, John, and George Scofield, and until the years following World War I, those three houses and their various outbuildings had marked the northern boundary of the town's residential section. Over the years, all three houses had remained occupied by one or another permutation of the Scofield family, changing hands within the family now and then, depending upon the inevitable deaths and births as the family carried on.

By 1928, however, Agnes and Warren Scofield sat out on the porch of the house where Warren had grown up; Lily and Robert Butler were just next door, reading the evening paper in the back study of Leo Scofield's house, and Leo Scofield himself and his brother George sat upstairs keeping company with Leo's wife, Audra, who was ill. None of them gave the fact much thought, but in the distance, each one of them could hear the youngest generation of Scofield children's voices mingling in a low-keyed, after-supper game of some sort.

"What do you think now, though?" Agnes asked Warren. "Do you still believe it? That you really left the ground? That you did walk on air?" Agnes watched the light withdrawing incrementally and bobbed her foot to make the porch swing sway a little. "Do you remember the sensation? How it felt exactly?"

"Of course I do! I know I made my way across that room absolutely . . . untethered. It was as if I could move one way or another by pure intention. Who else can decide that but me? I remember it as clearly as if it happened yesterday. More than remember it, really. I mean, I don't remember it just as something that once happened. It's the sensation of it I recall." Agnes nodded, because she, too, remembered the surprise of making a labored ascent into the air and then achieving the remarkable delight of sailing over the ground.

"I wasn't trying to walk on air," Warren said. "It was something I hadn't ever thought about. There's no question in my mind that it happened. I mean, after all, we all only know ourselves! When you come right down to it, we've really just agreed to believe certain things communally. Religion, for instance. Or good and bad. Who's good or bad. We've all agreed on the story. I suppose there's no other way we could live in a society."

He was quiet for a moment, considering what he had said, which he often did in conversations with her, whereas he rarely sounded less than certain with anyone else. "We've all agreed to live in a sort of . . . oh . . . a sort of cocoon that's shaped of other people's idea of us. Don't you think so? But maybe before we're really aware of other people . . . Before we have any idea that they're entirely separate from ourselves — when we're literally selfish. Well, maybe that's a time in our lives when we can do all sorts of things, since we don't know the rules. And since we haven't started yet to worry about other people's opinions of us. Think of what we might do before we become self-conscious."

Agnes couldn't make out Warren's features anymore as the light faded; she could only see his bright hair and the general shape of him as he sat tilted back in the rocker with his long legs stretched out before him. She was curious. "You think there ever is a time when we're not aware of other people? When we aren't bumping up against what they're like to find out just what we're like ourselves?"

Warren turned toward her, and the light from the kitchen illuminated his almost sheepish smile. "I think that maybe for a little while we're unaware. . . . Ah, well. No. I guess I don't believe that, exactly. I guess it wouldn't be possible. But I do think that we all have a private nature — not like any other person's. I don't mean just that we're all separate personalities. I mean the thing about us that I suppose some people think of as our soul. The essence of ourselves. Our whole lives are really just an effort to fulfill a sort of quest of that essential self. Don't you think the good things — any bit of apparent altruism, I mean — don't you think that's always suspect? I think everything we do is self-centered. Not on purpose. I just think it's a condition we can't escape," he said, but the note of persuasion had gone out of his voice.

"But it does take a lot of strategy," he said, but without his earlier urgency. "I mean to live to the very end of your life without killing yourself? Just to avoid the *fear* of dying. It's so tempting when you know you could outfox your own death. You could keep it from sneaking up on you. You could win, you see. Don't you think so?"

"Uhmm. Well, though. That doesn't strike me as

much of a victory," Agnes said. She thought that Warren intended to be ironic, that he was teasing, but it made her uncomfortable. "Killing yourself. Why, no. I don't think that's ever a natural human instinct. Or a natural animal instinct. Though I remember Mama saying they had a cat who just decided to die after her father died. I don't suppose that's the same thing, though. It was passive. He wouldn't eat. Wouldn't even drink water. But how else *could* a cat kill himself? I wonder if it's possible." She paused for a moment to retrace her thoughts; Agnes often seemed to stray from the subject, but it was a logical progression, and by now Warren knew how she had gotten from one thought to another. He didn't interrupt her.

"Killing yourself would be something you'd be bound to think about, I guess," she said, "if you were in terrible pain, or . . . oh . . . knew that you were going to die in some horrible way. But otherwise . . . why in the world would that be an alternative? What makes you say a thing like that?"

Warren was quiet for a little while, and then he turned more solemn. "Oh, I don't know, Agnes. I think it's sort of like what you said about flying. About it not being as easy as just soaring through the air. Living is a lot more tiring than people realize when they begin it."

"Oh," she said, eager to drop the subject, "I don't really think anyone has any expectations at the beginning," Agnes said. "And besides! Tiring compared to *what?*"

During the following few days, however, Agnes did remember feelings of grief and some variation of defeated resignation or exhaustion that had made her indifferent to her life for hours — even days — at a time. She never forgot her solitary flight; nor did that conversation with Warren ever slip her mind.

For as far back as she could remember, Agnes had managed to slide out from under the turbulence of thoughts that descended upon her as soon as she settled in bed for the night and tried to go to sleep. As a child, she had learned to construct bits of circumstances — not necessarily related to one another — and pile them one upon another until they became a narrative that encompassed her entirely, so that she was led from consciousness directly into a sort of waking dream and then, eventually, into sleep. When she was very young she had delivered herself to the vivid landscape of fairy tales: deep, dark woods, sudden, brilliant pools of water, ominous stone castles, or thatched-roof cottages, every object saturated with its own color to a degree not possible in the real world.

In her early teens, she distracted herself from the accumulated anxiety of the day by concentrating on all the aspects of the ongoing political complexities of her school life. Or she recounted time spent with her friends, in which she was free of worry about the sad domestic life of her household. Her unhappy parents and the fragile peace — like the delicate net of a spider web — that just barely held her family together.

As Agnes got older still, she took her mind off real life by imagining the man she would marry — never anyone she had met thus far — and the exhilaration of being desired by him. Once, she awoke horrified to remember that she had been walking across the field from the Damerons' house on the way home and had spotted Will Dameron's head over the crest of the creek embankment. He had heard her coming and climbed up the bank to meet her, seemingly unaware that he was stark naked. He was telling her something or other, and she stood listening casually as if he were fully dressed. She woke up dreading the moment when he would realize he didn't have on a stitch of clothes.

But after she met Warren Scofield, when he had come out to the house on Coshocton Road to talk over some business with her father, Agnes had begun to anticipate sliding beneath her blankets for the night and imagining all sorts of moments when Warren would reveal to her that there was no one as lovely to him as she was. That he liked her looks despite her unruly hair, her sallow complexion, her short, full figure that made her look coarse, her mother often said. Even though Agnes's waist was small, she had the obvious figure of someone of bad breeding, Catherine Claytor remarked now and then, in despair over everything in her own life but taking aim that moment at her daughter's looks.

But in Agnes's imagination none of that mattered to Warren Scofield. He didn't notice her flaws, and, in fact, he implied that she was beautiful, and that he was deeply in love with her. The tale became far more seductive than any sleep, and she often had dreams from which she awoke mortified, unable for a moment to believe they were confined to her unconscious self. It took several long, anxious minutes before she could convince herself that she was alone in her own room without witnesses to the lazy, sensual pleasure of her dream of Warren. She also found herself peculiarly embarrassed at having dreamed various sexual experiences she wasn't at all sure could actually happen.

After they were married, Agnes would find that she might be at a perfectly civilized social gathering of some sort, but if she happened to glance at Warren wherever he might be — sitting with their hostess, perhaps, accepting a cup of coffee or tea — she would notice his long legs and remember the flex of muscle along his thigh, and she was helpless against the heat that climbed her throat and turned her face a blotchy red. She would duck her head in an effort to become invisible, flushed as she was with the idea of sex.

Sometimes at the family dinner table she would lose her appetite completely when she looked across the table-cloth at her husband. What are we doing? she would think, helpless against her ridiculous outrage, wasting our time with lamp chops. Bothering with lima beans, with a plate of cake? The two of them made love whenever they could, and Agnes generally fell asleep contentedly sated. The intensity of that lust never dissipated, except during Warren's black moods, which nothing could permeate, but those bleak spells only made sex between them less frequent, never less ardent.

After Warren died, though, Agnes was unable to fall asleep in their bedroom for months and months. She couldn't divert her thoughts, and she would move to another room or wander the house in the dark, waking at dawn and finding herself huddled in a chair in the sitting room, or, in that first summer after his death, when it was so hot for so long, she sometimes found herself out on the porch, curled comfortably in the swing. It was no good turning her thoughts toward the children, because Dwight and Claytor had been eleven and ten years old respectively when Warren died, Betts just shy of six, and Howard barely three. To consider those children and her sole responsibility for them made her frantic and furious and also scared to death.

In early February of 1930, Warren Scofield and his uncle Leo were on their way to Arbor City, Pennsylvania, to work out the details of the merger of Scofields & Company with Arthur Fitch and Sons. Warren was driving Leo's big car, and he had rounded a descending curve in the mountains of Pennsylvania when he either hit a patch of ice or swerved, perhaps, to miss an animal. For whatever reason, that shiny black Packard had gone hurtling out of control across the brittle winter grass toward the precipice until it hit an old maple tree growing along the verge. Both men were thrown from the car.

Leo's youngest brother, George Scofield, and two of Scofields' top engineers were about a half an hour behind them. Every member of the family had heard George say, at one time or another, that just for a moment, when he came around the curve, he thought his older brother, Leo, and his nephew were playing a trick or had decided to rest, to stretch out and nap. George thought that Warren had braced himself against the trunk of the tree and fallen asleep. The Packard sat with its doors hanging open, canted toward a sheer drop off the mountain, but, except for a dent in the fender and a smashed headlight, it appeared undamaged. For one brief instant George thought Warren had parked it there. That's how surprised he had been; that's how peaceful Leo and Warren had looked as they lay where they had died among the fallen brown leaves and withered brush.

Not long after that, Uncle George had said to Agnes that if only Warren had lived a little longer, he might have turned into enough of a scoundrel that they wouldn't all miss him so much. And a few months or so after Warren died, Lily Butler, whose father, Leo Scofield, had also been killed, of course, swooped down on Agnes from her house next door and fetched her up like an owl snatching a field mouse by the scruff of its neck.

"You don't have time for all this, Agnes. You're only thirty years old! You've got such a long time ahead of you — you've got happy surprises ahead of you, too! You've got to get things in order. We're all grieved! I loved them, too! I loved them, too! My father . . . Oh, and Warren . . . but you've got to raise these children. And Robert and I will do anything in the world to help, but you've got to pull yourself together."

And that's what Agnes did. She had fallen into a state of guilty brooding and second-guessing, wondering if she could have prevented Warren from making that trip on such an icy day. She was miserable with regret and sorrow, as though she were bruised from head to foot, although when Lily confronted her, Agnes was embarrassed not to have better hidden her despair. She knew from experience the embarrassment another person's legitimate desolation calls forth, and she made a fairly successful effort simply to close down part of her sensibility.

Her grief, though, was a separate thing altogether. It was a gradual education, really, that served to delineate her by eliminating solace, paring away any mitigating circumstances of her life — the existence of her children, for example, was not a comfort in the immediate aftermath of Warren's death. Their inevitable transience in the world had been summarily brought to her attention. The ballast of her life had been jettisoned, and occasionally she had a brief glimpse of where she stood, now. In the first few years, it wasn't only Warren's absence that rendered her hopeless; nor was it only a crisis of mortality; it was also her newfound understanding of the loneliness of living all the way through the rest of her life.

By the time Dwight and Claytor were finishing high school and Agnes was in her late thirties, she lay in bed at night courting sleep by imagining the children's futures. How grand their lives would be with their good looks, their wit and charm and intelligence. Howard and Betts, too, although whenever Agnes began to imagine Betts's future, she got off track and began to worry once more. Nevertheless, her renewed and optimistic dreams for her children carried her through the years the older two boys were away at college and even the years Dwight and Claytor were in law school and medical school respectively.

The war in Europe hung over Scofields just as it hung over every household in the country, and as soon as Claytor received his medical degree from Johns Hopkins, he enlisted in the army, where he was made a captain after he finished basic training. Dwight, too, left in the middle of his second year of law school, in 1941, in order to enlist as an officer in the Army Air Corps. A college degree assured them an officer's rank, and each felt it would give him more control over his life than if he waited until the Selective Service began calling people up.

Of course, Agnes had anticipated Dwight's and Claytor's leave-taking — all over town families were seeing their sons off to various branches of the armed services. The two older boys had come home in order to go away again. Leaving home was something they thought they had already accomplished. While they were away at school, however, Agnes was always prepared for them to return — one or both for Christmas, for long weeks of summer; they hadn't departed for school in the same way that they were suddenly gone when they enlisted, and Agnes didn't allow herself to think of what might happen when or if either one was sent to Europe.

Agnes turned her nighttime reveries to imagining what she could do for Howard and Betts if only there were any extra money. She could send Howard off to college without any of the worry that had attended the financial arrangements she had made for Dwight and Claytor. Betts had no desire to spend any more years at school, but Agnes was drowsily specific, as she settled into sleep, in dreaming up the sedate and beautiful wardrobe she could furnish her daughter if only there were enough money to splurge a little. She would buy a soft blue wool coat with a fur collar to frame Betts's face, for instance. And Betts would be so surprised. Betts would see right away the sort of aristocratic good looks she could attain.

Agnes lulled herself to sleep night after night by imagining that out of the blue she had inherited a nice little sum of money. Because, to everyone's surprise, when Warren and Leo Scofield died, it turned out that not only had Warren's late father, John, sold some shares of his stock to Arthur Fitch, John had mortgaged most of his share of the company to him for a sizable amount of money — far more than it was worth at the time. He had sold to Fitch instead of giving Leo first refusal or, in fact, even consulting his brothers or his son. After his father's death only Warren had been informed of the situation by his father's lawyer, and he hadn't revealed it to anyone; he had been struggling to pay off the loan himself.

But Agnes was left stranded in a financially tenuous situation, because there had been nothing to inherit at all. The house had belonged to Warren's mother, of course, but after her husband's death in 1926, Lillian had the carriage barn just behind the main house converted into a cottage for herself, and Warren's family moved into the main house. Lillian had long ago given it over to Warren and his wife. That familiar and comfortable old house, though, generated a host of expenses all on its own, just sitting there through the seasons. It never crossed Agnes's mind to move, however; the house was where her children lived.

Lily had hurried to assure Agnes that she intended to make a gift to Betts of the tuition for the Linus Gilchrest Institute for Girls, and Agnes accepted with gratitude on Betts's behalf. Robert had helped Agnes find a job teaching at Jesser Grammar School, but her salary was modest, and she wasn't paid in the summer. Agnes had a little money from her mother's estate, and after the sudden deaths of Warren and Leo Scofield, when her father and his second wife had been in Washburn for the funeral, he had sat down with Agnes in private to see what would be best to do.

Agnes's father's youngest son and namesake, Dwight Claytor, was also, of course, Agnes's youngest brother, but since his birth he had also been the oldest child in Agnes and Warren Scofield's house. He had been handed over to Agnes the moment he was born, during the Spanish Influenza epidemic in 1918, just as the war was drawing to a close. His and Agnes's mother, Catherine Claytor, died of the flu less than two weeks after Dwight's birth, as had Agnes's younger brother Edson. Agnes hadn't even had sufficient time to contemplate the situation, nor had she had time to grieve. Not only had she found herself solely responsible for the baby, but she had also been pregnant herself with her and Warren's first child.

Eleven years later — right after Warren's death — Agnes hadn't even considered the fact that her youngest brother, Dwight, had a father of his own, that he had a safe welcome elsewhere and could certainly leave her household. Agnes's father suggested that perhaps that would be a help. "There are good schools in D.C.," he said. "Lots of things going on . . . Dwight and Claytor always enjoy visiting. And, of course, your brothers are in and out of town, and Camille likes having young people . . ."

Agnes seemed puzzled, at first, and then her expression took on a flat, shocked look as her understanding of what he was suggesting settled over her. He changed direction before she expressed outrage or dismay, which was the last thing he intended to cause. After all, the older Dwight Claytor had been away when little Dwight was born, away when so much misfortune befell his family. He had never seen his youngest son at a time when he was not under Agnes's care, settled comfortably, and made much of in the Scofield compound in Washburn. "In any case," he said, holding out his hands in a gesture of appeasement, "I had thought that it would be a help if I contributed a little more to your finances, Agnes. It's expensive to have a growing family, I know. Surely you could use some help?"

It was years later when she realized that if he had not stepped in, she would have been forced to sell the house, and it was largely through his help that Dwight and Claytor had financed their undergraduate college expenses. Even through her spells of resentment and anger toward her father — primarily on her mother's behalf — Agnes did appreciate his generosity to her and to all her children, not only to his son Dwight. With his help and Robert and Lily's emotional and sometimes financial support, Agnes got by pretty well, although there was never a time that a need for money was not on her mind.

Dwight and Claytor were gone by late January of 1941, and Betts graduated from high school that same year. She accepted a job offered to her by her great-uncle George Scofield, to manage his suddenly popular Mid-Ohio Civil

War Museum, which — as silly as both Betts and Agnes thought the whole enterprise to be — was a fairly demanding undertaking. Betts lived at home in order to save money, and she and her mother fell into a surprisingly pleasant domesticity. Whoever got home from work first would get something started for dinner and often put together a little plate of Ritz crackers with peanut butter, or celery stuffed with pimento cheese. Agnes loved smoked oysters or sardines on crackers with a little lemon juice. They both indulged themselves now and then by roasting pecans or walnuts, which Betts liked sprinkled with sugar and cinnamon but which Agnes preferred plain with salt, so they split the batch and made both. When the other one got home, they would sit together and have a cocktail or a glass of sherry.

"What a day," Agnes might say if she came in after Betts was already stretched out on the sofa with her feet up. "I tell you, I sometimes think Bernice doesn't have a brain in her head. All during recess . . . She was telling me something about a package she'd had from Will. I still don't have any idea what that was all about. She got off track trying to remember what she was wearing when she went into town to pick it up. 'Now, I had on my old brown coat, because my green coat needs new buttons. Or maybe I did have on my green coat, because I did sew on those buttons Wednesday . . .'" Agnes shook her head in exasperation and took a sip of sherry. "Sometimes I just want to shake her! But then she'll come into my classroom if she hears things getting out of hand. Just as if she happened to be passing by. Today she managed to suggest a new seating arrangement for reading aloud. Putting the good readers next to the ones who are going slow — it made such a difference." Bernice Dameron taught the third-grade class across the hall from Agnes, and although Bernice wasn't particularly beloved by the students, she was admired and respected. Agnes often resorted to a persuasive but cowardly charm to keep order in her classroom, and she was wildly popular but well aware that Bernice was the best teacher in the school.

Sometimes Betts would tell her about unusual visitors to the museum. "A woman came in today who's working on her doctoral dissertation. I don't think I know a woman who has a doctorate. She's mostly interested in the letters and diaries, though. I set her up in that little room Uncle George furnished like it would have been during the war. There's a desk, but I had to chase down a lamp. She'll be in and out all week. Maybe I'll see if she'd like to come to supper."

Howard was generally involved in something after school until almost seven, and then the three of them sat down to dinner. Their domestic regimen had a little of a make-believe aspect, as though they were playing house, establishing their small rituals, as they adapted to the absence of Dwight and Claytor. Of course, Dwight and Claytor had been away at school for years, but Agnes and Betts and Howard hadn't felt separated from them in the same way they did now that Dwight and Claytor were in the army. Now there was an entire official bureaucracy between those boys and their own family.

Everyone shifted roles a little bit, and life at Scofields carried on pretty much as usual until Betts began planning to leave. After a year working at the museum, she was heading off with her friend Nancy Turner to Washington, D.C., where Nancy's uncle, who was with the Office of Price Administration, had helped them find secretarial jobs in the mushrooming business of going to war.

Betts spent a few weeks putting things in order for Uncle George at the museum. She made up a calendar with dates and times of upcoming school tours, several garden club visits from around Marshal County, and the evening the Knights of Fithian were holding a banquet, catered by the Eola Arms Hotel, in the original dining room. Uncle George had urged her not to cancel any visits already scheduled — he would conduct those tours himself — but he had asked her not to arrange any further visits.

For the duration of the war, the museum would be open to the public whenever Uncle George could be available. It was housed in the building across from Monument Square that had originally been built in the 1880s as George's residence, where it was assumed he would live with a family of his own, but he never married, and since he traveled so much, he didn't set up housekeeping for himself but had always lived with one or the other of his older brothers. After Leo's death, George lived with his niece, Lily, and her husband, Robert Butler. He kept a bedroom furnished for himself in his own house, but otherwise he had turned his own residence entirely over to the display of his collection. He was toying, though, with the idea of inhabiting his own house permanently, just to keep an eye on things.

All the while Betts made arrangements for leaving, she was dishearteningly agreeable and cooperative and subdued. Hers was a gravity that did nothing to conceal the underlying current of her euphoria. In truth, she was genuinely thrilled with the legitimate and communal notion of being swept up into the full force of a solemn cause. But all at once the rooms felt vast to Agnes, even when she only imagined Betts's absence. Agnes began to study her daughter more carefully — to memorize her — when they were having coffee in the morning, when they were in any room together.

Betts had been taller than all of her friends during most of high school, and she had been angular and extravagant in her movements, her broad gestures, her long strides across a room. She had been an awkward girl, careening around Washburn as though she were herding her group of petite friends as they moved around town in a cluster. Trudy Butler was probably Betts's closest friend, and Trudy was considered very attractive, although Agnes had never thought she was particularly pretty. Trudy was small and dark-haired, with a complicated, pointed face which was serenely composed. Her emotions didn't fly across her features the way they did across the faces of all the other Scofields. All of Betts's friends were pert and vivacious, seeming even lovelier than they were, in fact, simply because of all the possibilities ahead of them. Betts could never be pert. Her gestures were wide and bony; her voice ungirlish, with a steely note running straight through her sentences, grounding her words in the category of drama rather than flirtation.

Agnes had worried about her, but Betts never seemed to care about her popularity one way or another; she was doted on by Dwight and Claytor — who were referred to as the "Tarleton twins" by all those friends of Betts's who had crushes on them, after the loutish but handsome young brothers in *Gone with the Wind* who rushed heedlessly off to war. Trudy objected to that. "The Tarleton twins were just dolts!" Trudy said. "Handsome, but stupid and coarse. That's not a thing like Dwight and Claytor!" Trudy always rose to the bait, but Betts just laughed and let it go, since it was teasingly meant as a compliment.

All through high school Betts was at the center of whatever was going on, and if there was no particular boy paying attention to her, it was true that all the boyfriends of the other girls liked and admired Betts. She was as talented an athlete as her aunt Lily had been, and she understood that games were never frivolous, which very few of the girls at school seemed to realize. And, too, she was witty and very smart, which always ensures popularity for anyone who is also endowed with some degree of social grace.

But not long after she graduated from the Linus Gilchrest Institute for Girls, Betts seemed to come into possession of her own height; she began to acquire synchronization. All of the separate parts of Betts suddenly fell into place. She was dramatic all of a sudden, with her blond hair and her characteristically Scofield large, dark brown eyes. She even appeared to move differently through the rooms of the house, across the yard — anywhere Agnes happened to catch sight of her. Everything about Betts's gestures and expressions had always seemed larger than life, had seemed amplified, somehow. But what had once seemed awkward now seemed sinuous, like the oddly sensual overanimation of *Snow White and the Seven Dwarfs.*

In fact, once Betts knew she would be leaving for Washington, and word of her eventual departure spread, she was in great demand. She rarely had time to join Agnes for a drink before dinner; Betts had dates night after night and attended one farewell party after another for other friends who were departing. Agnes missed her daughter very much even before she left, and, simultaneously, Agnes wished Betts were already gone, because the two of them had fallen back into the habit of being exasperated with and prickly toward each other.

Since there really wasn't an extra penny, and she had a good bit of time on her hands, Agnes spent her evenings sewing what she considered a career girl's wardrobe for Betts to take to Washington. Agnes had bolts of unused fabrics, some from as long ago as when they were her mother's and even some she had inherited from her great-aunt Cettie. Wonderful material that was no longer available anywhere and that was a pleasure to work with. Agnes was a passionate seamstress, and since she was making these clothes as a gift, she took the liberty of making wardrobe choices for her daughter.

She made two beautifully tailored suits for Betts. One a soft dove-gray wool and one of dark blue linen. Agnes took great pains to make the suits look like they had been bought at a fine dress shop. She knew about and even endorsed Betts's worry of seeming unsophisticated, a country girl at large in the chaos of Washington. Agnes spent a great deal of time blocking the padded shoulders over a wood form and steaming the sleeves into a beautiful drape from the seam.

"These are just amazing, Mama. I could never have found suits so well made anywhere. Or that ever fit me like this. But I'll be about as colorful as a sparrow!"

"Oh, well, Betts. With your blond hair . . . with your coloring! My mother always said that clothes should fit perfectly and show you off. That it shouldn't ever be the other way around! Mama didn't have a very happy life, you know . . . but she was famous for being so stylish. So beautiful. You remind me of her. She was tall and with blond hair, too. Well, of course, you've seen pictures. . . . But you have her look of . . . oh . . . of elegance, I guess. As if she were a member of some grand aristocracy. You've got that, too, Betts."

But Betts and her mother didn't agree about clothes. Betts loved brilliant colors and any sort of exaggeration of a style. She was always coming home triumphantly with great bargains she had found. "Betts," Agnes had said two weeks earlier, when her daughter came home with two pairs of open-toed, sling-back shoes — one pair a bright red leather and the other black patent — "the reason you can get these marked down so much is that no one else in Washburn would be caught dead in them. What I think . . . It just seems to me, Betts, that open-toed shoes are so . . . trashy!"

But Betts's enthusiasm remained unsquelched. The Saturday afternoon that Agnes had finished running up a simple pattern for Betts of a navy sailor-type dress with a white collar and red piping, Betts was overjoyed when she tried it on. "I'll wear this tonight!" She turned sideways and was delighted at how the dress nipped in at the waist, flattering her figure and drawing attention to her long legs, since the dropped-waist skirt was cut on the bias and had a slight flutter at the hem when she walked. "I look wonderful in this," she said. "Thank you, Mama! I love this dress, and we're going out to the lake for a dance to see John Hart and Billy Oliver off."

"You do look pretty, Betts. You'll leave a trail of broken hearts." And Betts grinned because she knew it might be true. Not broken hearts, but a few crushes that some of the boys in Washburn had developed when all of a sudden they looked around and found that Betts Scofield was a beauty. She had always been around town, but all at once she was mysteriously glamorous.

That evening, though, when Betts was dressing, she wailed from upstairs while Agnes and Howard were still at the dinner table. "My new red shoes! My new red shoes with the open toes! The sling-backs! Where have they gone? They aren't anywhere! Oh, Mother!" And Howard and Agnes had exchanged a wary glance.

"You've hidden them, Mother! Mama! I know you've hidden them!" But Agnes wondered how on earth Betts could ever find anything in her room. She was extravagantly untidy.

"I won't have you saying such things to me, Betts," Agnes had said. But Betts searched the house in vehement indignation, even taking the cushions off the couch, looking on the high shelf in the broom closet. Agnes thought that the navy blue pumps Betts had worn to work would be much more suitable, anyway, although she knew better than to say so.

Agnes cleared the table and scraped the plates while Betts searched up and down the stairs for those red shoes. The household had grown accustomed to weathering these scenes. And, to be fair, Betts was equally effusive when she was happy. Once, as Warren tried to restrain his three-year-old daughter, who was very nearly in a full-blown tantrum because she couldn't open the heavy front door for herself, he had said to Agnes that Betts would grow up into an adult who would be genuinely surprised to realize that many people considered emotional restraint a virtue. He had made that remark, but he had made it with fond exasperation; he had adored Betts, had adored all the children.

Betts finally appeared wearing her new dress and the respectable blue pumps, and she was so angry she didn't look at her mother. "I know you've hidden those shoes, Mama. Don't think for a minute that I don't know that."

Agnes had her hands in the dishwater, busy with the cups and saucers and dinner plates. She lifted her chin slightly, and her mouth was grimly set. She didn't make any reply at all, and, just then, Hal Railsback arrived. He had been Betts's favorite date for the last month or so, and Betts hurried to meet him at the door and leave the house before Howard invited Hal to come in.

Howard carried the garbage out to the compost heap before he left on his own date for the evening, and Agnes didn't even give a thought to that pair of red shoes, firmly wrapped in newspaper and at least three days buried under coffee grounds and orange peels. She couldn't bear to let Betts make a fool of herself, but Agnes had conscientiously slipped the full cost of the shoes — not even the marked-down price Betts had paid for them — into Betts's sequined evening bag. She would discover it when she went to the formal dance at the Eola Arms the following weekend. So, as it turned out, Agnes reasoned, Betts had profited from the situation.

The morning of Betts's departure had been predictably exhausting, and yet Howard and Agnes and Betts were all taken by surprise by the irritation each one felt at the other two by the time they got Betts packed and ready to go. Howard carried countless boxes downstairs and then was sent by Betts to retrieve them. Agnes tried to refold Betts's freshly ironed clothes using tissue paper to prevent their wrinkling, but that had only served to send Betts into a frenzy of anxiety. How would she manage? Would she seem as green as grass with her homemade Washburn wardrobe?

Agnes considered reminding Betts that she had declared she was going to Washington to help the war effort, to do her part. Betts had indulged herself in the idea of self-sacrifice. But Agnes knew that Betts's attack of uncertainty and her desire to do her part in the drama of the time could certainly exist simultaneously, and she kept quiet. When Nancy Turner and her father finally arrived to collect Betts and her luggage, Betts and Agnes were both teary-eyed with dismay and frustration, and it was with some relief as well as sorrow that they embraced and said good-bye.

Chapter Two

*I*T SEEMED TO AGNES SCOFIELD that the children left home all at once. By the end of the school year of 1944, only Howard was still in Washburn, but he and several of his friends arranged to take courses straight through the summer in order to graduate by January of the following year. They, too, wanted to enlist before they were called up. Howard and his friends presented their eagerness to enlist as the lesser of two evils, the alternative to being drafted.

The day after Christmas of 1944, when Agnes and Lily and Robert Butler saw Howard off on the afternoon bus to Columbus, where he would catch the train to Pennsylvania for basic training, Agnes came home to the empty house. She stood in the large center hall, taking off her hat and coat and gloves with an unnerving sense of being a tourist in her own home. Every familiar object upon which she cast her eye seemed to her as deceptively placed and misleading as if it had been arranged in a museum to illustrate an example, say, of a house in which Americans might have lived in the late-nineteenth through the mid-twentieth century.

Lily had invited her for supper, but Agnes had begged off, and about eight o'clock that evening she realized she had forgotten to eat anything at all. Finally she made a sandwich and carried it with her as she roamed the rooms, but there was nowhere in the house where she could remain settled. Something was amiss, and it awakened her vigilance. It was she who knew every nook and cranny of this house that had been built for her father-in-law, John Scofield, almost sixty years earlier. Ever since it had fallen under her care, she had made it her business to be on the lookout for evidence of its slow and inevitable decline, and then it was she who shored it up again, stopping any single bit of disintegration in its tracks. She tried to stay one step ahead; she tried to anticipate, but always there was unexpected deterioration nipping at her heels.

She had the pulleys replaced, for instance, and all the weights rehung in every one of the forty-six window casements, even though at least half of them hadn't yet broken. And while the carpenter was in the basement he had discovered a rotting bearing beam. "I don't know," he said, shaking his head in defeat even as he spoke. "Why, I just stuck this pencil all the way through. I'd been wondering why the things in that cupboard in the dining room shake so much. That corner of the floor's not resting on a thing. Might as well be sitting on a matchstick. I think you folks shouldn't walk anywhere around that north corner. That floor could let go anytime."

For almost a year Agnes directed everyone in the house to tread softly anywhere in the dining room, until she could afford to have the beam replaced. She found a fellow who could carve duplicates of the several rotting balustrades on the side porch, but he drew her attention to the fact that the latticework under the porch was in bad shape. She simply had to let it go for a while, and that winter, a family of skunks moved in, although they didn't cause any trouble. She oversaw the mason who tuck-pointed the old brick around the chimney where ice had blown it apart. "This mortar . . . Well, look here!" the mason said to her. He dislodged a rain of sandy mortar between the bricks beneath the window to illustrate. "It's not going to hold. Water'll get in and then if we have a hard freeze . . ." He continued to displace the crumbling mortar with the end of his pencil.

"Bert! Don't let's hurry it along!" Agnes said, and he stuck the pencil in his pocket and grinned in agreement. "I can't afford to do a thing about it until after Christmas. Let's hope the weather stays mild." Agnes lived in a state of waiting for the next little bit of reconstruction to become necessary.

"Mama, I think you're just making all these things up — forty-six windows repaired!" Howard once joked. "I think there's something going on. I think you have designs on one of those workmen."

"It certainly would be cheaper if I could just get one of them to marry me," Agnes replied, but it was clear she wasn't particularly amused. There was nothing much fun about the effort and expense of maintaining the house.

So in that early dark of December 1944, she investigated the rooms — looked into the corners, put her hand against the limestone hearths of all the fireplaces to test for dampness, but everything seemed to be all right. She put on her boots and took a flashlight outside to see if the gutters had backed up, because something in the house was not right. Finally she retraced her steps, shining the beam along the foundation, but she found nothing at all remarkable. Once inside again, though, she was disturbed still more, and this time she narrowed in on an odd scent in the air. Almost like stale smoke; a little bitter, like ashes tamped down and extinguished, but with a peculiarly sweet overtone.

She went up the stairs and into every room of all three floors, and then she realized that all through the house was the lingering odor of finally completed chores: clothes ironed, wool sweaters blocked and dried, then put away with moth balls, books packed up, shelves wiped down. It wasn't the smell of a temporarily empty house, where there would be dirty clothes waiting to be laundered, oranges or apples left out for the taking, the oddly pleasant banana scent of shoe polish and brushes left lying by a bedroom chair, the medicinal odor — which Agnes always tasted as well as smelled — of fingernail polish remover. The clothes were clean and starched and ironed, the shoes polished, the fruit eaten, the books gone — what had caught Agnes's attention was the vaguely sweet but sooty scent of her house from which the longtime occupants had permanently departed.

That particular night it had been so new to Agnes that she had searched for its source. But for months her children's absence manifested itself now and then through a waft of perfume from a drawer, closets that emanated a chilly drift of mothballs and damp wool. Even the scent of talcum from the nursery-cum-storage room occasionally wound its way through the upstairs hall and down and around two flights of stairs to startle Agnes as she was winding the tall clock in the front hall.

About eight o'clock on New Year's Eve 1944, Agnes realized that she had been sitting stone-still in the kitchen for almost an hour with a bowl of tomato soup and a turkey sandwich on a plate in front of her. She set herself briskly into motion before self-pity could catch hold of her, pushing back her chair and hurrying to the hall to telephone Will Dameron. "I know I thought I would just have a quiet night, Will, but now I'm feeling awfully sorry for myself. I begged off supper and bridge with Lily and Robert, too. Is there any chance we can still see each other tonight? All I can offer you is some dry sherry to toast the new year, but it's good dry sherry. I'll tell you, the house feels enormous to me — so empty! I'd really like to see you. I've got dry wood in. I could get a nice fire going."

In the bay window of the chilly front parlor she sat and watched for his car, only allowing her thoughts to browse across the glistening yard, where the snow had melted in the morning's sun and refrozen during the cloudy, windy afternoon into a pattern of flattened, overlapping waves. The tall trees lining the street had been painted white halfway up so that in blackout conditions drivers could see them, even with the top half of their headlights painted over. It had become a matter of civic pride that Washburn, Ohio, was one of the first targets the Germans would hit because of the production of Scofield engines, and the Civil Defense warden was very strict about even a sliver of unnecessary light escaping into the camouflage of darkness. Agnes couldn't imagine how German planes were expected to reach Ohio, and Robert said it was just a way to keep up morale, to let people feel as though they were doing something useful.

Gazing out the window, though, Agnes decided that it couldn't have been the local Civil Defense warden who thought it would be a good idea to paint the trees. It must have been someone in a place where it never snowed who had come up with that notion, because, with the white ground beneath them, the trunks of the trees disappeared, and their leafless crowns seemed to be suspended spider-like in the night sky. Will's car pulled in, and even without lights the radiance of the snow illuminated him clearly as he bent to retrieve something from the backseat.

Agnes and Will had known each other all their lives, had played together as children. The habit of knowing Will was so deep-rooted that it hadn't occurred to her in a long, long time that he was a nice-looking man, with pale arched brows which gave him a misleading expression of amused skepticism. He was entirely appealing, although not with the sort of striking good looks Warren Scofield had possessed. And, even though he had wit of a sort and a sense of humor, he didn't rely much on irony; he didn't have the slight cynicism of a man who is charming. He was easygoing and dependably kind.

As he crossed the yard and turned the corner of the house, however, Agnes was overtaken by weariness as she made her way through the darkened front rooms to let him in the kitchen door. It had been a mistake to call him so late. It had been a mistake to invite him. Now he and she would sit and talk and have a drink. She had forgotten all about that. She had only been counting on the pleasures and comforts of familiar sex; she had only been thinking of making love. The inevitable social aspect of the evening hadn't crossed her mind, and she despaired of the effort she would have to make. She thought it might be impossible to summon the energy to be alert and curious and hospitable. He greeted her with a kiss on the cheek and an apologetic laugh as well, because his arms were filled with all sorts of things he'd brought for her from the farm and from a recent trip to Cleveland.

She smiled at him even as she longed to tell him to go home — she longed to be able to turn him away without any explanation and without hurting his feelings. But she smiled on and, one by one, took the packages from him and exclaimed over and remarked upon each of them. "I feel guilty every time you bring me all these things," she said. "Not as guilty as I should feel, I guess, or I wouldn't accept them. Betts used to accuse me of being smug! She said people were going to think I was buying all this on the black market." Agnes was teasingly chipper and genuinely appreciative, too, but she was aware that her perkiness sounded forced. "I don't think I'd really mind if that's what people did think. It would give me a more . . .

well . . . it would give me a reputation." While Agnes put away the sugar and baking chocolate, the meat and the butter and eggs he had brought along, Will fixed himself a drink of the good Scotch he had bought in Cleveland, and he made a drink for Agnes, too.

Will had served on the board of the Midwest Agricultural Council since its inception, just after the start of the war, and it had become an onerous and time-consuming business. They sat at the kitchen table, and Agnes listened to him talk wearily about the three-day board meeting in Cleveland that had kept him out of town longer than he expected. ". . . I don't see how we can manage it with transportation compromised. We'll have a priority status, but not high enough . . . it may be we'll have to depend on trucks instead of the trains. Coordinated distribution of enriched fertilizer. And, I'll tell you, I don't see how else we're going to get our quota. There's more profit in other things. It won't go down well, but we're thinking we might have to make it mandatory to plant at least one-quarter acreage in hybrid corn."

He also filled her in on what was happening at the farm — which was a huge enterprise by now, and which Will had bought from Agnes's father. She had grown up in the house in which Will now lived. But Will was not a farmer, really, although he raised livestock and vegetables for the small local market and for himself. Essentially, though, he was the manager of a complex and thriving business that produced corn. Agnes was not uninterested, but her mind wandered, going blank for moments at a time until she dragged it back to attention once again.

". . . not the way I see things," Will was saying. "If they really don't have it, that's fine! But we stood there dickering over the price when we all three knew it was just sitting in the warehouse. Had been for a long time. They think I'm going to order that lumber again and pay the price it costs now. They think I'll do that. They think I'd fall for that kind of nonsense. It's disappointing, Agnes. What they don't know is I'm the kind of man who won't argue with them. Once I'm disgusted with a thing, I just don't fool with it anymore. So if I don't hear from them by midweek, I'll just go over to Grundy's, even if I have to pay more. That's just the kind of person I am. And I'll bet you that for a couple of months Andy won't even realize I'm not doing business with them anymore."

Finally they closed up downstairs and went to bed, and Agnes pretended an enthusiasm for the prospect of making love that she no longer had, although she felt perfectly amiable toward Will in the shadowy, snow-lit bedroom. And eventually she lost track of her initial indifference and fell into a loosening of concentration on anything other than his and her own physical selves. She fell asleep not long after he did, comfortable alongside him, and for the most part untroubled.

She woke up gradually when daylight only illuminated the rectangles of the windows behind their drawn shades and frilled curtains, and she watched drowsily as the various objects in the room regained their angles, were clarified for another day. Eventually, in a moment she failed to note, the floor, the braided rug, the chair where Will had neatly draped his clothes, her dressing table with its tall oval mirror, were marked by the faint tic-tac-toe shadow of the window mullions. If just once she caught that instant . . . But today she found herself oddly pleased that again that tiny flick of time had eluded her. It was a bit of magic thinking she indulged in every morning; if she ever observed that exact instant when the shadows materialized, then everything good she might have hoped for would come to pass; if she failed to catch it once again, she could only expect the unexpected. She decided this morning, though, that her failure to note the moment might augur nice surprises in spite of every-thing — the war, her finances, the empty house.

Not wanting to wake Will, she pulled on her robe and hurried downstairs to the basement in the morning chill and stoked the furnace, since Howard wasn't at home to do it. It wasn't a particularly difficult task, but it was a dirty one, and Agnes was always uneasy in the dank base-ment, where a large black snake resided, according to Howard, although she thought surely it must hibernate in the winter. Howard had also said that the snake was shy and harmless, and was a good sign that they wouldn't be bothered with mice, but Agnes had been unable to per-suade herself that she was glad it was there. In fact, she hastily clinkered the grate and shoveled in coal and decided it was worth paying the Drummonds' grandson, from across the square, to come in early and tend to the job before he was off to school. By the time she reached the upper landing of the second floor on her way back upstairs, she heard the thud and whoof of the heat coming up. She kicked off her slippers and stood barefoot on the hall grate in the warm rush of air. Her whole body, which had tensed against the cold, began to relax, and she stayed where she was until the soles of her feet became so hot that she had to step on and off the brass vent.

Will was still sound asleep, but he had turned and stretched and was splayed across the entire bed, and she didn't want to disturb him. With all the children gone, the night before was the first time she and Will had slept overnight in her bed. Anyone seeing him leave this morning would not have seen him arrive last night, and they would only think he had been in town early on some errand or other. It seemed to Agnes that his staying over was an intimacy greater than merely making love. In fact, she felt constrained somehow when she considered this development, and uncertain whether or not it was something that she would want him to make a habit of. On the other hand, this first morning of 1945, she was filled with more than her usual fondness toward Will. She wanted to be especially careful of his feelings; she felt an urge to protect him, though what hazard might be bearing down upon him she couldn't imagine. If he hadn't dropped whatever he might have been doing and come into town the night before, though, she knew that even the thought of going to bed with any expectation of falling asleep would have been hopeless.

And he had been as thoughtful as usual, bringing all sorts of things from the farm, even the winesap apples she loved so much, which he must have stored in the root cellar in the fall so they would keep. But as she quietly got dressed and went downstairs to make coffee and start the bacon, she realized that — although she was hungry —

the toast and jam, the bacon, the fresh eggs Will had brought from the farm, those apples — cored, sliced and slowly simmered in butter with a little sugar and cinnamon and nutmeg that she thought he'd like — they weren't going to satisfy her. They weren't what she was hungry for, although she couldn't think of anything else she wanted to eat.

There was plenty to do while school wasn't in session, and Agnes kept busy. There was so much closet space now, in the children's bedrooms, that she brought her spring clothes down from the attic, washed and ironed them, and hung them in Howard's closet. It was sensible and satisfying to have all her clothes at hand in case an unseasonably warm day came along. She prepared next term's lesson plans in the afternoons, and in the evenings she generally played cards next door at Lily and Robert's, or joined them to listen to the news or sometimes to a concert or variety show.

All through the few days at home Agnes instinctively — and as best she could — held at bay any moment of retrospection. What she intended for the time being was to let any ideas that might unsettle her simply float above her consciousness. She was dogged in her determination not to allow any disturbance to wend its way too soon into her stream of thought, believing that the longer she could simply acknowledge the concealment of sorrow and regret or remorse within the other, ordinary thoughts of any given day — well — the better off she'd be in the long run; the better off she'd be the more time went by.

Monday, January eighth, was the first day back at school after the Christmas recess. While her second-graders did copy work off the board, Agnes pinned up cutouts of animals that hibernate, which she had clipped from old calendars and magazines to decorate the cork-paneled strip over the blackboard. She stood stocking-footed on a chair, stretching upward almost on tiptoe so that she could use both hands to align the diaphanous wisps of paper satisfactorily before thumbtacking them in place.

In the familiarity of her schoolroom, though, and with her mind not wholly absorbed by the task at hand, her watchful discipline of mind simply slipped away, and she was ambushed by the melancholy that had shadowed her since Howard had climbed aboard the bus on his way to Indiantown Gap, Pennsylvania; had shadowed her, in fact, since her husband's death, but which the busy-ness of life with her children had ameliorated to a degree.

Before she could get hold of it — take account of and suppress it — that sorrow blossomed into full-fledged grief. Not sadness or any permutation of mere despondency. Nothing contained or governable. It inhabited the entire architecture of her consciousness. Just like that! While she was pinning up the cutout of a gopher. It was as if she had had the breath knocked out of her. Agnes had religiously rationalized the children's having gone, had told herself over and over that they would be safe, that they would all come home, but she lacked the information she needed to imagine their lives. Increasingly she seemed able only to conjure them up as no more than representations of themselves, like overexposed images in a photograph, or people remembered from a dream. But now, just at a moment when she wasn't paying attention, grief overtook her once again.

After Warren's death, Lily had offered bits of hopeful consolation now and then. She had said often that it was terrible for her and Robert, too, to have lost Warren. That she couldn't imagine what it must be like for Agnes. Agnes, though, discovered that the sudden blow of loss was terrible, but it was not as devastating in the moment as the slow hours and days, the weeks, and months of becoming increasingly convinced of the endlessness of that absence.

She stood in the over-warm classroom on the chair, helpless and mortified and unable to stop the sudden tears that slid silently down her face and then were accompanied by a sort of weeping she couldn't restrain. And, in fact, she was unaware of taking a sharp, teary gasp, in the same wholehearted way she had wept as a child.

She splayed the fingers of one hand across the corkboard to support herself as she hunched slightly forward and let go of the sheaf of clippings still to be arranged and tacked to the corkboard. They drifted away, riding the currents of heat rising from the radiators, settling widely over the classroom floor. With her free hand she covered her eyes, as if, in blocking the light, she might also disappear.

Agnes wasn't even aware of the new quality of silence in the room, where the children had stopped their copy work to look at her. Just for a few moments, in fact, she was bereft of faith in anything at all. Everything in the world was beside the point. In the chalk-powdered light of that second-grade schoolroom, Agnes temporarily lost the assumption of the reasonableness of human existence. She bent more deeply at the waist, her supporting hand well above her head as she still braced herself against the wall in an attempt not to fall. Nora Alexander, one of Agnes's best students, took it upon herself to go across the hall and get Miss Dameron from the third-grade class.

Agnes went home and spent the afternoon in bed, although she knew she wasn't ill. She was afraid, though, to turn around in her thoughts and face head-on the state of mind awaiting her. She remained in bed, and she did still feel fuzzy-headed and ill-defined, as though she were a person who has been crayoned into a coloring book by some child who can't keep within the lines.

The war itself was a horror she had already encompassed as much as that was possible. She shared the communal dread and appalled regret when people in town — when anyone at all — lost children and husbands. Two years earlier Lucille Drummond Hendry's daughter, who was Agnes's namesake, had been on a Red Cross transport that was sunk by German submarines, and their son was stationed somewhere in the Pacific. Lucille had been Agnes's closest friend since they were schoolgirls, and Agnes had spent two weeks in Columbus with Lucille and Davis Hendry after their daughter's ship was reported lost. Agnes hadn't been able to think of anything to do or to say that would offer Lucille even a bit of comfort, but Lucille had maintained an air of subdued but uncharacteristic serenity, in part, Agnes guessed, so that she would be left alone. A loss like Lucille's and Davis's was the most terrible thing that could happen to civilians during the war.

Claytor, Betts, and Howard were all still in the U.S., all three safe for the time being, but Agnes couldn't shake herself loose from dread on their behalf, and particularly on behalf of Dwight, who was stationed in England. It was beyond her to imagine an orderly life at Scofields if Dwight didn't return. After Warren's death, it was Dwight's stern expectation of family loyalty, of family responsibility, that held them in their early and fragile reorganized family orbit.

Agnes had come to grips with the fact that grief, unlike sympathy or even sorrow, is not selfless. The children had taken their leave without seeming to understand that they might not return. The three boys, at least, might not ever see Scofields again, might not see Washburn again, might not, in fact, ever see her again, and yet they had gone anyway. Agnes knew full well that such a complaint was absurd on the face of it, but it was one of those ideas she couldn't displace. She had tried to be stern with herself: Dwight and Claytor and Howard and Betts — any one of them — could walk out the door any morning of the world and be hit by a bus! It was foolish to borrow trouble!

Bernice Dameron had phoned Lily from school to be sure someone would look in on Agnes, and, of course, when Lily Butler came over from next door, Agnes didn't discuss anything about the anxious drama spinning through her thoughts. Nothing that Agnes might say along the lines of what she was thinking would be any surprise at all to Lily, and nothing Lily might reply would be the slightest help to Agnes. She and Lily knew instinctively never to admit the worst to each other. Lily was concerned and well intentioned but betrayed her impatience when it was clear there was nothing physically wrong with Agnes, that there was really nothing to be done to make Agnes feel better.

"Wouldn't you like me to bring you some supper?" Lily asked, in the very way of asking that made it out of the question for Agnes to allow her to do so. But Agnes wasn't hungry, anyway, and felt well enough to get something for herself if she wanted it. Lily could handle almost anything with flair. She organized bond rallies, the Ladies Aid Society, and Garden Club meetings with efficiency, and she presided over them with humor and an air of unruffled certainty. But she had very little talent for tolerating human weakness, and no patience at all if she suspected any sort of brewing sentimentality. She sat with Agnes for a little while, put a pitcher of water and a glass on the bedside table, then made her escape, and both women were relieved.

The next morning Agnes got up early and stepped back into the pattern of her days. She carried on as usual, teaching the second grade at Jesser Grammar School, eating lunch with Bernice Dameron, Will's older sister, in the cloakroom, where they sat on the boot bench with their cheese sandwiches and hard-boiled eggs, idly chatting and luxuriating in furtively smoking one of the few cigarettes a day they allowed themselves with the war on, fanning the smoke out of the high transom window so they wouldn't be caught breaking the rules. The days passed uneventfully, and after a while no one gave any thought to that strange little spell that had overtaken Mrs. Scofield at school — no one but Nora Alexander, that is. She was in love with Mrs. Scofield and believed she had saved her teacher's life. And Agnes moved through all the hours, working hard to make the time pass by.

Some days she stayed late in her classroom, reorganizing the supply closet, correcting workbooks, or just sitting unthinking at her desk, staring out the windows until she could scurry home too late to be expected to stop in at the Butlers' as she had been in the habit of doing. She was stuck in a state of incuriosity, and even the energy to receive Robert's courtly concern and Lily's briskly assuring cheer escaped her. Agnes saw Will now and then, although she didn't have the energy to display affection or feign interest in much he had to say. But sex was the one thing she did hunger for; she found herself dwelling on the idea of Will's hands touching her, of his pale torso and his long, strong legs.

Once, while she was chopping vegetables in the kitchen, the thought crossed her mind that Will was burly in the muscular way of the big dray horses still to be found on some of the farms in the county, whereas, although Warren had been about the same height as Will, he'd been built more along the lines of a jumper, a sleek thoroughbred. Agnes had been efficiently chopping chunks of celery and onions but suddenly she laid the knife flat down, opening her hands and bracing herself against the low chopping block as she leaned forward in surprised embarrassment at her own wandering thoughts.

She straightened and instinctively covered her face as she felt herself blush, but her hands were moist from the onions and celery. "Ah! Oh, oh," she said and made a small hissing sound of dismay. Finally she ran upstairs for the eye-cup and flushed her eyes as best she could. She had always been sensitive to onions, and it was hours before her eyes stopped tearing. But she was helpless against her imagination, and if an image of Will came to mind at some odd time or other, she found that she literally salivated, and it became her greatest pleasure — in a tangle of bedclothes — to abandon, finally, every other thought of anything at all.

In late February, Ernie Mullins came to school with a note from his mother asking if Mrs. Scofield would tell the class that the family was moving and had a good dog that needed a home. Agnes explained that she had to check with the principal before she could announce it to the class. That evening, however, after putting together a quick supper of sardines on crackers, which she ate standing over the sink, she put on her coat and went out herself to the Mullinses' house in a run-down neighborhood near the school, which looked all the more bleak with the last of the snow melted and windblown into yellowing patches that scabbed the stingy little yards like the end bits of soap floating in brackish bath water.

Mrs. Mullins didn't invite Agnes in, and Ernie walked her around back, where the dog was tied. It let out a single, declaratory bark of greeting and came forward to meet them. Agnes took one look at the animal standing alert at the end of his chain and was taken aback by an immediate welling-up of admiration.

The dog was a reddish-brown, medium-size shepherd mix, with his ears cocked forward at their approach, his strength leaning into his shoulders as he stood absolutely still except for a quiver of the silky fringe of his sweepingly curved tail. He approached them almost as far as his chain would allow, but that slight though definite arc of the chain's slackness — the dog's dignified refusal to pull it taut — was a bit of restraint that won Agnes over in less than a minute. This was too good a dog, anyway, she thought, to be subjected to the whims of Ernie Mullins or anyone of his family.

"Why don't I take him home with me, Ernie?" He merely shrugged his shoulders. Ernie was unnerved to have his teacher standing in his own yard.

Ernie's mother wanted the collar for some other dog her family would eventually have when they had moved away from Washburn, Ohio, and settled in Illinois. She stood leaning against the door frame, making it clear from her stance that she had other things to do. "Unless you want to buy it. It's good leather, and it might be hard to find one now. I just don't have the heart to ask you to pay for King, even though my husband says he nearly ate us out of house and home. Well, King never went hungry. I'll tell you that. Anyway, I said we should find him a home, though I don't know if he'll make a good watchdog for you or not."

Agnes looked at the dog, who stood calmly between her and Ernie, and she stooped down to unfasten his collar. "I'm sure he'll be just fine," she said. "And especially grateful, since he's going to cost me so much in groceries."

Mrs. Mullins put her hand on her hip and relaxed even her pretense of goodwill. She looked tired and hostile. "My husband said we should just leave him behind. That he'd make do for himself. But it seemed to me we could try to find a place for him."

Agnes searched through her purse, fishing out two dollars, which she handed over to Mrs. Mullins along with the collar. "I'd like to pay for him. I have a collar around someplace, I think. I'll be glad to have him," she said. "I'll take good care of him." She turned to Ernie, who was a scrawny little boy with a very round head too big for his body, and features so unassertive that Agnes was always unreasonably annoyed at him. "You can come visit your dog anytime you want to before you leave, Ernie. You can walk home from school with me tomorrow if you like." But Ernie looked blank, and when Agnes turned away and slapped her hand against the skirt of her coat to signal the dog to follow, the dog came right along by her side.

She and the dog moved away from the Mullinses' house and turned the corner onto Marshal Avenue, and still Agnes was floundering for the right thing to say. "Good boy! Good boy!" she said to the dog, finally, who moved along with her briskly. She was surprised to find that she was shy about addressing him at all, and she was especially embarrassed to think of calling him King, which seemed such a silly name for a dog, but she did want to encourage him. "Good boy! You're a good boy, Pup!" And "Pup" was as much as she could impose on this amiable dog. She glanced at him and thought that she had no right to invent a name for him. He seemed to be a dog who was perfectly aware of who he was.

When Dwight and Claytor were six or seven years old, Warren had come home one day with two puppies. Agnes had been baffled, but the boys were delighted, and she didn't say anything to Warren until that night when all the children were finally in bed. "I don't understand why you bought two dogs, Warren," she said. "They aren't littermates."

"Oh, no. I was at the Aldridge's in Coshocton, and they have a nice hound of some kind or other who just had pups. They only had that one left." Agnes eyed the puppy, and wondered what his father had been, because he already had coarse brown fur that stuck out all over. Not at all like any hound she'd ever seen. Maybe it wouldn't have a hound's personality, either.

"Hounds are hard to train, though," Agnes said. The other dog was about three months old, Agnes would have guessed, and looked to her like it might be part collie. It had a sweet face and tipped ears.

"I don't know how you do it," Warren said to her, his voice suddenly nasal and sharp, "but you manage to throw cold water on every surprise I come up with!" He shook his head briefly in resigned disappointment. But then his tone fell back into its normal, amiable resonance as he recalled his day. "I had to search high and low to find another puppy. But when I was in the bank and happened to say I needed one, one of the clerks spoke up and said his brother's dog had had pups a few months ago. I went on over there and there were three left, in fact. I thought that one was the best looking of the lot."

"He does have a sweet face," Agnes acknowledged. "But why two *males*? They might not get on together so well . . ."

"Agnes," he said, explaining to her patiently, "can you imagine how bad either Dwight or Claytor would feel if there was just one puppy and it took to one of them more than the other? I remembered how I admired Robert's dog when we were growing up. Ajax was devoted to Robert, of course. Sometimes I just couldn't stand that idea. It was hard to feel that dog wouldn't like me as much as he liked Robert. I was always with Robert. Always in and out of his house. Well, Ajax was really Mrs. Butler's dog. She didn't want him to roam. Robert and I would mark off twenty paces and then stand apart and both of us would call the dog to see who he would come to. 'Jackie' was what we called him. Mrs. Butler was the only one who called him Ajax."

Agnes waited for him to go on, but his attention had wandered back to the newspaper. "And who did he go to?" she finally asked, in spite of herself.

Warren looked up, raising his eyebrows in a question, and then he remembered what they had been talking about. "Oh, he always went to Robert, of course. He was Robert's dog. But with a dog for each boy . . ."

"But, Warren, you can't be sure with dogs. The dogs won't know who they belong to. You might buy two children two horses. One for each so they could ride together. That would make sense. But no one can tell who a dog's going to decide he belongs to. Well, at least if the dog has a choice," Agnes said, but she objected softly, because Warren's mind was made up.

He remained pleased with his gift to the boys. Dwight and Claytor named the semi-hound Tunney and the collie mix Dempsey, and the boys played with them and fed them and cleaned up after those puppies for almost two weeks, which was much longer than Agnes had imagined they would remain interested. Eventually, of course, when the boys started school and Warren was traveling in the field, those two dogs followed Agnes everywhere. Sometimes it seemed to her that she spent most of the day rounding them up and getting them out of the house only to have someone let them in again. They nearly drove her crazy hustling one past the other alongside her as she went up the stairs, each dog trying to be first in such a tumble that Agnes had to hang on to the banister. But she didn't really dislike them; she made sure they were fed and had water.

The two dogs were an odd pair from the start — the bristly hound had a squared-off terrier's head but with long, floppy ears, and the collie mix had stumpy legs that didn't match his body. And just as Agnes had expected, as those dogs matured, they became obsessed with one single desire: each one was bent upon killing off the other. She had to keep them outside and apart all day long, and she was constantly rushing out and dashing a pail of cold water over their backs, which usually broke up a fight if she caught it at the beginning. Finally she had Harold Ostrander, who helped around Scofields at all sorts of odd jobs, build separate pens for them out of sight of each other. Even so, Tunney, the hound, eventually very nearly killed Dempsey in a terrible, bloody battle. Agnes had done everything she could think of to try and break it up, but it continued in a moving, snarling, muscular tumult, and it was clearly a fight to the death.

The hair-raising yips and snarling that went on and on attracted everybody in the vicinity of Scofields, and Mr. Ostrander finally got the animals apart by smashing a wooden ladder down over their backs. Tunney let out a terrible sound — a dog shriek — and backed off but continued to circle Dempsey, who was down and bleeding. Harold Ostrander continued to yell at the dogs and wave the ladder at Tunney, so that his circle around Dempsey grew wider and wider until finally he raced out of the yard, crossing the street and then the park. The Scofields never saw him again, although when they came home from school Dwight and Claytor went out searching for him.

Agnes nursed Dempsey back to health, but then he, too, simply took his leave one day. He adopted for himself an older couple who lived a few streets away. Agnes only discovered where he'd disappeared to when she was downtown one afternoon and saw the couple walking him on a very fine leash. Dempsey was glossy with good health and didn't so much as glance her way; he seemed quite pleased with his situation.

Dwight and Claytor didn't appear to be unduly distressed over the abandonment, but Warren was amazed at such treachery. Agnes tried again and again to explain it to him, but he had never had a pet as a child, and this had hap-

pened before Agnes finally recognized a pattern to Warren's moods. She hadn't understood then that Warren's initial enthusiasm about the whole business would have
dissipated regardless of whatever happened to the dogs.

During their childhoods Agnes hadn't encouraged the
children to have pets of any kind, although there was
always some sort of creature in residence. Ernie Mullins's
dog, though, was the first pet Agnes had ever chosen on
her own. He came right along into the kitchen with her
and briefly investigated the downstairs rooms, and she fed
him the rest of the sardines mashed with some saltines
and an egg.

About nine o'clock she put him outside, but ten minutes later he gave out one quick, anxious bark at the back
door, and she let him in again. When she went upstairs to
bed, he followed tentatively but determinedly behind her
in an odd sort of crouch and with hesitant, nervous footing. Agnes watched him take the last two stairs up the
staircase and was surprised that his effort left her choked
up and teary-eyed. In all probability, she realized, he had
never been up a staircase before, but she was baffled to
find that idea touched off such an emotional response on
her part. She left her door ajar, but after standing at the
threshold for a moment and wagging his tail, Pup had
the good manners to choose Claytor's room just across the
hall. He stretched out full length on the single bed against
the wall.

Chapter Three

IN THE NEXT FEW DAYS, Agnes was both embarrassed and irritated by the consternation awakened on her behalf because of the company of the dog. One evening Robert came over after supper to drop off the newspaper and her mail, and the dog stood between the two of them, canted across the sill as Agnes greeted Robert at the door.

"Move away, now, Pup!" Agnes admonished but without any spirit of command, and the dog stood his ground.

"I have to say, Agnes, that appears to be a mighty fine dog. He's not going to let any strangers walk into this house." Agnes relaxed her tense hold of the door and swung it wide to invite Robert in, and as soon as she gave an indication of welcome, the dog eased back and lay down in the hallway with his chin between his paws.

"Can you come in for a cup of coffee, Robert? I've just made some. Or would you like a drink?"

"I'd like that. A glass of that good sherry."

"I've got Scotch and bourbon, too. Will brought it back from Cleveland."

"Bourbon, then. Bourbon and just a splash of water. With ice if it's not any trouble." Robert handed her the paper and mail and a package wrapped in butcher paper.

Agnes led the way through the house with Pup close behind. "Lily's off to her Ladies Aid meeting," he said, "but she sent along what she tells me are very good soup bones she thought the dog might like."

"She won't want them herself? For soup?"

"Oh, I imagine Lily was very glad not to tackle it."

Robert and Agnes smiled in mutual acknowledgment of Lily's grudging, harried attitude toward cooking, for which, in fact, she had developed a real talent over the years of her marriage. "My mother always told me that a person would love the things he did well," Lily had once said to Agnes, when they were putting up preserves in Lily's steamy kitchen. "But it's not true! It's never been true for me, anyway. Not with mathematics and not with cooking."

Robert took his place where he always sat, in the brown velvet curved-back rocking chair next to the radio, both of which Agnes had moved into the kitchen once she occupied all the rooms of the house by herself. She gave Robert his drink and poured another cup of coffee for herself. It was laced with chicory because of the shortages, and it was pungently acrid, but she had developed a passion for it, and it was all she could get, anyway. She savored the dry, clean, ashy feel of her mouth after she swallowed. Robert went through the little ritual of filling and lighting his pipe and settled back comfortably.

He shifted in the rocker as he reached for his drink and studied it a moment before he took a sip. "Lily and I have been wondering if it might not be hard for you to keep a dog with the food shortages. The rationing and so forth? It's pretty safe around here, I believe. I wouldn't think you'd have much need for a dog."

Agnes was surprised. Will Dameron kept the houses of Scofields fairly well supplied from the farm with poultry and eggs and even a nice roast of pork or beef now and then, although Robert so disapproved of Lily accepting these gifts during rationing that Agnes became the conduit through which all sorts of things made their way into Lily's household. And she and Lily had always put up plenty of fruit and vegetables from the garden Robert had tended with absorbed passion since long before the war began. In fact, one summer day she and Lily had been so engrossed in a two-handed game of canasta that, until they finished and moved from Lily's screened porch into the kitchen, they hadn't realized that the top had blown off the pressure cooker, plastering the ceiling and walls with bits of peeled tomatoes. But maybe Robert really didn't know that Agnes had ample food for herself and one medium-size dog.

"Oh, the dog won't make any difference. You know that! Not a bit. I always have leftovers."

"Well, Agnes." He sat at ease for a few moments, drawing on his pipe. "But a dog can be a good deal of trouble. They can get so attached to a person. You might find that he'll want to follow along with you anywhere you go."

"That's true. That's exactly what he did this morning. I felt like Mary and her little lamb! I didn't even know he'd followed me, and I don't have any idea how he got into the school. I suppose he slipped in behind one of the children. When he found me in the office, where I was turning in the midterm attendance . . . the evaluations, too, I had to explain to Mrs. Daniels that he'd had a bath before I even gave him breakfast. And that's a good deal more than she could say for most of my pupils. But it was peculiar, Robert . . . he doesn't want to play with the children. He didn't even go outside with them at recess." She was perplexed once more, as she remembered it. "Not even little Ernie Mullins. You know that family? They live down toward the end of May Street? They're moving in a few days. He was Ernie's dog, you see. But Ernie didn't even seem to notice the dog was in the classroom. Well, Ernie's not very noticeable himself. He doesn't have much character . . . or substance, I guess I'd say. To tell you the truth, there's not much to Ernie one way or another. He's not any trouble. In fact, I have to remind myself to call on him now and then. Oh, I always have a child or two like that. Transparent children. I really think the dog wasn't attached to that family a single bit. He just came right away with me without any sort of persuasion. Just came along as if he'd been expecting to go somewhere."

They both glanced over at Pup, who was watching them talk about him with his ears flat back in entreaty, and who thumped his tail and looked out from under his brow imploringly.

Robert had done the best he could. Lily had charged him with persuading Agnes to return the dog to wherever it had come from or at least to give it to a family with children. "I'm afraid it will end up running wild around Scofields," Lily had said at breakfast. "I don't know what's the matter with Agnes. Except for her horses when she used to ride . . . I never thought she had any patience for animals. Pets. I can't imagine why she brought that dog home. It's not like her. She's never been . . . You remember it was always Warren who was bringing home some pet or other. I always thought it was the only time Agnes ever was really annoyed with him. Well, angry. But he always thought it would be wonderful for the children. And then he'd be off traveling and Agnes would end up dealing with one disaster after another. Why would she borrow trouble for herself?"

Robert had agreed with her. Agnes was a practical woman; she never struck him as sentimental. But after another drink and a comfortable, wide-ranging conversation in Agnes's company, Robert thought he had said all he could say about the dog within the bounds of good manners.

After Robert went home, Agnes lit the last cigarette she would allow herself for the day and savored the little shiver of guilt that accompanied that first, lovely inhalation. She hadn't made much of an objection when first Dwight and then Claytor had taken up smoking; all the college boys seemed to smoke. But she and Betts had had tearing arguments about it when Betts — still in high school — brazenly sat with her brothers, casually holding her own cigarette.

"No nice girls smoke, Betts! You have no idea how you look. I know you think you're as glamorous as anything, but you just look . . . cheap!" Which wasn't exactly how Betts looked; it was more that she looked silly, but Agnes would never be so cruel as to tell her so. Betts started smoking when she was still awkward, her elbows sharp angles, her collarbone too prominent. She looked like a student in a school play pretending to be a woman who smoked as she gestured exaggeratedly with her cigarette, and Agnes was embarrassed for her. "Why would you want people to think of you as fast?"

"Mother, I swear to you I'm not going to disgrace the family! I won't run off with the milkman or turn into a home wrecker. I'm almost eighteen years old. I should be allowed some privacy in my own life. And don't think I don't know that you throw away my cigarettes whenever you can find them! Don't think I don't know that!"

Agnes was always caught trying to save Betts from herself and then being shocked at Betts's ease in confronting her. Shocked at Betts's utter failure ever to accede gracefully to anything at all Agnes might say. It was clear to Agnes that often Betts debated an idea with her that, had it been put forth by Dwight or Claytor, or either one of the Butlers, Betts wouldn't even have remarked upon. It was hurtful, and when Betts accused her mother of confiscating her cigarettes, Agnes had merely lifted her head slightly and pressed her lips together in an expression of exasperation.

She hadn't thought she owed Betts any answer in the face of such rudeness, but, in fact, Agnes never threw those cigarettes away; she simply thought that if they were out of Betts's sight, they would also be out of Betts's mind. At first Agnes only hid them in a hatbox in her closet with the vague idea that she would return them to Betts eventually. Then she had taken to smoking a cigarette now and then when she couldn't sleep, or when her students had been especially tiresome that day in school, or just to relax after having the whole family to Sunday dinner. Usually she would stand at her window in the dark, but sometimes she would steal a moment in broad daylight, slipping from the kitchen out to the shed, or strolling along the alley beyond the hedge at the bottom of the garden.

Lily smoked, and no one thought twice about it. When Robert remarked once that smoking might be bad for her health, reminded her that the doctor had warned her of "smoker's cough," Lily, of course, pointed to the fact that he smoked a pipe himself. And she always said airily that she never inhaled, anyway, that she just enjoyed the opportunity to do nothing; she liked the excuse of a cigarette. "It's one of the greatest pleasures of life!" she said. And Agnes had no real reason to hide her own habit of smoking, except that she would lose the high ground in her ongoing struggle with Betts, and Agnes also truly savored her surreptitious and inconsequential rebellion.

With the house empty, though, Agnes had no need of any subterfuge. Pup sprawled on his back under the kitchen table, and she poured herself another cup of coffee, sitting on in the kitchen for a little while, just leaning her head back against her chair, doing nothing at all for the time being but inhaling and exhaling.

Without ever discussing it between themselves, Agnes and Will fell into the habit of his arriving late at night at least two or three times a week and staying over. Either he left before dawn, so that no one would notice his car, or he waited until midmorning and delivered freshly dug new potatoes or a nice plucked hen to the Drummonds' house, too, across the square, and no one thought anything about his comings and goings. Pup no longer barked when he heard Will come in the back door after the Scofield houses appeared to be shut up for the night. Lily had said to Agnes once that Will was the sort of man you only had to look at to know he liked dogs — to know that he liked animals, liked children. There was something about his ease within his own body; he moved with confident efficiency, no nervous hesitations. Agnes was always glad to see him, and he always had a treat in his pocket for Pup.

Agnes had been surprised to discover that in her early forties she experienced the same full-fledged lust that she had during her marriage, but she was far less concerned about Will's opinion of her. She never bothered to pretend anything with Will. In fact, some of the most sensual moments in her life were those she spent smoking a cigarette with Will while they were both still lazy and sated with sex. Or just before he touched her, as she undressed, when she insisted that she wanted just a moment to relax — it was mysteriously thrilling to her to light a cigarette while wearing nothing more than her plain white slip. And thrilling to him, too, even though he didn't approve of women smoking.

Once, when she had finished taking her hair down while sitting at her vanity and lit a cigarette before carefully unbuttoning her blouse and sliding it off onto the back of her chair, he had said she should at least come over and keep him company where he was stretched out on the bed. As soon as she was near enough, though, he slid his hand between her thighs and she stood still exactly like she was, with her feet slightly apart. He had held her there — long after her cigarette had dropped and burned a long scar in the floor — stroking her, but not letting her move toward him or away from him, and she had been near tears but also ecstatic by the time he released her. She was privately ashamed of her own arousal — which seemed wrong, somehow self-abasing, and she never got herself into that situation again, but she was helpless against the memory of it.

Agnes enjoyed sex with Will, and she enjoyed his company in the evenings well enough, but she was distressed more than she allowed herself to say when he began talking about getting married. In fact, she was surprised at the depth of her own consternation. She had made a light supper and they were sitting together at the table in the kitchen, taking their time over coffee and listening to the news, the first time he brought it up.

"I think we ought to begin thinking pretty seriously about getting married," he said and reached over to turn off the radio. "I'd like to ask you to consider it, Agnes, if you think you can put up with me." He was teasing her, which was disquieting, because the humor in his voice rested on the premise that she would accept without question, would possibly be relieved that finally he had brought it up.

"We could live in town or at the farm. We could keep both if we like. We'd have lots of room for the children . . . grandchildren," he said, but just matter-of-factly, in the way people ask a question when they already know the answer.

Agnes had shut the whole idea of the future out of her involvement with Will and found herself unable to think of what she wanted to say. "Oh, Will. Let's not worry about it right now," she said and got up and began stacking their plates in the sink.

Will sounded surprised, even injured. "You must have been thinking about this, too, Agnes. I didn't want you to think for a minute that I didn't intend to be honorable. Well, I didn't want you to think that I didn't feel about you . . . With how things have changed, now. The way we feel about each other. I didn't want you to think that it was only . . . ah, only about —"

"I never thought that," Agnes interrupted. "I haven't been worried. Will, I haven't really thought about it. Let's not talk about it tonight. You're so busy with the Agriculture Council . . . and all the children. Even if they meant not to care, they might be upset. I don't see any reason to make things more complicated."

"Well, my girls are only at home now and then, with their husbands, and Helen has the baby. Our children are all pretty much grown up. And why would they care?

They'd probably be glad," Will said, and Agnes uneasily entertained that idea for a few moments. The children probably would be glad. Agnes would finally be relieved of any financial worries — she wouldn't even have to teach unless she wanted to. And, also, if any one of her children felt responsible for her happiness, it would relieve him or her of that burden. But, still, she couldn't quite imagine working through the intricate convolutions of a marriage with Will, the constant adjustments as you find out more and more what the other person is like. She knew she didn't have the energy to deal with the inevitable guilt, to work up the patience, nor could she ever summon the eventual sustained state of forgiveness that's required in a marriage when each spouse proves to be not quite what the other expected. Agnes didn't have the desire to regain the emotional flexibility essential in a marriage.

"Well, Agnes. You know we can't keep carrying on like this," Will said. "Running around in secret. It makes me feel like a fool. That's just not the kind of man I've ever been. It's not the kind of person you've ever been, either. You're not at all like that."

"No? I'm not?" she asked, because she hadn't given much thought to being any particular kind of person, and she was intrigued that — at least in Will's opinion — she had become one.

"You know, Agnes, I honestly thought that of all the women I've ever known, you'd be the last one to be coy. Women always feel they have to pretend . . . I don't know . . . modesty? Or like they aren't really aware of what's happening. . . ." He was soft-voiced and musing, but also annoyed. She wondered if it would hurt Will's feelings that it hadn't crossed her mind to pretend any particular state of mind when she was with him, and, too, it occurred to her just now that her lack of pretense was probably because she wasn't at all in love with him.

"You aren't the sort of woman," he said earnestly, "who could possibly be so . . . well . . . It's not that I'm any expert, but no woman in the world can enjoy herself so much in bed and not be in love. And you must know that on *my* part . . ." He paused to gather his words carefully, and Agnes was shot through with a spike of amused irritation as he maintained a didactic solemnity.

"I'm feeling just as foolish as I did before I rushed off to Canada before we entered the first war. I even asked your father's permission just to say good-bye to you. Lord, I was a wreck! But what your father wanted to tell me was that I was a damned fool to go to Canada. That I'd have plenty of time to get killed for my own country. I had to press him to get him off the subject, because he was only telling me what I'd started to think myself. I'd lost all my courage overnight, and I —"

"That was perfectly natural," Agnes interrupted, but Will went on.

"No, I really had. And I wanted to talk to you. . . . When I finally got through to him that I wanted to see you before I left, he didn't turn a hair. 'She's down at the house, I think.' He hardly gave it a thought. I'll never forget him looking up at me for a minute, like he hadn't ever thought of that," Will went on.

"'Will Agnes care?' he said to me. But not . . . He

wasn't being sarcastic. Not unkind, I mean. I think he was just curious." Will paused for a moment, musing over Dwight Claytor's peculiar detachment.

"And you made me feel so much better. I'd gotten myself into a real fix, and I was homesick before I even left. But you told me I would be fine, that everyone admired me for what I was doing. Your brothers . . . Lord! I was relieved more than I can say. It's the thing that made it possible for me to get on the bus that night. But that's the sort of person you are, Agnes. I wouldn't have taken the liberty of saying good-bye to you without asking permission."

She looked at him for a minute, thoroughly astonished. She didn't remember a single thing about any of this.

"For goodness sake! I'm almost forty-six years old, Will! I've had a husband! I have children! What you're remembering . . . It wasn't ever like that . . ."

"Oh, it was. You were sitting out by the croquet court. You were sitting in the swing. I thought you looked so pretty." He paused for a moment. "Of course, I hadn't even gotten to know Sally yet. I don't want you to think that I would ever . . . But it was through you that I did get to know her eventually. She just seemed out of reach to all the boys in Washburn. We were afraid of her, she was so pretty. We didn't know anything about her, since we never dreamed we'd have a chance," he said.

Agnes had been uneasy the moment Will began to relate this tale, but at least for a few minutes it had been flattering. Now she was simply annoyed, and yet, she wasn't any good at letting someone else realize he'd made a mistake. Had put a foot wrong. Said something remark-ably stupid, given the point he was trying to make. She followed her inclination to save him embarrassment.

"*Wasn't* Sally so pretty! And she was smart, too. She was funny. You were a hero to her when you went off to Canada." In fact, it surprised Agnes as she spoke to remember that Sally had thought of Will as a hero. Sally Trenholm had been a good friend of Agnes's, and the prettiest girl in their class at Linus Gilchrest, but she had died only five years after she and Will were married, before she was even thirty years old.

"But, Agnes, you'd been there all my life! Right there next door. I knew you so well. I really believed you were the most serious love of my life. I so much wanted to have someone waiting for me. Not just my family. My mother. I wanted someone to talk about. I didn't want to seem so young, and I wanted to believe I had someone to make plans about." He ran his hand over his hair, pushing it off his forehead, which was a gesture he often made when he was perplexed.

"But it was Sally who wrote to tell me you got mar-ried," he went on. "I was surprised. You'd married War-ren Scofield! He seemed to me to be one of those men already . . . oh, out of our lives. In the same category as my father. As *your* father. Established, I mean. Someone who was all done. Who wasn't still becoming something. He was already doing what he had grown up to do. It seemed to me that you'd married into another life. Well . . . But to get that letter from Sally . . . that was a surprise. It was a sweet letter. She didn't want me to feel bad. That was something. That did set me up for a while. I didn't even know she remembered who I was."

Will was looking at her, and she realized he was expecting her to say something. "I'm sorry, what —"

"You must have known how I felt about you, though? Back then? When I joined up early, it was you I was hoping to impress. You'd always been right there, and then you'd grown up. . . . I think you've been in my mind one way or another all my life. If a disaster happened, for instance. Say, a tornado . . . Well, or this war. I always think, Is Agnes all right? So, you see what I mean?"

"I didn't have a single notion of how you felt, Will. I think you're just not remembering it right. You and I didn't even write to each other. Mama and I used to get news of you from your mother. And your grandmother. But, Will. You're making something romantic out of . . . just out of circumstances. We *have* always been friends. Of course we have. But that's not . . . It isn't like needing . . . Oh — I don't know. This is upsetting, Will. Let's not talk about it right now. Let's just let it lie for a while."

Will looked at her quietly for a moment, and Agnes knew immediately what he would say next. She was annoyed that she'd left herself open to it.

"Come on, Agnes. We're more than friends, for God's sake. I know you like being with me. I've never felt so at ease with anyone. I always worried . . . Well. I don't know . . . it was almost like I found out that you're an entirely different person than I thought I'd known. It's been a surprise. This has turned out to be a good time in my life, despite everything else. It's been a nice turn of events I never imagined. After Sally died, I knew that good things would happen still. I knew there'd be times I'd be pleased about something or other. But I didn't even guess that I'd ever feel the way I do."

Agnes startled herself by standing up with her hands clenched in the folds of her skirt. "I don't see why you insist we're more than friends, Will! We're not hurting anyone. I've thought about that. You're wrong about the children. They'd think I was betraying Warren. Why would we get married? It would just be too complicated. What you're saying . . . What you seem to mean . . . Will, it would be like getting married because we *dance* well together! Or . . . oh, because we made good bridge partners. It —"

Will had risen, too, and he shook his head wearily and rubbed his hand over his face as though he were waking himself up. "No matter how much you try to convince me, Agnes, I don't believe for one minute that you're comfortable with the situation the way it is now. I know you think I feel that it's only the honorable thing to do for us to get married. And I do think that! But it's more than that. What's happened with you and me . . . Well, to tell you the truth, it seems to me like something sacred! Not even Sally had the sort of trust you do. . . . But to listen to you . . . You make yourself sound like a sort of . . . You make yourself sound *careless* of your reputation. You aren't at all like the person you think you are."

Everything Will said made Agnes miserable. It was so unlike anything she thought herself. And, too, she felt peculiarly embarrassed for him, because he had revealed a kind of sentimental sanctimony that made him seem a little foolish to her. Agnes remained resolute in refusing to discuss it further, and Will didn't stay over. She knew she was at least a little like the woman she thought she was; it was Will who was not the person he believed himself to be. He hadn't thought out all the dailiness of marriage, he had only considered the propriety. His sense of honor annoyed her, even made him seem less attractive altogether. She supposed that made her less virtuous, certainly, than Will was, but Agnes realized that she wasn't especially concerned with honor. Or at least she wasn't interested in preserving the sort of respectability imposed by society. She had never thought of herself as dishonorable in the slightest, although, now that she considered it, the idea was unexpectedly exhilarating.

The most seductive aspect of seeing Will — the marvel of the sex between them in the face of a long-standing and dispassionate friendship — was that no one knew about it. It wasn't only another ordinary thing; it wasn't what people ever thought about if they saw either Agnes or Will just walking down the street alone, or even together. Or if the two of them ate dinner at the Monument Restaurant on Sunday night, greeting so many acquaintances. The knowledge that she was walking along in a tidy dress, her coat buttoned, her gloves adjusted, her hair combed, a little powder on her nose, when perhaps a half hour earlier she had been in bed with Will — well, it delighted her over and over again.

She did know that Will meant to save them from becoming a scandal. Of course she understood that she and Will were walking a fine line between respectability and licentiousness just by crossing the square together. She also knew, though, that if they were discovered, it would be she who would be held accountable. And it was that very tinge of edginess — the constant risk of being discovered and disapproved of — that was all that came between her and the hopeless feeling of inconsequence that had befallen her when she was standing on that chair in her schoolroom decorating the corkboard.

After the first few years of Agnes and Warren's marriage, Lily had thought Agnes was unbecomingly attuned to Warren. "Just let him pull himself together," Lily said. "Of course it upsets you. It worries me and Robert, too. Warren's a grown man, though. I don't think it helps if you indulge these . . . these *spells* of gloominess."

But Agnes resented Lily's implication that she had the inside track on Warren's nature, and, too, that Agnes was incapable of wrenching her attention away from Warren if he removed himself from her — or from the household itself — emotionally and sometimes actually. Getting up one morning and, out of the blue, hastily packing for a trip, for instance, and telling her very little about it. "You know I promised Uncle Leo I would go out to Chicago," he would finally reveal, as Agnes trailed behind him while he gathered shirts and ties.

"But we planned . . . What should I say to Lily and Robert about Thanksgiving?" And her voice would become plaintive.

"If that's all you're worried about . . . Good God, that's not like you, Agnes! Don't nag at me like that. . . . Damn!

I don't have my ticket. I've got to get going. . . . Oh, I'll be back by then." And Agnes would watch him escape once more from his own house. When the children asked where he was, she adopted Warren's strategy, because otherwise she was too vulnerable; otherwise it might seem to the children that their father was running away from her.

"He had to go out to Chicago. Uncle Leo depends on him. . . . Your father is very good at the sort of diplomacy . . . could talk the birds right out of the trees. . . ." They never asked further; they were never especially worried, only curious. When he remained at home but fell into weeks at a time of a paralysis of sorts, Agnes had a harder time altogether. During those spells Warren was less irritable, but it was as if every word he spoke had to be dredged up from a well, and his mouth seemed too stiff to properly fashion the few sentences he managed to articulate. He often retreated to his office at the Company until late at night, but now and then he was unable to do even that. He would stay in bed and sleep on and off through several days and nights.

During those sieges, Agnes simply said to the children that their father wasn't feeling well, or that he had too much responsibility, had been working too hard. She was left, however, caught in the middle of pity for and fury at him, and her unspecified anxiety vibrated through the household like a plucked wire.

It was during these occasional episodes that Agnes would astonish and frighten the children with a sudden outburst of inexplicable rage. She became crazed over some little thing so insignificant that the children scattered, if they could, and let her wear herself out roaming up and down the stairs because, say, all the umbrellas had disappeared. She would be seemingly inconsolable that none of the children had put them back in the umbrella stand beside the front door. And how could they possibly know that their perceived forgetfulness made her feel betrayed? How could they know that under duress their mother considered them her only allies against the rest of the world?

Agnes lost track of how young the children were, forgot that even if they had been outside with the umbrellas, they would certainly have been under her supervision. Or under some adult's watchful eye. Dwight and Claytor were each separately grief-stricken when Agnes fell into these odd spells of enraged despair. Betts only became angry and indignant herself and persistently complained about the unfairness of it all.

"I never took an umbrella, Mama! I never did!" She would follow Agnes all around the house until Agnes acknowledged her.

"Well, all right, Betts. I know you didn't mean to lose it, and you probably don't even remember. . . ."

Howard, since he was so young and had the three older children translating his experience for him, generally didn't realize that anything unusual was going on.

Agnes had fallen back into dependable stability after Warren's death, and she mistakenly believed that her children would remember serenity and competence as clearly, and for as long a time, as they would remember injustice or grief. By the time the children were grown, Agnes didn't even recall having been angry at or ever behaving with less than the best intentions for the children. She assumed that her children would never forget how much fun they had in their parents' house. There was no one in the world who was as much fun as Warren often was, Agnes thought, in spite of whatever dark moods occasionally overcame him. And her children would have agreed with her, but Agnes did realize that his popularity had come at the expense, to some degree, of her own reputation within the family. After all, she was still there at Scofields, whereas their father had long ago become someone mythical.

After Will first brought up the subject of marriage, he kept at it; he pointed out all sorts of benefits that he thought perhaps she had neglected to consider, and when she failed to succumb he was annoyed. "You're not being reasonable, Agnes." Agnes never admitted to Will that for months she pondered exactly that notion, thinking that Will might be right. Perhaps she was unreasonable. There was no question that Will was an easier person than Warren. Will always went along pretty much on medium speed; he was dependable and good-hearted. Being married to Will would be much easier than being married to Warren had been, but she dreaded the idea of all the unsurprising days they would spend alone together.

In any case, no matter how much she worried at the bone of that idea, she always concluded that she didn't love Will, really, even in the way she did love Lily and Robert. She liked Will, but she didn't worry about him. She wished him well in every way, but her own happiness wasn't contingent upon his welfare, and, she thought, as good-natured as he was, he was also a little boring. Nevertheless, the continuing fact of the otherness of the people she and Will became when they were in bed made Agnes feel as if she were visiting somewhere exotic without even leaving home.

Chapter Four

DURING THE EARLY YEARS of the success and expansion of Scofields & Company, even before it became Washburn's primary employer, the town as a whole conferred upon the Scofield family a particularly American idea of nobility, which had to do with an ill-defined combination of power, money, good looks, and temperament, and almost nothing to do with heredity. And, even though other industries had grown up in Washburn and were flourishing, the Scofields' prominence, in particular, remained an integral part of the identity of the town.

The Scofield family engaged the imagination of the people of Washburn. After all, Leo, John, and George had humble enough beginnings, but they had managed to develop an enterprise that began as no more than a small foundry into a major engine manufacturing company. And then, too, Leo and John had married the beautiful Marshal sisters, whose family had settled the area that was now Marshal County, which encompassed the town of Washburn. The communal legend was that Leo Scofield had been shrewd and incomparably wise, whereas his handsome brother, John, was a notorious but endearing scoundrel, although anyone who had dealt with one of those two brothers in the flesh had come to terms with each man's complexity. But any myth is contingent upon generalities, and the town had taken custody of the characterization of those early Scofields.

The largely affectionate regard in which the members of the Scofield clan were held relied largely on the townspeople's knowledge of the details. Leo Scofield, for instance, had maintained that all the Scofields were born on the ides of the month, just as he had been. Just as his youngest brother, George, had been. It was of no consequence to anyone that *John* Scofield's birthday fell on February fifth. That was an inconvenient fact that was either ignored or reinterpreted. After all, birth records of the early nineteenth century, as far west as Ohio, were notoriously unreliable. Somewhere along the way John's birthdate may have been mistranscribed. Lily and Warren had been born on September fifteenth, within eight hours of each other, as had Robert Butler — born before either of the others but on that same day in 1888 — which conferred upon him a tentative *Scofieldness* in the communal subconscious of Washburn, which Robert unwittingly legitimized when he married Lily Scofield.

In the next generation the same coincidence had proven true in every case except for Claytor Scofield, who had just barely missed being born on the fifteenth of April. He arrived two days earlier on the thirteenth. But everyone in town said that he was clearly so much a Scofield that it was probably just the case that he was born early. Everyone knew that Scofields were born on the ides, and no one took any account of those two days. No one except Claytor as he grew older, and birthday after birthday, he was reminded by the other children in the house that he couldn't be a real Scofield, which was what he suspected, anyway, with Dwight always right there ahead of him, accomplishing everything with brilliance. Of course, Claytor was only being teased — fondly, his mother insisted — but he dreaded the celebration of each new year of his life.

Certainly there were other families far wealthier and also closely watched, but the Scofields were so numerous and more attractive en masse — more interesting altogether. And because of their collective charisma, this second generation of children contended with more than average attention even from relative strangers, but they were also the subjects of collective pride of a sort. The people of Washburn expected them to excel — expected them to be far more publicly successful than any children from the prominent families of Coshocton, for instance, or Palmyra, or Centerburg. Those children living in the Scofield compound incurred the same variety of loyalty in the community as did the Washburn High School Wildcats, who were counted on year after year to have a winning season at the very least. It was simply assumed that Dwight and Claytor, Trudy and Betts, and Howard would be respectably accomplished — the boys, at least — and that Betts and Trudy would be uncommonly attractive and make wonderful marriages. All of them were expected to live productive and happy — though virtuous — lives.

In April of 1943, however, when word spread that Dwight and Trudy had gotten married, those very townspeople proprietarily rooting for the welfare of those children were quick to be appalled by that union. It was unthinkable that first cousins would marry. People wondered to each other if the marriage would even be recognized in Ohio, where it was, in fact, illegal to form so close an alliance. Trudy and Dwight had gotten married somewhere in Texas, and, well . . . Texas wasn't even as respectable as, say, Charleston or Savannah. No one in Washburn knew anyone who was held in particularly high regard who also lived in Texas.

And, too, hadn't it always been the case that it was *Claytor* and Trudy who were in each other's company all through their teens? Each a shadow of the other? If first cousins *could* marry . . . what had happened behind everyone's back? It was upsetting and hurtful not only to people who knew the family well but even to people who had never met them. And the two had gotten married so far away from home — and no wonder! In the South almost anything was legal between family members. Dwight and Trudy's families hadn't even known until two days before the ceremony when Trudy telephoned her father to break the news, and then Dwight called his family. Trudy was on an extended visit to a friend from Mount Holyoke who lived in Austin, Texas, near Randolph Field, where Dwight was stationed.

In Washburn the main sticking point was probably the confusion caused by those two boys' names. Agnes and

Warren Scofield had settled on the idea of using Agnes's maiden name for their first son before Agnes's little brother, Dwight Claytor, was even born. When Agnes had her own child, only five months later, it hadn't crossed anyone's mind to worry about future misunderstandings, when Dwight Claytor's last name was also Claytor Scofield's first name. After all, they were still infants to whom no surname yet adhered.

Since most people in Washburn hadn't considered the nature of the Scofield-Butler-Claytor connections for years and years, it took more than a week for everyone finally to conclude that Dwight and Trudy were not, after all, the first cousins they had come to be thought of. In fact, it seemed to be the case that they weren't related in any way at all. It took a few weeks more for most people to unravel the exact relationship between Dwight Claytor and Trudy Butler — as it had been previous to their marriage, of course. Dwight Claytor was Trudy's mother's — Lily Scofield Butler's — first cousin Warren's wife's brother! No one could sort out if that made Dwight some sort of distant uncle or cousin by marriage to his own bride, but most of the furor died down when everyone decided it was certainly not a blood relationship.

The whole upheaval might have been resolved much sooner, though, if the older generation of the family hadn't remained silently uneasy about the marriage themselves. For one thing, they all remembered very well that during their adolescence it had been Claytor and Trudy who had spent hours and hours together. "But it was because they simply were complements of each other,"

Lily insisted. "Like ice cream and cake. Or . . . rhubarb and strawberry. Like peaches and cream."

"Well, now," Robert said, "you're whetting my appetite for a little something sweet. I believe we ought to have some dessert." Lily, Robert, and Agnes were seated around the Butlers' table after supper, and Robert was merely making an effort to lessen the sense of urgency about what was, after all, a fait accompli. But Lily waved him off with only a whiff of a smile.

"But when you think of it? Isn't that the way you see it?" Lily asked, leaning forward with determination. "Trudy and Claytor would talk for hours about nothing at all, but I never thought it was anything romantic between them. Did you? They were like brother and sister. Don't you think so? I mean it always seemed to me just good luck that Trudy had a cousin she liked so much."

Neither Agnes nor Robert commented, though. For a while, when the four older children entered the highly charged years of their teens, it had been impossible to be in the same room with Claytor and Trudy and not feel the physical attraction between them, no matter what they were talking about. Once Agnes had passed Claytor on the staircase, where he was standing at the window of the first landing, and it was clear to her that he hadn't even realized she was in the vicinity. He had been standing very still, with his fists pressed against the glass panes on either side of the one through which he was gazing as if he had been frozen in place.

Upstairs Agnes had looked out her own window in the same direction. Across the way, Trudy and Betts were lying on the porch roof outside Trudy's bedroom, sun-bathing. The girls had talked about it earlier, because Betts wanted to try her theory that if each of them put a rubber band around her feet to hold them together — so that they would stay upright without any effort on the girls' part — it would make it possible to tan the fronts of their legs.

They were in their bathing suits lying on separate blankets. Betts had still looked like a girl growing up. She appeared to be tenuously connected, as if she might fly apart, might not hold fast at the joints; she had the thin, attenuated look of a praying mantis, and she was holding a book up over her head so she could read. She had gotten bored with the effort of vanity and wanted to get back to *Villette*. Trudy lay next to her, and the contrast was startling. Trudy was all of a piece, rounded and sleek like a little house cat; she was so still she almost appeared to be asleep as she lay with the straps of her bathing suit unhooked and her arms lying lax at her side. Her skin had turned golden after weeks of summer, and her state of seeming entirely self-contained and quiet — while Betts shifted this way and that, fidgeting and clearly uncomfortable — made even Agnes want to reach out and touch Trudy. Grasp her wrist, tap her lightly on the shoulder, in order to become the object of her reflective, particular attention.

Agnes moved away from the window and experienced a long, clear moment of recognition. She remembered being unable even to look at Warren without thinking of all the ways his body could accommodate her. She literally couldn't take his hand without a sort of swoon washing through her, and it had been miraculous to Agnes that

Warren had been subject to the same obsession with her. But until she had seen Claytor gazing fixedly at Trudy, Agnes had never thought to imagine lust from a man's point of view. Trudy was so petite. She was small and delicate and completely feminine. Claytor would want to protect her at the very same instant he would want to have sex with her, and there's nothing dainty about having sex. The contradiction of Claytor's imagination where Trudy was concerned would be considerable. The tension of those opposing desires, Agnes thought, would be uncommonly erotic.

And, in fact, Claytor did feel protective of Trudy just in everyday life at Scofields. She was so slight among the tall Scofields, so easily lost track of in the muddle of family. She was subdued in the face of debates and arguments and opinions that flew freely among Dwight and Claytor and Betts, and eventually Howard, if they were all sitting in Trudy's garden after a tennis game, for instance, or if they were out at the lake, swimming. Among all the light-haired, fair-skinned family, Trudy's dark hair and olive skin made her seem foreign. Her quietly observant composure seemed mysterious, seemed to be a kind of indulgent wisdom with which a foreigner would observe a clutch of noisy Americans. And probably not the least of the attraction between Claytor and Trudy was the fact that each was the other's forbidden country.

The only person Claytor confided in was Dwight, when they happened both to have retreated to the porch to read one summer afternoon. The second summer they were home from college, Dwight headed out to the porch with a stack of assigned reading on a perfect day. One of those rare days the family always referred to as "Goldilocks" days — a family shorthand that stemmed from Betts's childhood observations. He found Claytor already in the swing with a book propped on the armrest so that he could look down from his slouched position and read.

Dwight put his small stack of books on the table beside the rocker. "Looks like you're reading for the pleasure of it," Dwight said, gesturing to the books he had just put down along with a notebook and a fistful of sharpened pencils.

"No, not really. Well, I guess I am," Claytor said. "This book's assigned, but I've gotten interested in it. Probably I'm going to have to read it again. I forgot to take notes about forty pages ago." Claytor righted himself, closing his book by grasping it so that one finger held his place. He leaned forward, resting his elbows on his knees. "I don't know what to do," he said. He was earnest and spoke softly as if he might be overheard. "Can I ask you something? Do you have a minute?"

"Sure," Dwight said. "Fire away. I don't know that I'll be much help, but I'll be glad to give it a shot."

"It's just that I don't know what to do, Dwight. Probably I can't do anything. I don't think there's anything *to* do!" Claytor admired Dwight more than any other man he knew, with the possible exception of Uncle Robert. And Claytor was wrung out by the several years of his secret, overwhelming devotion to and desire for his cousin Trudy Butler.

Dwight listened with careful attention and was surprised. "But you haven't even been dating anyone else! I'd been wondering why. You aren't giving yourself a chance. You need to give yourself a chance to . . . overcome this. Well, I suppose that's a little dramatic. After all, it's only Trudy. Good Lord! You've known her all your life. We all love Trudy. But I think you've confused perfectly natural feelings for her. . . . There're some terrific girls at school. There're some terrific girls right here in town."

Claytor looked at Dwight despairingly and moved his head just enough to signify the impossibility of what Dwight proposed.

Dwight tried not to sound annoyed. "You'll get over it. Trudy will, too. After all, you hardly see each other except over school breaks. You probably shouldn't come home so often. You could find some sort of summer job at school. Don't brood about it! Nothing's worse, and it's just Trudy, anyway. It's probably mostly a habit —"

"It's not a habit," Claytor interrupted. "If you'd ever felt this way about anyone, you'd know that it's about as far from being a habit as anything can be. It's nothing I could change by just making up my mind to do it. I thought you'd pretty much fallen for Cleo Morris. You spend a lot of time —"

"Oh, Lord, Claytor! Cleo's just . . . She's just a friend. We're just friends. We like each other, but not . . . I don't want to feel the way you do about Trudy! I like so many girls. Any girl with a sense of humor. A girl to flirt with. To have fun with. I don't want to feel serious about a girl right now. Good God! And I don't want any girl to feel serious about me. I don't have time. I have so much debt. . . . And it seems to be pretty miserable, anyway. It doesn't seem to me that you and Trudy are having any fun."

Claytor considered this for a little while and sighed. "I guess you're right. I should stay away from here when Trudy's home. And you're right, too. We're not having fun. Not fun, exactly." Claytor sat quietly for a moment, still perplexed, but then he smiled a defeated thanks at Dwight and went back to his book.

Dwight, however, had trouble concentrating on his own reading. Trudy as an object of desire had never crossed his mind, and as he sat on the porch reading, trying to break through to the meaning underneath the clotted text of Peterson's *Honor or Justice in America: The Making of American Law,* his mind drifted back to the idea of Trudy and Claytor. It was an impossible situation; he couldn't think of any satisfactory resolution to offer Claytor. And, oddly enough, the rest of that summer, Dwight could scarcely keep his attention from resting on Trudy whenever she was among them. He had never thought of her as someone who was more than attractive, but she was, he came to see, quite lovely in an unusual way. "Pretty" wasn't exactly right, because it was everything about her manner and looks taken in context that was so compelling. She was a dark, inflexible exclamation point set down in the middle of all the wheeling blond asterisks of the rest of her family.

Over that summer and through the next year, Dwight found that he, too, was enormously attracted to Trudy, although he would never reveal it; he wouldn't cause either Claytor or Trudy any further worry or unhappiness. He was taken aback and ashamed of himself. By necessity, he adopted an avuncular attitude toward her, which — to his surprise — allowed him absolute freedom to seek out her company. When he came home for Christmas, for instance, he stopped first to greet Agnes and Betts and Howard, putting their presents under the tree, and then went off to deliver his gifts to the Butler family. Dwight had come home without Claytor, who had accepted an invitation to spend Christmas with a friend in St. Louis. "It wouldn't be Christmas without finding out what sort of situation Aunt Lily's gotten herself into now," Dwight said.

Betts and Howard and even Agnes urged him — for heaven's sake! — to hurry on to the Butlers', in a high-spirited bit of teasing, because Dwight was alluding to the year before: he and Claytor had arrived at the Butlers' house when only Lily was at home. She had called loudly for them to come in. Had told them to hurry. They had found her in the sitting room decorating the Christmas tree, but trapped stock-still in a swath of spun-glass angel hair caught all around her. "If you two don't get me out of here soon, I'm going to wet my pants! Robert won't be home for at least two hours, and Trudy's off somewhere."

Christmas of 1939, though, Dwight had scrupulously bought both Betts and Trudy the same gift, a large stuffed bear with an Oberlin sweater and pennant. Trudy was delighted to see Dwight, delighted when she opened her present, embracing the bear and sinking her face into its warm fleece. Before Dwight could stop himself, he spoke up. "I wouldn't mind trading places with that bear just now."

Trudy raised her face to gaze at him in surprise, and then she laughed. "You're already missing whatever girl you're in love with right now, aren't you? Honestly, Dwight! You've probably been pinned to every pretty girl at Oberlin by now." Dwight showed up at home off and on with one girl or another, while Claytor came always on his own. And it was a great relief to Trudy to have Dwight as a confidant, although she never mentioned Claytor at all unless it would have seemed strange if she remained silent. And, even then, she changed the subject as soon as she could. Dwight began to think that she wasn't much interested in Claytor anymore, and he wrote Claytor that reassuring news as tactfully as possible.

In 1943, however, in light of Dwight and Trudy's marriage, Robert and Lily Butler, and Agnes Scofield, too, separately revisited memories of various childhood incidents involving Dwight Claytor, Claytor Scofield, and Trudy Butler. Possible misinterpretations of past events popped into their heads at odd hours of the day or night. But eventually each concluded that it was inconceivable that either Dwight or Claytor would ever in his life knowingly do anything that might cause the other so much distress — and certainly not something as momentous as marrying a girl the other was in love with. Lily's and Robert's anxiety was for Trudy, herself, who was the soul of moral propriety — not of virtue necessarily, but of honor. She would never have put herself between two men she had always been fond of.

The whole thing, though — the surprise of the marriage, what seemed to be its furtiveness — left Agnes and the Butlers and Uncle George Scofield unsettled, even when they factored in the difficulties of transportation and the uncertainties of wartime life. None of them spoke of their misgivings, however, because it would have been traitorous in some way they couldn't quite pin down. Claytor and Trudy wouldn't ever have married each other in any case, since they were related. But none of the family knew if Claytor had transformed his infatuation with Trudy into no more than a cousinly affection.

A month or so after the news of the marriage, Uncle George approached Agnes where she sat alone on the small side porch, doing nothing at all other than trying to stay cool one hot afternoon. George was the last of his generation of Scofields still living, and he was the only Scofield of his generation with whom Agnes had ever been comfortable.

She had admired Warren's uncle Leo but had always felt shy in his company, and she had done her best to stay out of the way of Warren's father, John Scofield, whose attentions toward her had been secretively sly and lecherous, disguised by a pretense of affectionate teasing. But George Scofield, the youngest of those three brothers, with his eccentricities, his gentle curiosity, his elegance — Agnes had always liked him. When she saw him crossing the wide yard in her direction, carrying with him some object or other, her spirits lifted. She looked forward to being distracted from the heat by one of Uncle George's reimaginings of a Civil War battle or some new intrigue he had inferred. He often brought along items from his collection of memorabilia to illustrate one or another of the incidents he described. This afternoon he carried an old jar of some viscous, murky brown substance.

"It's just a jar of peaches," he said when he was about ten feet away and saw her look with apparent apprehension at what he was carrying. "Can I join you here for a little while?" he asked, just as Agnes had gotten up to dust off and reposition an old wooden rocker that had been abandoned to the elements.

"Would you like some lemonade, Uncle George?" But he was declining even as she asked.

"No, no. Just some shade. I don't require another thing. Don't trouble yourself." He put the jar on the table between them. "A jar of peaches put up by Adelaide Murry in June of eighteen sixty-one," he said. "They were in the basement of a farmhouse that was right in the middle of the battle of Gettysburg. Now that's a fantastic thing, isn't it? Her husband was a captain in the Union Army. But he was with Grant's men, fighting in Mississippi. Out in Tennessee, as well."

"You'd think it would have been broken somewhere along the way," Agnes said. "That is amazing." She gazed at the peaches that had turned to a muddy sludge over their eighty-odd years, and she reminded herself that she and Lily needed to rotate the fruit and tomatoes they put up every year so they would use up the older ones first.

"When I used to be able to travel more easily . . . while Leo and John stayed home making my fortune . . . Well,

Leo did, anyway, though John was the best salesman I ever knew in my life. Because he liked to listen to people. Liked to hear all the stories they wanted to tell about themselves. At least for a while. . . . Well. *I* spent all my time searching those battlefields. . . . But, in any case, on one of my last forays I came upon these peaches. And I found out the story of Adelaide and Edward Murry. It's always interested me. I haven't ever been able to decide in the end if it's a happy or a sad story."

He leaned back in the rocker, stretching his long legs out almost to the edge of the porch, crossing his arms comfortably over his chest. Even now George Scofield was the handsomest man Agnes had ever seen. Tall and lean and patrician to such a degree that his good looks had never had any emotional or visceral effect. It was as though he had been so perfectly invented that his appearance didn't engage the observer's imagination. Or that's what Agnes concluded. It was how she'd always felt, and George had never had any romantic involvement as far as she knew; he had never married.

"What is the story, Uncle George? What happened to them? The Murrys, I mean. Not the peaches."

"Oh, well . . . I wouldn't say it's exactly that something happened to them. But it was three years that Edward Murry was in the war before he was wounded pretty badly and had to make his way home in the summer of sixty-three. Adelaide had put up these peaches two years earlier." He picked up the jar and turned it in his hand to read the label she had affixed. "You see here," he said, holding it out to Agnes so she could see it for herself.

"'Pickled Peaches, June, eighteen sixty-one,'" he said aloud and then turned it back to read it again himself, pondering it a moment before he put it down again.

"Those peaches were waiting for her husband — no one had opened them when Edward Murry came home from the war ... when he walked up the steps, crossed the porch, and didn't stop to knock on his own front door. Even though he'd been wounded, Agnes, just imagine the sort of gladness he was feeling! Then, the story goes, he was greeted by his wife, who was right at that moment nursing her infant baby."

Agnes was looking out at the hot, thick light beyond the porch, waiting for him to continue. She gave a start when she realized he hadn't said a thing for some moments and that she had nearly dozed off.

"Ah! Well! It's a happy story, then," she remarked.

"Oh, I don't think anyone can know that. Who knows what happened when Edward met that baby? But he seems to have adopted him as his own child. I did check the documents in the courthouse. That baby, Duncan Murry, was born April of eighteen sixty-three. No other child was born to the Murrys as far as I could find out, and it was a Duncan Murry who eventually sold the place, so he must have inherited it. The parts of the story I turned up do seem happy enough. Adelaide and Edward lived there with little Duncan — eventually with Duncan and his wife — almost twenty-five years longer. But that baby was born in eighteen sixty-three. Edward was out west then. He'd been out west with Grant for two and a half years."

Agnes turned her attention to Uncle George's expression, but it gave no hint of whatever he was getting at. "Well, then he must have been glad to be home, Uncle George," she finally said, thinking that he was waiting for her to draw a conclusion. But he didn't say anything, and he, too, merely gazed out at the waning day.

"Wasn't he?" she asked. "I don't — Oh! Oh, you mean you don't think the baby could have been Edward Murry's son? But that's just silly. One of those stories! Edward Murry could have come home on a furlough . . ."

"He may well have. I couldn't find a record of it."

"I'll tell you what I think," Agnes said, eager to change the subject, which she found distasteful and melancholy. "I think that whatever had happened, Adelaide and Edward just never even mentioned it at all. I think Adelaide jumped up to meet him as he came in the door and that Edward Murry was delighted to have a son! He had lived through those battles. He had seen men die . . . he had killed men. What difference would it make where that little boy had come from?"

"I hope you're right. I hope that's how it was. I wish I knew a man that would feel that way. Well, though, Agnes, the reason I've been thinking about it . . . I've been turning it over in my mind since Dwight and Trudy got married. I want you to consider this, because all sorts of trouble can come of people not knowing things. Then again, I think that sometimes ignorance . . . Well, I wouldn't say it's bliss, but sometimes you might say that ignorance is required to sustain contentment. And I don't plan to mention any of this to anyone but you."

"For goodness sake! What? What is it, Uncle George? Is there something serious that's happened?"

"It's Warren's father I've been thinking about, Agnes. Ever since Dwight and Trudy got married. I wonder about him every time my eye falls on this jar of peaches. John was my brother, and there were times when I was young that there was no one else in the world I liked so much. Leo seemed awfully stern, you see. John was full of . . . oh . . . energy. Full of fun. But, then, you knew him, too. He turned into a man who seemed to be trying his best to make himself miserable. By the time he was your father-in-law, I don't think there were any traces left of his . . . well, I can't think how to describe it. He wasn't ever able to get back his happiness. He couldn't handle his drinking. It was a sad thing, because he wasn't even good at enjoying it. His drinking and all that carousing, I mean. By the time he died, I had been thinking that it was only a matter of time, anyway. . . . I was sorry about it, of course. No. No, I was sad. I missed him so much the way he'd been when I was growing up. But I have to say that when I think back about it, now, I was relieved, too. I didn't know I'd been expecting something terrible to happen to him. But when it did I thought, Oh, yes. Well, now we've crossed that bridge," George said, stretching his legs so that the rocking chair canted backward alamingly.

"But, you know, Agnes, the year or so before your mother had Dwight — oh, you were probably still at Linus Gilchrest — John was just full of how beautiful your mother was. He claimed no woman north of the Mason-Dixon line ever could have her kind of beauty.

He'd say that anytime. Of course, his own wife was considered a beauty all over Marshal County. Lillian, and Leo's wife, too. Audra. The Marshal sisters ... I used to hear people who hadn't even seen them talk about how good-looking they were thought to be.

"I went with John and your mother — and two of your brothers, I think — out to Judge Lufton's to watch the harness racing. We went a few times. John was right about your mother. She was a beautiful woman."

"She was. She certainly was," Agnes agreed. "It's nice to think of Mama going to the races. She loved them. Before Warren and I were married, he and Lily took me and Mama and Edson out to Judge Lufton's. But I don't remember Warren's father being there. I guess he might have been. I always thought later that it might have been the happiest day of Edson's life. Lily made a big fuss over him. That must have been nineteen seventeen. And, you know, neither Mama nor Edson lived even another year." Edson had died just two days after he came down with the flu, the very day after Agnes's mother had given birth to Dwight. Not much more than a week later Catherine died of the same thing. She had never even held her youngest son. In fact, Agnes wasn't sure her mother had ever understood that she had given birth to him.

"Yes. Of course I know that. I remember that," George said. "It was a terrible time. John was drinking too much by then, and carrying on. Although it was your mother he raved on about. I've been remembering it more than I like, Agnes. John was out at your place whenever he could get away. He wouldn't come into the office, and Leo would be beside himself. And his poor wife. Poor Lillian. But I don't believe Warren had any idea. Neither did your father. He was making a name for himself in the legislature then. He wasn't at home much, of course."

Agnes leaned back in her chair and looked out at the light as it had narrowed to a slant in just the time of their conversation. She carefully noted the crisp edges of the shadow of the house as it elongated over the yard. And she tried not to think of anything else except the tall chimneys, as their shadows lengthened disproportionately across the lawn in contrast to the softer, mutable shadows of the trees.

"Oh . . . ," she finally said in a long, downward-falling breath of dismay. "Oh! You can't think that my mother and John Scofield! Mama wouldn't . . ." But Agnes felt a flickering ignition of anger at her careless, careless mother, and also a reawakening of fury at her lecherous father-in-law, John Scofield. "Well. I don't believe anything at all happened between my mother and John Scofield! I just don't believe it. I don't even remember her mentioning John Scofield! I don't know if she even knew he existed! Mama was so . . . She wasn't connected to the town, really. To any people . . . She didn't ever like living here, and she pretty much disapproved of anyone who did like living here. She counted it as a mark of . . . oh . . . of mediocrity," Agnes said.

"Besides," she went on, after a pause during which she waited for Uncle George to recant what he had just said, to say that of course she was right, that now he saw it much more clearly. But George didn't say a thing. "Besides!

Uncle George, you're just wrong! You're just wrong about all this, and it's truly unbecoming of you to tell me you suspect my mother . . . suspect her and your own brother! You never should have imagined a thing like that. It makes me really angry. . . . You know it can't be true. It would mean Trudy and Dwight . . . why, they'd be related, too. It's only Trudy and Claytor who're cousins, Uncle George. It's beyond me to understand why in the world you told me about it. Trudy and Dwight are married! Of course they're not cousins! Otherwise why not *Claytor* and Trudy . . . ?"

"Well, you're right about all that, Agnes. I do think that John . . . I know that John carried on a flirtation with your mother. But it could have been that it was entirely platonic. It's certainly possible that Dwight and Trudy aren't connected by anything but circumstance. Well, and now by marriage, of course. It's all conjecture, after all. Not worth worrying about. No one ever knows why two people get married, anyway. Claytor and Trudy probably grew out of their whole romance. And even if Dwight and Trudy have children . . . Well, I don't think it'll make a bit of difference."

The notion, though, that John Scofield and her mother might have conceived that baby — that infant who was Dwight — took away any other words Agnes might have said to George Scofield, who didn't seem to expect conversation as he sat alongside her for another ten minutes or so. She was speechless with anger at him, not because he was the messenger, but because all at once it was clear to Agnes that George Scofield's love of history, his pursuit of artifacts, stemmed from his own lack of involvement in life as it was lived day in and day out. She decided in those few minutes that she had never really liked him after all; he seemed to her now no more interesting than a person whose sole obsession was collecting butterflies, chloroforming them and arranging them carefully in exhibition cases. There was a morbid quality about collecting; she was appalled at the thought of the isolated, secret, prurient glee Uncle George must have felt when he discovered Adelaide Murry's signed and dated jar of peaches.

Finally he began to gather himself together to go home. "People make such a mess for themselves," Uncle George said, with no particular emphasis, just as an observation. "You know, in the South people often marry cousin to cousin. To keep the land. Or to gain more land. Not the Negroes, though. Even when they were slaves. It's against what they believe. It's a taboo. And, of course, as you say, your father was at home now and then. Maybe there's nothing to it at all, Agnes." He stepped cautiously down the stairs onto the grass. "In any case we'll never know one way or another. But it didn't seem right not to tell you once it was in my head. It seemed you ought to know of the possibility, at least. But I guess we ought to assume things are just as they appear to be."

Agnes looked after him as he made his way tentatively along the path of stepping stones. She was shockingly enraged; she didn't dare allow herself to say a word, but when he was all the way across the yard, Agnes noticed the jar of peaches still sitting on the table. She picked up the jar and examined it once more, turning it in her hand.

And then she just let it fall to the paving stones — she did not fling it — and it made a satisfactory crack and gurgle when it hit the ground, although it also gave off such a sweet and concentrated odor of decay that Agnes turned away and went inside.

When Dwight Claytor was assigned as a navigator with a B-17 bomber crew and was eventually stationed in England, at Deopham Green, no one except Agnes thought any more about Dwight and Trudy's marriage, except to be surprised that Trudy didn't come home when she was pregnant or even after she gave birth to a daughter. Trudy had decided to share an apartment in New York with the wife and baby of one of Dwight's crew members so that the two of them could trade off nursery duties, and she took a secretarial job at Merriman Oil Corporation.

By the time the war ended, their marriage seemed always to have been the way things were. Trudy and Dwight had a little girl, Amelia Anne Claytor, and Trudy was pregnant again by the time Dwight was finally demobilized. By then Claytor, too, was married, although no one had been able to attend the wedding because he was only briefly stationed in Biloxi, where he met his wife, and which was too far to travel during the war.

By the end of the war, Betts and Howard, too, had both had enough adventures of their own that they thought their childhood was behind them, and they thought their growing up was comprised entirely of those years they had lived at Scofields under Agnes's supervision. All of them but Dwight — who wanted nothing more than to take his family home — were wearied by the prospect of adjusting once again to the naïveté, the provincialism, of their hometown. They were uncomfortable with the pity they felt for those people they loved who had spent the years of the war just going along as usual. They felt sorry that they could never explain real life to their parents or their aunts and their uncles, who no doubt believed that the important things that happened to them were whatever had happened in Washburn, Ohio.

Part Two

Chapter Five

DURING THEIR CHILDHOOD, and when they were away during the war, Dwight and Claytor, Howard and Betts, and even Trudy Butler considered the houses and grounds and fences and sheds of Scofields to be entirely Agnes's domain. Robert Butler tended his garden but was otherwise taken up with his writing and teaching, and he was frequently invited to take part in literary conferences, and sometimes to receive honorary degrees or a prize of some sort. Lily saw to her own house in a sort of slapdash way, an easiness with her household that her nephews and niece admired.

Their mother had always been finicky about domestic things: making slipcovers for the furniture to protect it from the summer sun, worrying over the shabbiness of the curtains — waiting until fabric went on sale and then sewing new ones herself for weeks of evenings, during which she was defensive and irritated, as if she had been wronged somehow, as if her children had commented on the state of the draperies, or, in fact, had even noticed them.

Agnes went about the days with certainty and maintained an efficient household in which there were no untoward surprises. There were never the sorts of amusing disasters in Agnes's house that befell the Butler household, and with which Lily often regaled the rest of the family. The time, for instance, when Robert and Lily had been out of town and their housekeeper, Mrs. Harvey, had taken it upon herself to remove and dust all the books and thoroughly clean the bookshelves. She hadn't reshelved those books alphabetically, however, as Lily and Robert had arranged them; Mrs. Harvey had set them back on the spotless shelves in order of height and color. "So," Lily said, "if I'm looking for a short, green book, I know exactly where it'll be, but if I don't know what the book looks like . . ." She made a helpless, palms-up gesture. "We can't find a thing! And neither of us has worked up the energy or, really, the courage to rearrange them."

Dwight and Claytor, who remembered Warren Scofield, thought of him as the keeper of all there was about their family that was not tangible — the idea of them all, the epitome, somehow, of their very "Scofieldness," for which they were much celebrated in Washburn, Ohio. Betts had bits and pieces of memories of her father, but Howard had no recollection of him at all, so the younger two counted on Dwight and Claytor as interpreters. And now and then they also picked up a nuance from some casual reference Aunt Lily or Uncle Robert might make, or their great-uncle George, all of whom reinforced the notion of glamour and dash with which they had imbued the idea of their father.

Their mother, of course, never hesitated to speak of Warren, always amiably but without a hint of any emotion they could discern. The older three children weren't aware that they held Agnes's apparent serenity against her, as if it were an insult to Warren Scofield himself. Howard didn't think much about it one way or another — Dwight Claytor filled the bill for Howard as an example of an admirable man, as did Claytor to a lesser degree. But the very fact of Agnes's relative silence on the subject made Dwight and Claytor and Betts wary and defensive. Without ever acknowledging it to each other, the older three were alike in not wanting to know whatever Agnes might have to say. They already knew from scraps of conversations picked up here and there among the adults of the three houses that with Warren Scofield's death, his family had been unexpectedly strapped financially.

Dwight and Claytor remembered vividly how relieved their mother had been to get her job teaching school. Those two boys didn't want it to be the case that Warren Scofield had let her down, had put any of them at risk. Certainly Agnes had never implied such a thing, but, nevertheless, Dwight and Claytor and Betts, too, held against her the possibility that it might be true.

The children of Agnes's household certainly believed they loved and admired her, but it had occurred to the older three separately that a woman like Agnes, lacking any hint of underlying sensuality, a woman who had watched the housepainter like a hawk, who kept a cynical eye on the coal deliveries, the plumber, and the yardman, a woman who kept such a tight rein on trivial particularities, well, they thought a woman like that might not be a reliable witness on the subject of their charismatic father.

Their mother's low-to-the-ground practicality, her determined frugality, the little snap of satisfaction with the dailiness of her life — a brisk nod of her head as she matched coupons to her shopping list or balanced her checkbook — was not at all what the children considered Scofield-like. They were enthusiasts; she was a skeptic; they were very nearly greedy in their anticipation of the future, whereas she seemed no more than resigned to it.

Those children had spent a great deal of energy, of course, courting Agnes's affection and approval; they were in full flight, though, from the idea of "taking after her." And this whole notion of theirs was reinforced around town, where early on most people had forgotten that Dwight wasn't, in fact, a Scofield at all and took to calling those two little boys — Dwight and Claytor — the "Scofield twins." There was rarely a time when the boys were out in public at age four, or five, or six years old, with only five months' difference in their ages, that some adult didn't bend over them admiringly and exclaim at just how remarkably the two of them resembled their father.

And Agnes never said a word; she was perfectly comfortable the first time Dwight had looked up at her from his crib and said "Mama." It never crossed her mind to instruct him to call her anything else. Of course Agnes had explained to Dwight that his parents — who were

her own parents, as well — were the older Dwight Claytor and the deceased Catherine Alcorn Claytor. When
Dwight was growing up he saw very little of his father,
and whenever the older Dwight Claytor and his second
wife, Camille, were visiting, the children in Agnes and
Warren's house all referred to them as Granddad Dwight
and Aunt Cammie, which suited everyone just fine.

Agnes couldn't see any particular merit in insisting that
Dwight continually grasp the idea of who his parents were,
as long as he knew the truth of the matter. Even though she
had been terrified when the responsibility for Dwight had
been so matter-of-factly thrust upon her immediately after
his birth, to all intents and purposes he *was* her and Warren's first child. By the time she gave birth to Claytor five
months later, she was ferociously protective of Dwight,
even resenting the new baby the first few days of his life for
usurping Dwight's place as the center of Scofield attention.

And, as it happened, Dwight had not incorporated the
idea of who his parents *were* as much as he understood
who they were not. Day to day he did think of Agnes as
his mother and of Warren as his father, but as a little boy,
whenever his guard was down — in that elongated trance
between wakefulness and sleep, for instance — Dwight
grieved deeply for that self he protected so arduously, the
self who was an orphan within his own clan. Being part of
his own family — being, in effect, the archetype of a
Scofield — was a task he had instinctively undertaken
when he was no more than two or three years old.

When Claytor became more than an infant, when he
began to walk, and then to talk, and then to have opinions

and desires, Dwight understood — with far more certainty than would a mere sibling — that he had no choice at all but to relinquish some part of his place in the family to Claytor. Dwight never acknowledged or allowed himself later to investigate those occasional spells of fury toward Claytor so overwhelming that, even when he was very young, he had known to suppress them. In fact, he realized instinctively that the only recourse open to him was to cultivate what was, as it turned out, genuine affection for Claytor. As a result, of course, during his childhood Claytor practically worshipped the ground Dwight walked on. There was so little apparent rivalry between those two boys that it was often remarked upon by members of the family and the family's close friends.

"They're devoted to each other! Those two!" Uncle George Scofield often said when the boys were little. "They put me in mind of Warren, when he was a boy, and Robert Butler. They were just as close, and Lily was always tagging along with them, too. They were more like brothers than friends. But they didn't look so much alike. Sometimes I see Dwight and Claytor at a distance — not far, just across the yard, say — and, I tell you, I can't tell the one from the other. And do you know what? They do look like Warren, but more than that, they look like my brother John. They look more like Warren's father, really, than they look like Warren himself."

Tut Zeller, whenever he came by, and Mrs. Drummond, across the square, and her daughter Lucille, naturally, when she was in town, and Sally Trenholm Dameron, Will's wife and Agnes's old school friend, when she was still alive — anyone who visited Agnes and Warren's house, or saw the boys out and about — remarked upon their resemblance to one another as well as their likeness to Warren Scofield. Almost everyone, too, generally commented on their unusual, endearing, and unshakable camaraderie.

When Agnes and Warren had a daughter, it was just assumed around town that she would favor her mother, but by the time Betts Scofield was no more than two years old, she — and little Howard, too, a few years later — looked like the Scofield side of the family through and through. As a result of being told so often how much they were like all the other pale-haired, brown-eyed Scofields who had gone before them, not one of the children in Agnes's house compared him or herself to her. They didn't even see Agnes, really, since she was always right there.

In fact, if they had been pressed to describe their mother, they would have named the ways in which she was unlike the Scofields. She was small, like Aunt Lily was small, but Agnes had a round, softer figure as opposed to all the Scofields' lanky, athletic frames. Nor did Agnes have the fair Scofield skin that burned so easily, and she claimed that the unruliness of her dark and curly hair was the bane of her existence. The children could have said that much, but otherwise they only knew her as their mother; they had never had occasion to consider that perhaps that wasn't her sole identity. Around town many people considered Agnes Scofield quite pretty and remarkably sensual even as she aged, but Agnes's allure, in particular, was something her children didn't even notice. Agnes's maternity, like her cautious householdery, was taken for granted and had generally been dependable but never particularly seductive.

Howard had benefited from coming last and being raised as much by the older children as by his mother. He and she had enjoyed solitary hours together during which Agnes told him stories about Uncle Tidbit and Miss Butterbean — stories her own mother had told her, she said. But he, too, subscribed to the idea that their mother would conspire against her own children whenever possible to make their lives ordinary and tediously safe. They counted on her for it.

After their father's death it was Uncle Robert with whom the older children discussed at length their sudden, sometimes sweeping reinterpretations of the world as they grew into it. Or they sought out Aunt Lily to tell her about some grand scheme that occurred to one or the other of them, and with which he or she was infatuated for a time, each in turn assuming that such an idea had never before been considered. The nature of evil: Did it exist at all? Wasn't it dependent on context? And was that idea itself only relative or was evil an absolute? Could there ever *be* evil intention? Or religion, for instance. Each of the older boys wrestled with the idea and with the nature or existence of God. Dwight and then Claytor had served as crucifer at the Episcopal church. It pleased Agnes a great deal to see either one of those boys proceed solemnly down the aisle, carrying the cross and leading the processional.

At some point, though, each of them — and Betts, too, when she wanted not to attend church any longer — had tried to determine how seriously Agnes took all this. She didn't argue the point with Betts; Agnes was perfectly willing to let her attend church or not. And to Dwight and Claytor she only answered lightly, along the lines of saying that having to go to church was the only incentive for her to get all the ironing done by Saturday afternoon, or that it was reassuring to see people on a Sunday morning on their best behavior. "No matter whatever else is going on in their lives," she remarked, "they get up and brush their hair and put on their best clothes. At least for a few hours all the people at church have to behave as if they're the people they mean to be every day. It feels so safe, I always think. So calm." It didn't occur to Agnes that she was being asked about the nature of God or of religious belief — hers or anyone else's.

Uncle Robert, though, listened to any of the children with deep consideration, responding to their ideas thoughtfully, even as early as when they were only seven or eight years old. He never interrupted a child who was struggling to put words to an idea; he listened with the same deliberate courtesy he extended to his students at Harcourt Lees College. Robert Butler was the son of a Methodist minister, but he and Lily rarely went to church at all. As the children got older and their questions more complex, he told them he would never deny any man his comfort, but that, for himself, he couldn't say that he was traditionally religious. Although, certainly, he said, he believed in religiousness.

He cautioned Betts against intolerance when she declared that she didn't think that any intelligent person could really believe in God. He assured her that wasn't the case and advised her to keep that opinion to herself. "Religion is the most controversial subject I know of," he said to her. "I think it should be a subject that's entirely personal. Not bandied about as if you're discussing . . . oh . . . taxes or politics, Betts. You don't want to seem to be insulting people." His daughter, Trudy, kept her own counsel and rarely asked him any questions that weren't simply factual.

Those boys debated and mulled over Uncle Robert's idea — the notion of not being religious oneself but believing in religiousness — off and on for years, and each one considered it a startlingly frank, profound, and generous answer. An answer so sophisticated was a remarkable concession, a courtesy, and a great compliment to a child. Neither of them realized that Uncle Robert's careful, articulate explanation and the reasons for going to church that Agnes had offered were essentially the very same thing.

Neither Dwight nor Trudy had been back to Washburn since their marriage, and as they came into town, Dwight slowly drove twice around the full hexagon that was Monument Square, taking note of any changes and suddenly being struck with amusement at the statue of Daniel Emmett in the center of the square. It seemed to him endearingly ridiculous that the author of the song "Dixie" was the most celebrated citizen of what had been a Union Army town. He remembered the excitement of the first "Dan Emmett Days," when he and Claytor were about ten years old, and the thrill of the inauguration of Hiawatha Park out on the edge of town with its Ferris wheel and swimming pool. All the concerts and speeches — a few made at the foot of that statue. "I've even missed old Dan," he said to Trudy.

"Hmm? What do you mean?" She was combing her hair and straightening her skirt and blouse.

"The Dan Emmett statue," Dwight said patiently, "that statue of him." He slowed the car so she could see. Trudy gazed out briefly, and then turned to look at Amelia Anne in the backseat, who was sound asleep.

"Oh, no, Dwight. That's not a statue of Dan Emmett. The Historical Society only had enough money to preserve his house. Over on Mulberry Street . . ."

But neither Dwight nor Trudy was paying much attention to the other at the moment, and when Dwight pulled into Scofields he was swept through with relief and surprise at the delight with which he was filled at being back in familiar territory. He found himself overwhelmed for a moment with a lessening of anxiety, an ecstatic headiness he had only ever felt before as a child in these same surroundings. He couldn't remember any particular incident in childhood that had brought about that quick wash of pure gladness; he couldn't remember any particular incidents, although he clearly recalled his astonishment at the intensity of his brief euphoria.

He pulled into the seldom-used, shallow semicircular drive on which the three houses of Scofields fronted. Generally all the family and most everyone else used the separate drives of each house that ran in back of the property, where it was easy to park. But Dwight wanted to get a look at the houses as they must have been envisioned by Leo, John, and George Scofield before the turn of the century. They were handsome Greek Revival–style houses, large by 1940s standards, and garnished, now, with later ideas of a porch here or there, a gable where light was needed. They were nicely spaced, one from the other, given their proportions.

Agnes's house had originally been built for John Scofield and was positioned sturdily between the other two. Leo's house, where Trudy had grown up and where Robert and Lily Scofield Butler lived, was its original white painted brick, set farther back and on the western flank of the compound. Uncle George's tall white house, to the east of the others, still served as his Civil War museum, and Dwight's and Trudy's first impression was that nothing had changed in all the time they had been away. The grass was vividly green in the unexpectedly fierce June sun, but the leaves of the old trees that lined the drive were so dense that no light at all interrupted their shade, and Dwight's initial euphoria embraced the lush beauty of this small Ohio town. When he was growing up in Washburn, it had never occurred to him to compare it with anyplace else.

As soon as he and Trudy stepped from the car, though, Dwight was confronted by a medium-size dog that came hurtling around the corner of the house, followed languidly by Will Dameron, who whistled for the dog. "Pup!" he said. "Come on back here! Pup!"

Agnes hadn't expected Dwight and Trudy until dinnertime, and she opened the wide front door — which was used so seldom that it always stuck — and hurried across the front porch and down the steps to meet them. Will had stayed over the night before, and he and Agnes had been sitting drinking coffee when she heard the car and saw that it was Dwight and his family. It had annoyed Will to be hustled out the kitchen door. "For God's sake, Agnes! Why would anyone care? We're just having some breakfast!" But Agnes had learned caution in what she revealed to her children. She was concentrating fiercely on collecting herself. She didn't even notice Pup's persistent growl, which erupted into frantic barking when Dwight gave her a hug, although the dog didn't seem as distressed when Trudy, too, came forward to embrace her mother-in-law.

Amelia Anne was leaning against her mother's knees, not yet having shaken off her heat-drugged and intermittent sleep. Her face puckered as she came completely awake, and she turned and reached up mutely to her mother in that universal gesture of children when they want to be picked up. Trudy bent automatically and scooped her up, propping Amelia Anne against the convenient ledge of her body created by the baby who was due in less than three months.

"Oh, let me help with all this," said Agnes, but she didn't offer to take Amelia Anne, who still buried her face against her mother's shoulder. Agnes thought it was likely the little girl would become hysterical if she were handed over to anyone else. Agnes had seen it happen more than once. When a tired or crying child was put into the generously open arms of a stranger and then became even more disconsolate with terror. Generally that hapless do-gooder was immediately viewed with annoyance and slight suspicion. Agnes had seen it happen even with school-age children now and then.

She began to collect various items that Dwight had put out on the grass, and Dwight continued to unpack the car while keeping a close eye on the dog, who watched him with equal attention. Will Dameron finally relieved Trudy of Amelia Anne, who let out a loud whoop of surprise as Will swung her in an exaggerated arc and settled her comfortably on his shoulders. She became quiet and somber as she clung to Will's hair and looked down upon them all.

Finally the whole group managed to straggle into the front hall, the dog as well, who became frenzied with barking when Dwight crossed the threshold with an air of authority. "Mother. The dog. Does that dog come in the house? Maybe Mr. Dameron could leave him out back." He had always liked Mr. Dameron well enough, but it seemed to Dwight that he was taking a lot of liberties — was assuming an unusual intimacy with the family and with the household — that his mother wouldn't usually have permitted. Especially allowing his dog to make itself at home in her house, where she had never welcomed any animals or pets. Dwight thought that Will Dameron should know to go home, or wherever else he had been headed in town.

Will clapped Dwight on the back. "Now, Dwight! 'Mr. Dameron'! Well, that would be my father. Let's don't have any more of that! I'm 'Will' to you and your family! I hope you'll do me that courtesy! But I've got to get a move on," Will said, "and Pup will follow me out, I imagine." He looked at Agnes for a moment. "So supper is about six o'clock?" he asked, and she nodded. "Just let me know if there's anything else I can bring," he told her and then turned his attention back to Dwight. "I wanted to bring your mother the last of the beefsteak tomatoes and some fresh corn. A new hybrid. You can see what you think of it. It *is* sweet," Will said.

"You don't need to worry about the dog," he added. "I don't think Pup would hurt anyone unless they really did threaten your mother. He's part collie, I think. Or some part working dog. Wants to herd everything, and he's been protecting the place long enough now that he's just feeling important with so many strangers. Just showing off."

Will carefully lifted Amelia Anne up and over his head, handing her to Trudy, who smiled her thanks. He leaned forward to give Trudy, then Amelia Anne, a kiss on the cheek each and a kiss for Agnes, too. He offered a quick handshake to Dwight before taking his leave.

Dwight was relieved to see the dog trot alertly out the door with Will. A few minutes later, though, as Will's car pulled out of the drive, Dwight was offended to see the dog at the screen door once again, and even more annoyed when his mother opened the door without hesitation to let him in.

"The dog's staying here?" Dwight asked. "That seems to me a real imposition. He's really made himself at home."

Agnes was distracted and guiltily assumed Dwight meant that it was Will who was too comfortable in her house. "Oh, well. It is nice to have him around the place. It's nice to have a little company, especially since Robert and Lily are out of town. And I suppose he must feel pretty isolated out at the farm. He's been a good friend."

"Well, I'm glad, Mama. I'll tell you . . . we're all just tired out from being in the car so long," Dwight said more calmly, realizing that he had been ungracious to Mr. Dameron, ungracious to Agnes herself. But he made the mistake — as he was speaking — of gazing in the dog's direction. Pup tensed immediately and began anxiously issuing a successive two-bark warning.

Dwight's voice became strained once more. "But, Mother, even if the dog's good company when you're by yourself, I don't think it made sense for Will Dameron to leave him here this particular day!" While Dwight had turned to speak to Agnes, Pup quieted and backed away a few steps. After a moment or so, however, he barked twice more and then kept it up at regular intervals.

"Oh!" Agnes said. "I thought you meant . . . No, Dwight. He's not Will's dog. He lives here. He's my dog. Honestly, he won't hurt you," Agnes said, waving in the dog's direction. "He just doesn't know you. Go on, Pup! Scat! Scat! Will's right about that. Pup's just showing off." But the dog stayed where he was, just inches from her skirt; he canted his head toward Dwight and continued to issue warnings in staccato bursts, his front feet shifting in excitement. Agnes remonstrated halfheartedly. "No, Pup! That's not a good dog!"

"He doesn't look like a pup to me," Dwight said matter-of-factly. "I think he's pretty much full-grown."

It was a dazzling day with a pure blue sky and such clarity that the sun streamed into the front hallway exactly like a children's book illustration of sunbeams falling from heaven. And Agnes was dazzled herself at the sight of Dwight's bright hair glossed white by the glare, and at this first look at Amelia Anne, who had her father's coloring exactly. Agnes stood looking at them with a small, shocked smile on her face, because this little girl could have been one of her own children. Amelia Anne burrowed her head into her mother's skirt under Agnes's scrutiny.

Agnes was in sole charge of seeing to the homecoming of Dwight and Trudy and their daughter, with Robert and Lily away, and she found herself uncomfortably and surprisingly bashful. Dwight and Trudy had seemed grown-up but not adult, exactly, when she had last seen them. Trudy was busy with Amelia Anne, but on Dwight's part, he, too, felt oddly ill at ease.

Agnes Scofield's competent jurisdiction over the Scofield compound was so ingrained an idea that not one of the children who had grown up there gave it much thought at all. But each one, as he or she returned to Washburn after the war, was taken aback. On that Sunday in June 1947, Dwight had been euphoric when they had finally reached Scofields, but gradually he began to feel a dismaying letdown. He and Trudy had decided at the last minute to trade off driving while Amelia Anne slept so that they could drive straight through without stopping, and they arrived home at Scofields about eight in the morning, anticipating baths and breakfast and fresh sheets. It hadn't occurred to Dwight to let Agnes know about their change of plan. After all, he and Trudy were going home, and, also, he had wanted to leave open the possibility of stopping somewhere overnight if he and Trudy got too tired to stay on the road.

The dog continued to stand with his head raised and his forelegs slightly splayed, barking to warn Dwight off and refusing to back down until Agnes finally gave his collar a jerk and spoke to him with clear annoyance. Pup didn't want Dwight on his territory, and he obeyed Agnes with reluctance. Dwight was affronted; it seemed to him not only uncharacteristic but unkindly secretive of his mother to have acquired this dog behind his back, without consultation.

Their father had brought home all sorts of pets when Dwight and Claytor were young — cats, turtles, birds, and dogs, too. Dwight couldn't remember that his mother had ever been swayed by his father's enthusiasm for any one of those pets. In fact, it struck Dwight suddenly that, even in the face of their father's delight — and a pleading eagerness on his own and Claytor's part — she had steadfastly refused to admit their charm, although, of course, she had never neglected them. But the animals had all come to a bad end, as if his mother's adamant indifference to them had been toxic.

Turtles escaped their shallow bowls only to be found months later, their empty, overturned shells swept out from beneath a chest of drawers, so that the frantic pedaling of their short, spatulate turtle legs — as they must have tried to right themselves — was only too easy to imagine. One morning Dwight had come down to the kitchen, where the canaries' cage was suspended from the ceiling as a precaution against cats, and found the tiny metal door ajar with nothing inside but two pairs of small, reptilian bird feet. Not even a feather was left.

But cats also disappeared sooner or later, or were discovered flattened in the road two streets away. Pet rabbits died mysteriously overnight, and not a single dog had developed a loyalty to the household and become a family pet. So Dwight was both bemused and irritated by the presence of his mother's dog.

He and Trudy and Amelia Anne followed as Agnes took them through the house, the dog nearly hobbling her at the knees and barking alertly as they crossed each threshold, although Agnes didn't pay any attention to the noise. The dog preceded her as she led them along the back hall, where she opened the doors to the dining room and the little study to let light into the hall. And as they made their halting circuit of the rooms through one door after another, Dwight observed furniture rearranged, wallpaper faded, a water stain on the dining-room ceiling. All this was an insult to his affectionate memory of his life in the house, to his idea of his own place in the world. His discovery that everything was not as he remembered made him feel foolish, duped, gave him an injured feeling of somehow being betrayed.

After all, this was Agnes presiding over the property; this was the one person to whom he felt entirely known, and here she was, preoccupied with some strange dog. This was the person he thought of as his mother but who was inviting people to dinner left and right on Dwight and Trudy and Amelia Anne's first day home, not considering the fact that they might be tired, that the three of them might only want to see the family. And what did it signify that — upon close inspection — the house had a worn, disheveled look about it, that the yards had gone to seed?

Agnes seemed to have let the rooms become shabby, even threadbare. And although the children had dreaded Agnes's persistence when she got a bee in her bonnet about getting some little chore attended to, Dwight was disturbed that so many things around the place appeared to need repair. Trudy glanced at him curiously when he spoke to Agnes with a clear note of petulance.

"You know, Mama, you never wrote a thing about getting a dog. How old is he? He can't be a puppy! How long have you had him? I'm surprised Aunt Lily never mentioned it . . . or Uncle Robert. You never said a thing."

"I didn't? I imagine I just never thought of it when I wrote you. Well, it wasn't important, Dwight." But he still looked at her expectantly.

"Oh, well . . . a pupil of mine was moving and had to get rid of his dog. . . . Pup's probably about . . . Well, I didn't even ask. I never thought about it, but I don't think he's very old. . . ." The dog became agitated when Dwight's attention shifted his way once more. "Hush, now, Pup!" Agnes said. "Hush!" And, once again, when he heard the real annoyance in her voice, he subsided.

Agnes cocked her head up toward Dwight with an unself-conscious smile of deep pleasure. She had been astounded at the sight of him, the tall, blond sweep of him. She was so surprised by her own intense joy that she knew it had made her shy and foolish. She was amused, too, by Dwight's determination to know about the dog. It was exactly like him to run some fact to ground. Even when he was a little boy, his face would take on that insistent expression — his mouth drawn out straight and his eyebrows slightly raised. She finally reached toward him and grasped his arms just above the elbow so that she could hold on to him, so that she could take a good look at him.

"I'm so glad to see you!" she said, still gripping his arms, still watching his face, while Trudy looked on, Amelia Anne sucked her thumb, and the dog momentarily relinquished his vigil and sat down to see what would happen. But Dwight was unnerved by her ingenuous delight — all his life it seemed to him her affection had had to be caught on the fly. It had seemed reasonable to him that it was bound to be Claytor whom she favored. And Claytor was so likable, so easy in his idea of who he was, where he belonged; never considering his entitlement to a place within Scofields. Dwight had always kept in mind that although Agnes Claytor Scofield had mothered him all his life, she was not, in fact, his mother. It would be nearly impossible, he always thought, not to love your own child most of all.

Dwight smiled, too, but with a tightness around his mouth that he couldn't overcome. She released him and turned away, and the dog began to bark once more. Dwight was relieved to see Agnes's expression lose its oddly threatening and fond intensity. But she did give a brief, soft laugh and trailed a little poem behind her as she led them into the sitting room:

"James James
Morrison Morrison
(Commonly known as Jim)
Told his
Other relations
Not to go blaming *him*.
James James
Said to his Mother,
'Mother,' he said, said he:
'You must *never* go down to the end of the town
without consulting me.'"

Dwight had bent to pick up Amelia Anne, who was finally overtaken by weariness and was sitting on Trudy's feet. With the dog barking again intermittently, Dwight didn't hear all of whatever his mother was saying. "What's that, Mother?"

"— if you want to put Amelia Anne down for a nap," Agnes was saying to Trudy. "I've got a cot and a crib, too, set up in the sewing room. She must be tired. Oh, Dwight. Don't you remember that? It's just a poem you used to like. It suddenly popped into my head. You know it! It's in one of those Christopher Robin books," she said. "It's just that little poem. About the little boy who's so cross at his mother? His mother gets into all sorts of trouble — gets lost, I think — because she doesn't consult him? You and Claytor loved all those books. Lucille Drummond sent them from England on her wedding trip. Don't you remember? I've still got them packed away somewhere. Mostly they were about Christopher Robin?"

Amelia Anne was reluctant to be picked up as Dwight

lifted her, pushing away from him, stiff-armed, turning this way and that when he tried to calm her. "I'll show you where we'll put our little Orphan Annie, here," he said to Trudy. "Come on, Ammi-Annie, Ammi-Annie-Nannie, come on, Annie," he crooned to his daughter, who finally gave in and went limp, her legs hanging slack and her sandals bumping against his side. But when Dwight approached the doorway, the dog stood firm once more, barring his way, and suddenly Dwight's voice inflated with exhausted frustration.

"Out, Christopher Robin! Out! Out! Get out of the way! Now! Out of the way!" And Pup moved backward in surprise. "Mother, maybe you could put the damned dog outside until he's used to us!"

Trudy followed Dwight up the stairs, glancing an apology toward her mother-in-law, and Pup looked toward Agnes doubtfully, his whole skeleton giving way under the weight of his own inherent uncertainty. He sank in upon himself, looking overflexible and cowed, his head hanging in consternation and humiliation, and Agnes suddenly found herself fighting back tears, as if it were she upon whom Dwight had unleashed his unasked-for, patronizing, absurdly proprietary disap-proval. She tilted her head back fractionally in a slow inhalation of the musty air of the sitting room and care-fully unclenched her hands, stretching her fingers out into upward arcs so that she could feel the tendons pull as she cautiously released her held breath.

"Come on, Pup! Come to the kitchen while I make sandwiches." But the dog lagged back, and Agnes knelt down and wrapped her arms around his neck and laid her cheek against the top of his head, which gave off a clean scent, like warm wheat. "You're a good dog, Pup," she said, embarrassed to hear her voice break tearily. She held on to the dog and spoke softly. "You're a good dog! You're my good dog, Pup." She hugged Pup to herself — swaying back and forth as though she were comforting a child — for a long moment on the slightly gritty, old Persian rug. And when she rose and moved along toward the kitchen, the dog went with her, reassured.

Pup had settled down by the time Amelia Anne got up from her nap, and he became enamored of and devoted to Dwight and Trudy's daughter as she moved around the house or ran across the yard, calling to him delightedly. "Bobbin!" she said. "Here Bobbin! Come here! Bobbin-Bobbin-Bobbin!"

"She can't quite handle 'Christopher Robin,'" Trudy explained to Agnes, who didn't reply for a moment.

"Oh, no. Of course she can't. Well, Christopher Robin's not his name, anyway. I never could get around to giving him a name. Just 'Pup.' I just call him Pup. That's what Warren always was good at. Just the right name, so that you knew from the sound of it . . . Well, I always thought whatever name Warren came up with had just been hanging out there in the air waiting for the person or the animal to come along and have it." She paused a moment, suddenly thinking not to dwell on Warren. Not to say to her own daughter-in-law, even though it was only Trudy, whom she had known since the day Trudy was born, that Warren had said to her one night, just after they were married, as he lay over her, most of his weight supported on his hip, but his head propped on his hand as he looked down at his wife, that she wasn't ever meant to be an Agnes. "You should be . . . uhmm . . . Celeste," he said. "Or maybe Guinevere. Or Lady Elaine! Those heroines I imagined when I read *The Knights of the Round Table*. Or Marian from *Robin Hood*. A beautiful maiden who would give you her scarf to tuck in your sleeve as you rode off to battle."

Agnes didn't say anything about Warren; she turned her attention to Amelia Anne. "But whatever Amelia Anne wants to call him, it looks to me like Pup will follow her." Trudy smiled and nodded, but she hadn't really heard what Agnes said, because Amelia Anne and the dog were heading toward the screen door, and Trudy moved at once to follow them outside so she could keep an eye on her daughter.

Chapter Six

*I*N RETROSPECT, when she tried to sort it out, it seemed to Agnes Scofield that her children had come home for good from their years away all at the same time. There had been a wave of children, friends, and family returning in the summer of 1947. Dwight and Trudy and their little girl, Amelia Anne, arrived in June, and Howard and Betts had shown up unexpectedly that same month. Claytor had been home briefly on leave at Christmas of 1946, but his wife and her daughter hadn't been able to accompany him and meet the rest of his family until the annual Scofield Fourth of July picnic the following year. Agnes had lived in the house by herself since 1944, and all at once, there was scarcely room for everyone to find a bed. It seemed to her a jumbled, shortened rush of time that brought Dwight and Claytor and their families back to Washburn permanently, and Betts and Howard, too, more or less.

Dwight and Trudy, of course, had both grown up at Scofields, and Agnes hadn't imagined that their return would be much different from any other of their home-comings, although, naturally they would have their little girl to worry about. Not until they arrived, however, had she recognized that it was altogether different to adjust to Dwight and Trudy as a couple, bracketing little Amelia Anne with a family's focused intention, as opposed to having them around as separate entities, each with his or her own idea of what was entailed by being at home. And then there was Betts, back and forth in stages, arriving on the bus and often bringing a friend along, or borrowing a car to come home for a few days at a time. Howard was still serving out his tour of duty, although even he was home on leave with some regularity.

Her household had emptied gradually, and Agnes had looked forward to the return of all the children since the dreary December afternoon in 1944 when she had seen Howard off to Pennsylvania for basic training. She had come back to the empty house at Scofields, longing for nothing more than Dwight's and Claytor's, Betts's and Howard's return; she had now and then been sick with yearning for their company, or even for the knowledge that they were around town, in and out of the house, arguing, joking, eating, sleeping, breathing. But when there was a sudden convergence of nearly everyone — some of whom she didn't even know — on the very day she had expected only Dwight and Trudy and little Amelia Anne to arrive, Agnes found herself nearly overwhelmed. Howard had appeared unexpectedly, arriving just after lunch, having caught a ride with another soldier who lived in Zanesville, but Howard insisted that the fellow stay through dinner at least, and Agnes was in bed before he left. He seemed quite nice, but Agnes hadn't expected to be feeding so many, or to be rushing to hastily make beds — borrowing sheets and towels from Lily's house. Agnes certainly hadn't expected the day to turn into an event so burdened with slap-dash hospitality.

Late on the afternoon of that same day, Sam Holloway, an army friend of Dwight's, had called to say he was in Columbus on business and had missed his train connection and would be staying over until he could make other arrangements. He hoped Dwight and his wife would be able to join him for dinner. Dwight urged him to get on the first bus to Washburn. "There's one leaving every two hours," he said. "There's plenty of room to put you up."

Agnes declared she was delighted, of course, when Dwight told her Sam was arriving — Dwight had written that Sam knew his and Agnes's mother's family, the Alcorns, some of whom still lived in Natchez. Agnes looked forward to hearing all about it, she told Dwight, and that was true enough; she wasn't uninterested in what her cousins had been up to in Mississippi; they had lost touch with each other even before the war. But Agnes had to rethink the accommodations, and she put Howard in Betts's old room on the second floor and Sergeant Holloway in Howard's bedroom, down the little hall off the kitchen. He would have more privacy there, and if he and Dwight, and the fellow from Zanesville — if any of them — wanted to stay up late catching up with the others, they wouldn't wake Amelia Anne.

Howard and Dwight and Sam Holloway — along with Bob Treadway, before he set out near dawn to reach his parents' house in Zanesville by breakfast time — did sit up long after Agnes and Trudy had made their excuses and gone up to bed. Agnes could hear the low rumble of their conversation off and on all night as she made a futile attempt to get to sleep. They weren't keeping her awake; it was only that she couldn't stop herself from trying to rearrange all the plans that needed changing in the next few days in order to accommodate the unexpected guests.

Sam Holloway and Dwight Claytor had been assigned to separate bomber crews, but they were both stationed at Deopham Green, and they had first met each other simply because of the small-world syndrome, which occurred so frequently in the armed forces that it had become a morale booster of sorts. It often created instant camaraderie, but more than that — and illogically — it heightened the notion of being part of a huge but unified force. If a man you met in the service knew someone you knew yourself, for instance — or came from somewhere with which you were familiar — and yet neither of you had even had an idea of the other's existence, well, then, who in the world was not fighting your same fight, enduring the same boredom and terror and surprise?

Agnes and Dwight's mother had been born and had grown up in Natchez, and remnants of her family remained there still, where Sam, too, had lived for a year or so. Sam and Dwight knew many of the same people. It was the damnedest thing! But then, as they remained friends, they also realized that, after all, it wasn't really that unusual, and eventually they rarely thought about their original connection.

After the war in Europe, Sam Holloway was stationed

in Washington, D.C., assigned to the Office of Housing, which sought to ease the shortages of living quarters for soldiers who were streaming back into the country with enough money to own a place to live but who had no choice but to move their new wives and children into their parents' houses — if the parents were willing — all of them crammed together like sardines. Some men couldn't find any place at all to live, and, all over the country, there were veterans living out of their cars, veterans and their families making do in Quonset huts that had been hastily thrown up before the war to house soldiers during basic training.

Sam became fascinated as he traveled here and there to assess conditions. There were new ideas popping up all over. By the time he telephoned Dwight Claytor, he had been demobilized and was in Columbus to see about a job with Lustron Homes, with whom he had worked when he was assigned to the Office of Housing. He was in town at the request of Carl Strandlund, the company's founder. Sam planned only to see what the prospects for a job at Lustron looked like before he headed south, following his worldly possessions home to his mother's house in Louisiana, and he and Dwight and Howard, as well as Bob Treadway, who had been a mechanic in the service, stayed up late discussing what they were thinking of doing in the future. Trying out ideas as they spoke and bouncing possibilities off one another, and all of them were increasingly delighted by the plans they made with each beer they drank. When Agnes came downstairs in the morning, Sam and Dwight had only gone to bed two hours earlier, and Sam was dead to the world. He didn't hear a thing, even though his bedroom was no more than ten feet from where she was starting breakfast in the kitchen.

Agnes had come downstairs in the quiet house about five o'clock in the morning with the idea of getting breakfast under way before she left for school. She had just started the bacon and begun to set out the ingredients for pancakes when a convertible turned into the long drive that ran along the back of the Scofield property, branching off in the three separate driveways that disappeared discreetly behind hedges planted around what had originally been unplanned parking areas. By now no one even remembered that they hadn't always been there, and every year, fresh stone was put down, the hedges trimmed, and the brick borders reestablished if need be.

Agnes leaned forward at the kitchen window and admired the sight of the creamy-yellow convertible and the glamorous woman in dark sunglasses who was behind the wheel, driving slowly and steering with only one hand while she ran her fingers through her blond hair, trying to untangle it where it was windblown. Even after Agnes had been surprised by the fact that the car turned into her own drive, it was at least another minute before she realized that the woman driving that car was Betts. Agnes hadn't expected Betts to be able to get home at all for the rest of the month.

She pulled into the parking area but left the motor running while she leaned over to check her face in the mirror, applying lipstick and taking a comb from her handbag to attempt once more to untangle her hair. While Agnes still stood gazing at her from inside the house, Pup was outside and regarding this development with extreme suspicion, dancing with urgency as he barked at the peculiar vehicle. He was using every tactic he knew to frighten it away, dodging toward it with ferocious intentions and then retreating with a yip when the thing didn't move. Betts gave up the struggle with her hair, turned off the engine, and began gathering various things together, looking at Pup and laughing with her wide grin that called forth a responding smile from Agnes, whose senses finally came back into the moment.

She headed out to corral Pup so Betts wouldn't be afraid to get out of the car, but it wasn't necessary; Betts simply stepped confidently into the drive, leaving the door wide open, while she rushed toward the dog, startling him into silence. She kneeled to embrace him. "Oh! You're a fierce boy! Don't you remember me? No one's going to sneak inside this house while you're on the job. What a handsome boy! I bet you were glad to meet Amelia Anne. Let's go find her! Let's go find Amelia Anne!" She stood up abruptly and swiveled toward the house, nearly colliding with her mother, whom she hugged exuberantly, explaining her unexpected arrival as the two of them made their way to the kitchen, having to dodge Pup, who was completely won over and euphoric as he bounced along beside and in front of them across the stepping stones.

Although everyone but Agnes was asleep, Betts darted through the house, waking them all, followed by Pup, who had given up the idea of protection and become ecstatic. "I just can't wait, Mama!" she called over her shoulder when Agnes tried to stop Betts, who rushed through the kitchen and down the little hallway to Howard's room, where Sergeant Sam Holloway was sound asleep with the sheets drawn up around his head, until Betts tickled his ribs through the bedclothes. He grasped her hard by the shoulders in the same instant he sat up, and they were face-to-face for a bewildering moment.

"Ah!" She was kneeling on the side of the bed, and she drew back in retreat, although he was still holding her tightly by the shoulders. "You aren't Howie!"

"No. No. I'm sorry," he said reflexively, because it felt to him as though not being the person she expected him to be was rude, and when he realized he was still holding on to her, preventing her from moving, he let her go immediately and apologized again, but she had backed out of the room before it occurred to him to explain who he was. She looked so much like Dwight that it was no mystery to him who she was.

Betts was undaunted; she had grown up in a houseful of boys and had long ago redefined the bounds of modesty. She hurried up the stairs, looking for Dwight and Trudy and Howard, wanting to see her niece Amelia Anne for the first time. "I couldn't wait!" she said as she burst into the rooms, hugging anyone she could find. And in no time everyone was milling about in pajamas, although Sam Holloway had gotten up and was fully dressed and standing off to the side, trying to stay out of the way. Trudy had slipped a robe over her nightgown and was holding Amelia Anne, who looked on blankly, her face still creased from her pillow.

It seemed to Agnes as if the household as a whole moved in accord with Betts's tidal pull as she approached, broke over them, and then receded. She deposited a cage containing two lime-green parakeets on a table in front of a south-facing window in the front room. "Don't worry, don't worry! These are a gift for Aunt Lily," she said to whoever might hear her as she dashed back and forth to the car to retrieve things she remembered she had brought home for her mother or little Amelia Anne, perfume for Trudy, or something she needed herself.

Her brothers traipsed after her, trying to lend a hand. But finally Betts wheeled at the top of the stairs, her eyebrows raised in astonishment as she put a hand to her hair, and stopped her mother and brothers, who were trooping up the steps in her wake, carrying various boxes and pieces of luggage. Agnes was halfway up the stairs, carrying Betts's little train case.

"Oh, Mama, that's what I need!" She swooped down two stairs to take the case in which her toothbrush and shampoo and cosmetics were packed. "A bath! Good Lord! I must be a mess. I drove all night, you know," she said with mildly surprised indignation, as though she had just found this out herself. "About four-thirty, when it started getting light, I stopped to put the top down. Oh, Lord, I need my cigarettes and a good long bath. I must look a wreck . . ."

"Well . . . Oh, goodness, Betts!" Agnes said. "Your hair does —"

"Nope! Betts, you look like a million dollars! You look like you own the place!" Dwight laughed, edging past his mother to deposit Betts's suitcase on the landing. "I'd say you're a sight for sore eyes. Our own Baby Betts!"

Dwight suddenly adopted a caricature pose, like a vaudeville singer, his arms spread, his torso canted back, and launched into song:

> "Beautiful, beautiful brown eyes,
>   Beautiful beautiful browwwn ey-ey-eyes."

He infused the notes with exaggerated vibrato. Howard laughed and joined in, singing harmony:

> "Beautiful, beautiful brown eyes,
>   I'll never love blue eyes again."

Their father had established the tradition of *Beautiful Brown Eyes* being Betts's theme song, so to speak, and it had stuck. Dwight and Claytor had cajoled and teased Betts all through her childhood, in the midst of one of her tantrums, or just out of the blue, singing the song at the drop of a hat and sending Betts into enraged but irrepressible fits of laughter. Lifting her out of her darkest moods.

"Oh, stop it!" Betts said. "And Howie! For God's sake! Parading around in your pajamas. Mother, make these boys get dressed!" she said, mock scoldingly, and Agnes realized she herself was being teased, and she smiled a little, unexpectedly remembering her own bafflement so long ago at the seeming knowingness of all the other students on that first day she had arrived at the Linus Gilchrest Institute for Girls when she was thirteen years old. But she told Betts where to find fresh towels.

"And just put your things in my room, Betts," she said. "We'll get everyone sorted out later on —"

"I can sleep on the couch —," Howard began, at the same moment Trudy spoke.

"Aunt Agnes, Dwight and Amelia Anne and I can certainly go next door if —"

It was almost an hour after Betts's unexpected arrival that Agnes got back to thinking of breakfast. Even though she had turned the flame off before going out to greet her daughter, the kitchen was filled with the bitter scent of burned bacon. The heavy skillet had retained enough heat to thoroughly blacken the edges of the thick slices. She contemplated the greasy mess in the brightening day, and all at once fatigue caught up with her. She recognized the first tiny deflation of what had been this early morning's energetic contentment; she recognized the fragility of what she imagined was her reputation for bounteous, easy, competent hospitality.

She had no idea that the children and her daughter-in-law never thought of Agnes's hospitality one way or another; they were merely at home. Whenever they came home, the sheets were always crisp and fresh, meals were served with dependability, clean towels were folded and plentiful. There were always new bars of soap, talcum powder, extra toothbrushes, any toiletries anyone had forgotten. Just as it had been all of their lives. They would only have noticed if this had not been the case.

Dwight appeared over her shoulder while she was considering what was left of the slab of bacon and trying to decide if there would still be enough for everyone. "You let me fix breakfast!" he said. "I know you have to get to school. I'll give that knife a good edge, and, I tell you,

you'll be able to read the paper through a slice of that bacon."

Agnes moved aside, unnerved a bit. She had forgotten Dwight's way of teasing: an authoritative, good-natured sort of bantering. "Listen, I've become an old hand at this," he said. "Trudy'll tell you that pancakes are my specialty. Well, waffles, really. We use that waffle iron Aunt Lily gave us all the time. But I've perfected them. I know the secret now. You see, you can't beat the batter so much. It's better to leave some lumps. These'll be light as a feather!" So Agnes sat down uneasily at her own table.

When Howard joined them, scissoring around the room, his long legs and new height startled her as she watched him carefully navigate the same space that had held him comfortably all his life. Every few moments she winced inwardly, wanting to warn him that he was about to hit his head on the door frame, knock a glass off the table, step on the dog. But Howard was, in fact, quite graceful, just as he always had been. The best athlete among her children, a gangly child and then a lanky man who moved with an unexpected, elastic ease, as though his hands and feet caught on to his intention in far less time than it took other people to achieve coordination.

Agnes looked on while her children milled about, as unfamiliar with these people as if it were she who was the newcomer among them. Amelia Anne wandered in, tentatively trailing after Betts, whose wet hair was wrapped turban-style in a towel. Sergeant Holloway came to the table spruced up and carefully polite, and finally Trudy appeared. "Amelia Anne! There you are!"

Agnes made a quick count and realized there wasn't enough room at the kitchen table; she had planned to serve breakfast in the dining room, but it was no longer in her hands. She vacated her own place, and Sam Holloway scraped back his chair and stood when she rose, but her children didn't notice. They were all talking at once, engaged in an immediate, familiar, and passionate conversation about all sorts of things. Agnes paused for a while, out of the way of all the commotion, looking on from the doorway.

Pup sat alertly at Betts's feet when she finally came to rest on the edge of the chair where Agnes had been sitting. Howard settled next to Betts, his long legs stretched out under the table all the way to the other side, taller than all of them now. He had been a little under six feet when he left Washburn, and he was nearly six feet four inches when he returned. Betts had only seen him once during the war, and she couldn't get over it. "You're taller than God, Howie!"

"For goodness sakes, Betts . . . ," Agnes objected from where she stood in the doorway, but Betts didn't hear her. She lit a cigarette, restlessly rustling the paper between her long fingers as she exhaled.

"Oh, you look wonderful! Like a good-looking pole bean," she said. "Long and lean . . . you've turned into one of those interesting, angular men. I know you've got girls falling all over you!"

Howard just laughed, and Betts cocked her head at Sergeant Holloway, who was probably ten years older than she was and very attractive himself in a mismatched way. He looked as though his face had been assembled too quickly, so that head-on his angular features didn't quite match up side to side, but the whole effect gave him a jaunty, amused expression. But then Betts was off again — there was no interrupting her when she was on a run. She was leaning over, petting the dog while collecting Amelia Anne with her other arm and giving her a hug, although Amelia Anne was intimidated by Betts's wide movements and dramatic pronouncements and stood transfixed but rigid within her aunt's embrace.

"But here's this sweet thing! You are our beautiful brown eyes, sweetie. Just look at you!" And Betts's voice dropped, becoming gentle and almost seductive. "Your aunt Lily — your grandmother Lily, I guess. She must think she's looking in the mirror, you know. Looking at her own scrapbook. Now, she was the great Scofield beauty. People came from all over the world for her wedding," Betts went on while Amelia Anne studied her intently. "You just can't imagine!" Betts said. "Her father had an avenue of flowering trees planted to keep the sun off her skin — it's as fair as yours is — just to protect her during her wedding procession and for the ceremony in the garden! And Aunt Lily is so much fun. Let her show you the silver bird that lives on her mantel and comes to life! He's full of ridiculous advice, but he always brings you at least a quarter. Sometimes a present."

"They're at a literary conference in New Mexico," Trudy explained. "My parents haven't seen Amelia Anne since they visited after she was born. She was only about six months old. They'll be back day after tomorrow." Amelia Anne ducked her head and smiled a little. Dwight, who was making pancakes, smiled, too, and Trudy was relieved. She had thought that Amelia Anne looked alarmed enough that she might burst into tears.

Betts edged back in her chair and hoisted Amelia Anne onto her lap, where the little girl settled back unresistingly, sucking her thumb. "Ami-Annie, Ami-Annie," Dwight sang out softly from the stove. "Orphan Annie! Don't suck your thumb, sweet pea," he said to his daughter from across the kitchen. "Don't ruin those pretty pearly whites, Annie Fannie." Amelia Anne didn't pay any attention, and Trudy said, "Oh, Dwight, one of those silly nicknames is going to stick . . ."

But Betts spoke above them both. "Dwight, look who's fallen in love with your daughter," she said, nodding toward Pup, who had settled on the floor and was gazing soulfully up at the little girl. "He's such a good-natured dog. A good watchdog, too." As she reached down to scratch the dog's head, her voice immediately dropped into the same note of wheedling endearment she had used when speaking to Amelia Anne. "Yes, you are! Good dog . . . you're a good dog!"

Agnes slipped away, retreating to her room to put on a skirt and blouse to wear to school, and then she just moved around the edges of the kitchen, packing a lunch for herself. Even Pup didn't get up as she edged out the back door, trailing behind her the information that she would borrow a cot from Inez Jordan or Bernice Dameron so that Howard could share the downstairs bedroom with Sam Holloway and that Betts should go on and move into her own room.

Only Howard, though, sitting near the door, heard what she said and grinned up at her. "I'll get my things out of Betts's way, Mama. Don't worry about a cot, I can sleep on the sofa. I'll get Betts to let me pick you up in that yellow car she brought home —"

"That's not mine, of course. A friend loaned it to me," Betts interjected.

"We'll leave the top down and impress the whole school with how glamorous you've become!" Howard finished, and Agnes tried to smile gamely at the fun he was pretending that would be.

Dwight was putting plates of pancakes in front of Sam Holloway and Howard. "I'm making another batch. Betts? But you know what, Betts? I didn't even know Mother *had* a dog —"

"No pancakes for me, for God's sake! But coffee. Coffee. Real coffee! Can you pour me a cup? If I don't watch my girlish figure . . . Well, who else will? But could one of you hand me a cup of coffee? I don't want to disturb anyone here," she said, indicating Amelia Anne, whose head was nodding drowsily against Betts's shoulder.

Agnes's spirits sank even lower at Howard's good cheer toward her, his kindliness, but she stepped out the back door with a quick nod and a smile in his direction. For the first time since she had brought him home, Pup was not alongside her, so she rounded the house and took a shortcut along the alley behind Lily's house. It was a shortcut she avoided with Pup along, because generally there were cats sunning themselves on back steps and a few dogs who protested Pup's infringement on their territory. She

clicked along down School Street with the sudden realization that her house was at last returned to what she had
long considered normal, and yet she held that idea at
arm's length, approaching and retreating from it, slightly
astonished and worried at having gotten what she
thought she wanted.

Before the war, the growth of the town of Washburn,
Ohio, had been unplanned but predictable; new houses or
commercial buildings went up where they were needed,
so that, for instance, when BHG Glass consolidated their
West Virginia and Ohio operations in Washburn, several
new buildings went up at the manufacturing site on River
Road, and houses sprang up nearby, extending a neighborhood that was already established. Gradually a residential area had grown near the industrial section of town
between Mulberry Street and River Road in tidy rows,
exactly as if the houses had been set down in their loca-
tions by a giant typist who came to the right-hand margin
and flung the return lever — setting the roller one space
down and moving the carriage back to the left to start all
over on a new line. But that growth was gradual enough
that very little attention was given to it as a trend or a particular phenomenon. Mulberry Street was eventually par-
alleled by Hickory Street, then Walnut, Maple, and,
finally, Chestnut.

The most desirable neighborhoods remained those
anchored on Monument Square by big, old two- or three-
story houses built in the late 1800s or the early years of
the 1900s. For decades those houses were the idea of
home that everyone in Washburn held on to no matter

where else in town he or she actually lived. After the war, however, the grown children returning to the area found they no longer yearned to acquire or to remain in the spacious, shadowy rooms of those tall houses standing among even taller trees. Shrouded in shady repose, those handsome buildings embodied an old-fashioned approach to living one's life that nullified the clean rush of postwar urgency. The clipped gables, the spear of a conical tower, the vari-patterned, beautiful but brittle old slate roofs, the gingerbread of a Victorian porch — all the elaborate details — bespoke careful consideration and a ponderous progression that put a damper on a newly roused enthusiasm for getting on with things.

After the war, too, it was not so easy to find a woman who would take a job cooking or cleaning in another woman's house. New industries had moved to Washburn, which had gained a reputation for having a skilled workforce, and any women who did want jobs could generally find secretarial or clerk positions in the low-slung brick administrative offices of BHG Glass, or Hazelman & Company, out past Marion Avenue, as well as at the Bestor Nellmar Flexible Packaging Company, which employed nearly seven hundred people, and, of course, there were jobs to be had at Scofields & Company, too.

But even though those tall old houses — the sweeping lawns to be maintained, the tall, groomed hedges and flower gardens, the beautiful brickwork often in need of tuck-pointing — were relics of another world altogether, Sam Holloway enjoyed the hospitable impression they made. He relished the notion of resting on a shaded porch or seeking out the tower room to peer down upon the town through the tops of trees. He spent his second day in Washburn touring the town and admiring those old neighborhoods. It was a hot and sunny Monday morning, and he strolled the downtown streets on his own, taking note of the good-natured bustle of the thriving business area.

He stopped in to have lunch at the Monument Restaurant and then crossed the street to sit in the square, slouching a bit against the wooden slats, stretching his arm along the back of the bench and enjoying the sun. He looked straight up into the heavy canopy of tall trees through which the cloud-puffed sky flickered and formed momentary patterns, as if he were turning the barrel of a kaleidoscope. He thought that not enough good could be said about this agreeable and prosperous community.

In the afternoon, while Dwight and Trudy and Amelia Anne resettled themselves in Lily and Robert Butler's house, Betts Scofield drove Sam around the countryside, showing him Harcourt Lees College and driving back the long way around, where the new Green Lake Golf Course and Tennis Club was going in. "But it's in the middle of nowhere," Betts explained. "I guess people might play golf when they come out to the lake, but it's quite a drive. I think most of the people in town who play golf are still going to play at the country club, even though it's only nine holes." And at that moment, Sam Holloway began thinking about the town's other needs and if there might be the possibility of implementing ideas he'd been considering during the time he had spent in Washington.

Agnes insisted Sam remain at Scofields until the end of the month, when he would be moving to a room he had arranged to rent in a house on the corner of Main Street and Vine, just a block off the square. He sent a telegram redirecting his trunk and several other boxes to the Vine Street address instead of to his mother's house in Alexandria, Louisiana.

Sam Holloway had been on the lookout for a good job opportunity since the day he had returned home to Alexandria, after his third year at Vanderbilt, in 1935. Without a penny in his pocket he had taken a taxi from the train station to his house, run up the steps while the cab waited, greeted his mother with a quick kiss on the cheek, and asked her for fifty cents to pay the driver.

"Well, Sam. We don't have fifty cents," his mother said.

"No. Come on. Come on. I'm serious. The man's waiting out there. I don't have any money left," he had said.

"I'm serious, too," she said. "We don't have fifty cents." Finally Sam had turned his little sister's savings bank upside down — had literally shaken it for all it was worth — and managed to pay the driver, but the income from the investments his father had left his mother had evaporated, and Sam's college days were over, as they were for nearly half of his class.

He ventured into New Orleans and managed through a friend to find a job at Wohrley's, a local grocery store chain. Since he owned a dinner jacket, he was able to volunteer in the evenings as an usher at the theater, or the opera, or the ballet, where he could generally slip into an empty box seat and enjoy the performance. More often than not he ran into old friends of his family and was invited to all sorts of events once it was discovered that he was living in town. He was living the life of a popular and sought-after young bachelor while spending his days cutting the rotten parts out of last week's cabbages and wiping the white, slimy mold off wieners.

Eventually he found a better job working at Teche Greyhound Lines, which was certainly a step up from sorting and arranging the inventory at Wohrley's, and early in 1937, Sam was transferred to Natchez, Mississippi, to manage the bus station there. Sam expected to miss New Orleans, but Natchez turned out to be a big party town, and he enjoyed himself. Even though he was just the boy at the bus station, Sam was invited to everything, since he was attractive and amusing and came from a good family.

He was disappointed the following year to be put in charge of the new, larger bus station in Baton Rouge, because by now Sam knew that even if he became the president of Greyhound Lines, it was a job he couldn't tolerate forever. He had always managed to land on his feet, and, within less than a month, he happened into a sales position at a new radio station in Baton Rouge, WJBO, that had only been on the air since 1934. He had agreed to a salary of twenty dollars a week, which was less than he made from Greyhound, but he was delighted to leave the bus business behind forever.

One mild December day when he had the day off, he had driven to Alexandria to spend the day with his mother, and the two of them were having lunch on the enclosed sunporch when his sister arrived in a rush, still dressed for church. "The Japanese have attacked Pearl Harbor," she said, "and Bobby thinks that's where his cousin Lawrence is stationed!"

"I'd better get back to Baton Rouge," Sam said. "It'll be coming in on the wires." He was already up and around the corner when he turned back to give his sister, Joan, and his mother a kiss. Then he was off again, only turning back briefly. "Joan, where *is* Pearl Harbor?" he called from the yard, but with a shrug and a shake of her head, Joan pantomimed ignorance.

Sam enlisted in January of 1942, but he wasn't called up until the following year, and he filled in at WJBO, doing a little bit of everything, and he had decided during that year that radio might be the career he wanted. By Tuesday afternoon, June 10, 1947, within only two days of arriving in Washburn, Ohio, Sam found a job at the town's first radio station, WBRN, which only had authority to broadcast during daylight hours.

The little station was in a hopeless competition for listeners with KDKA in Pittsburgh, although Sam pointed out that WBRN was the only station that covered local news for eleven counties as well as Marshal County, and he and the owner, Clifford DeHaven, resolved to secure the authority to broadcast around the clock.

Sam was immediately popular, and various young women developed crushes on him. He was very attractive, although — or because — he wasn't run-of-the-mill handsome. He had a quirky kind of appeal. He was one of those men about whom a childhood self could scarcely be imagined, which gave him an air of world-weariness that was engaging. He was nothing at all like someone who had grown up in Washburn.

Almost everyone in town assumed that Betts Scofield and this new fellow, Sam Holloway, would gravitate toward each other, although there was another school of thought that held to the idea of a lost romance, a broken heart, Sam's need for a new start. As much as the people of Washburn were pleased to live where they did, it seemed strange to some that Sam chose to avoid the region of his youth, his own family, or even Chicago or New York, with their inherent excitement and adventure.

Betts Scofield and Sam were often together, but the thought of a romance with Betts never crossed Sam's mind, and, for Betts's part, she was still reeling from an intense wartime love affair. She did find Sam attractive, however, and they were thrown together so often that they began to take each other's company for granted.

Shortly after Betts and Nancy Turner had arrived in Washington, where they stayed temporarily with Nancy's aunt, the two of them and Evelyn Ramsdale, who worked in the same office as they, finally found a cramped but decent enough apartment they could afford to share. Betts had insisted that they treat themselves to a celebratory dinner at Bob and Jake's Restaurant and Club, which was considered pretty swanky. "As top-notch as any restaurant is in Washington," Betts had said, having caught on to the fact that people from New York City, and Los Angeles, and even Chicago, considered Washington, D.C., distinctly unsophisticated.

A group of officers arrived and were seated several tables away, still in the middle of a lively discussion of something or other, and Nancy was sitting facing their table. "There's a good-looking group of men I wouldn't mind meeting," she said. "But almost all the men I see in uniform look handsome to me. They look so earnest and sure of themselves. It would be fun to have someone to dance with, though. I miss the parties at home."

"Do you really want to meet them?" Betts asked.

Both Evelyn and Nancy laughed and said there was no way to do that without being considered too forward. But Betts bet them each a dime that she could get those officers to seek out their company. "And we'll be so taken aback and modest. Our reputations won't suffer a bit."

Betts had on her beautifully fitted blue linen suit and a wide-brimmed hat tipped down over her forehead, and she thought briefly of her mother's dictum that clothes should show off the woman, not the other way around. She looked like a sophisticated young woman from what must surely be a family of some consequence, and she knew she looked older than she was and very pretty. She spared a brief, kind thought for her mother. Betts was delighted not to look like a girl who had recently arrived from the wilds of Ohio.

She leaned across the table to consult Nancy. "Which one is the best-looking? Where's he sitting? Lean across toward me and act like you're telling me a secret! Something private . . . serious."

Nancy did lean closer to Betts, although she was smiling without the least bit of solemnity. "Stop that, Nancy! If you want me to get those men to introduce themselves." Nancy did her best to appear serious, and Betts turned her head to see the man Nancy chose, and, just as Betts imagined would be the case, all the men at the table were clearly aware of the three young women across the room. Betts glanced obviously but briefly at each man at the table with her mouth slightly open in the expectant beginnings of a smile, but then an expression of disappointed resignation settled over her face, and she turned back to Nancy, shaking her head so that her thick pageboy swung from side to side. "No, it's not Dwight, Nancy."

"Well! Of course not!" Nancy began, "I would have known . . . Oh! Are you sure, Betts? Are you absolutely positive it's not Dwight or Claytor?"

"*Who* do you think it is?" Evelyn asked. Evelyn was from Oklahoma and hadn't yet mastered the names of Betts's and Nancy's various siblings. Betts turned so that her profile was to the table of crisp-looking officers.

"Oh, Nancy thought one of those men was my brother," Betts confided to Evelyn.

"Really? Which one?" Evelyn asked, glancing toward the table across the way, and Betts, too, turned to regard a tall, brown-haired major for a solemn moment, and then she shook her head slightly as she turned back to Evelyn. "Don't look at their table again," she instructed Evelyn and Nancy. "Just sit back in your chairs and look concerned and . . . look like you're let down. Like you thought something nice was going to happen but that you were wrong. You're disappointed."

And Nancy and Evelyn played their parts; those three pretty girls somberly ate their dinner with the most exquisite manners, buttering their rolls on their plates and breaking off just a morsel at a time to pop into their mouths, spooning up their soup away from themselves, carefully bringing it to their mouths without bending forward, without a sound, and with their other hand demurely in their laps. They used just the corner of their napkins to dab away a nonexistent crumb, and they bent toward each other now and then, talking softly. They were each startled when they were interrupted by the very polite major whom Nancy had mistaken for Betts's brother.

Betts demurred when Major Henry Abernathy introduced himself and asked if any one of them would care to dance. Would they allow him to introduce them to his friends? It was the Billy Horace band, he said. That's why he and his friends had come.

"Thank you, Major Abernathy, but I don't think —"

"Oh, Betts! I hardly think we have to give up dancing!" Nancy said. "We were just saying how we missed all the parties back home. . . . And goodness knows the place is full of people. It would be fun to . . . relax a little. Nice not to worry about anything else for an hour or so."

"You see," Betts explained to the major, "my friend mistook you for my brother. But he's stationed in England, and suddenly we all thought about our brothers and cousins, and . . . Well!" Betts made a frantic plea to fate that she and Nancy hadn't traitorously brought down a curse on Dwight by invoking his genuine peril for a frivolous cause. After all, Betts thought, she did worry about him. She adored Dwight and Claytor and Howard.

Eventually Betts more or less moved into Major Henry Abernathy's apartment, and they had lived as though he didn't have a wife and two teenaged children waiting for him in California. On Sunday mornings Hank went out for coffee and whatever pastries or doughnuts he could find and all the newspapers, and they often sat in bed without even getting dressed and read the news. They ate the rolls Hank had brought back and drank their coffee and eventually became uninterested in the sections of newspapers strewn across the bed. Now and then Betts would find a readable sentence of newsprint on the back of her thighs, or on her forearms, and Hank found they were both printed upon in unusual places, which amused them both.

He was a career army man, and when the war in Europe ended and he was reassigned, he bought Betts a lovely, gold-link bracelet inscribed with the words "Forget Me Not," but it was he who broke down when he gave it to her. "I'm almost twenty years older than you are, Betts. You'd be bored in ten days. And I love Judith. I do. And the girls. . . . We knew this was temporary."

Betts remained cool-headed. "I know. I believed we could do that at the beginning. I thought I was so sophisticated. . . . I thought how romantic you were, and that what harm could it do. But I don't think this will be temporary, Hank. I just don't think it'll be possible."

And Betts saw him off, feeling certain she would one day be together with him for good. Hank Abernathy harbored the same secret belief and yearning all the way across the country until he was met on the base by his pretty wife and his two gangly teenaged daughters. His memories of Betts Scofield slowly dwindled in intensity, and he wasn't at all proud of himself whenever they came to mind. It had never occurred to Betts that to be remembered guiltily by a nice man was almost certainly the fastest way to be put out of his mind entirely.

Chapter Seven

IN JULY OF 1947, Mary Alcorn was only a few months past her fourth birthday, too young, still, to be able to make abstract comparisons, too young to know she was hot in the backseat of the car, on the third and final day of the trip from Texas to Ohio. It had been ninety-six degrees when they got under way at eight in the morning. Even the idea of a trip had escaped her three hours into the first day, and by now the motion of the car had become an existence in itself; she had closed down her other sensibilities.

The heat had made them all three nearly mute for the past few hours. Claytor rested his elbow in the open window and steered with one hand while he smoked one cigarette after another, and Lavinia lifted her heavy hair and dabbed at the nape of her neck with her handkerchief, which she had soaked with cologne. Both the cigarette smoke and Chanel No. 5 swept out the front windows and into the backseat, where they rendered Mary limp with nausea, but she had lapsed into a mindless endurance and gave no thought to singling out the various sources of her discomfort.

Claytor sang bits and pieces of songs, humming mostly to himself, but then he glanced back at Mary and made his voice bigger, louder, infusing it with amusement to indicate Mary's inclusion:

> "To Grandmother's house we go,
> To Grandmother's house we go,
> Heigh-ho the Derry-o,
> To Grandmother's house we go!"

He made the song a kind of joke in an attempt to engage her, in the same way he would come and find her in the mornings and say, "Give me a kiss, Mary! I'm off to the horse-pee-tal!" That always struck her as outrageously funny — for a grown-up to say such a thing. But with the wind whipping through the car, she scarcely even heard him. She remained stuporously quiet with her head flung back against the seat where she sat next to the galvanized tub that held a block of ice that was beginning to wallow in its own puddle.

A narrow ring of dirt encircled Mary's neck just where her flesh creased when she bent her head forward, and there was a thin tracery of grit in the bend of each elbow. In an effort to cool the car, Claytor bought a fresh block of ice each morning before they set out, but within an hour or so it was furrowed and gray where the dusty, incoming air rushed over it as they drove across the country.

When they stopped for gas, Lavinia moved to the backseat, and Mary scooted over. "We'll be there in about six hours," her mother said. "That doesn't seem so long, does it? It seems like nothing after driving this far." Mary didn't reply; she didn't realize that her mother had asked her a question.

When they were back on the road a while, Lavinia poured black coffee into the cup of the thermos, and Claytor turned on the radio and sang along now and then. ". . . just say good night but not good-bye . . ." Snippets of lyrics drifted into the backseat over the rush of wind. ". . . fireflies and the moonlight's glow . . ."

Lavinia finished her coffee, recapped the thermos, and lit a cigarette, looking out the window as they passed through a small town with tree-lined streets that seemed appealingly cool; the houses had deep front porches with ceiling fans. She shifted in her seat, finally, turning to sit slantwise against the window. "Mary," she said to her daughter, "there's something I've been meaning to talk to you about." But she was still working out exactly what she was going to say. Lavinia had read here and there in Freud's *The Interpretation of Dreams,* had just read the new book by Dr. Spock, had thought a great deal about sibling rivalry.

She had read enough to be convinced that if she approached this issue the wrong way, it could be terribly damaging to Mary. Her daughter's sense of security might be ruined. The ramifications of Lavinia's getting this wrong might be felt throughout Mary's whole life. Might possibly shape Mary's own maternalism, perhaps even affect her idea of her own sexuality, although Lavinia couldn't remember exactly why that was so. She respected her daughter's intelligence but also believed that anyone aged four had a necessarily limited sophistication. Lavinia had considered for some time how to broach the subject, and Mary recognized her mother's gravity and dredged up a drowsy attentiveness.

"You see, after you were born, Mary . . . Well, you and your father and I were very happy. We were so glad to be together." She paused to be sure Mary was listening, and then she continued, gazing just past Mary's shoulder and collecting her thoughts. "Well . . . now . . . I want you to think of us all — the three of us — sitting on a park bench. And we're so lucky. What I mean is . . . just think about the Armenians, and the French, now, of course, and poor England . . . Well. Anyway, the bench we get to sit on is in a beautiful park with fountains and gardens everywhere. And maybe a reptile house. Right near the zoo. We've all been walking through the park together, your daddy and me and you. We've been to see the animals, and we've been through all the gardens. You got to ride on the merry-go-round." Lavinia had become entranced with her own idea, and she spoke rapidly and with enthusiasm, leaning toward her daughter and gesturing with her hands to describe the images she conjured up in the rushing air of the backseat.

"On a blue horse with a gold mane . . . then, well, we were all pretty tired. We decided to sit down on a bench. One of those green benches with the wrought-iron armrests . . . Anyway, we sat down in the sun. Just the three of us. The ice-cream man came by . . ."

Lavinia noticed her daughter's expression and paused. Mary had that swollen-lidded look she always had if she was feverish, and Lavinia reached across her and soaked a handkerchief in the ice water and then wrung it out. She gently wiped Mary's face and neck and then took up her daughter's hands and cleaned them front and back with the cool cloth, trying to make Mary more comfortable.

"Of course," Lavinia continued, curbing the urgency in her voice, "you don't remember your daddy, because he was in the war. He died when you were just two months old. You remember I've told you about your daddy? About Phillip? Tall and awfully good-looking? All the Alcorns are good-looking. And, oh . . . he could dance! The first time I met him, we'd come with different dates, but we danced at least every other dance with each other."

Lavinia was assailed by the sudden notion that perhaps she had married Phillip because he was such a wonderful dancer. Could that possibly be true? Was that the one final thing that tipped the balance? Being in love was much different than being married. And Claytor! There were all sorts of reasons she had fallen for him, but one of those reasons was Claytor's idea of what she was like. He had been delighted when they first met and had ended up sitting together at the Officer's Club for hours discussing books, defending their favorites and discouraging the other's enthusiasm if they didn't agree. And, then, the first night she'd gone out with him, he'd picked her up in a borrowed car, and they'd stopped to give a ride to a soldier hitchhiking in the pouring rain. The radio was on, and a romantic piano concerto blared against the onslaught of weather in the desolate, flat Texas landscape.

"Now, that's nice," the soldier had said into the clammy silence of the front seat, where they were all three crushed together. "You don't hear music like that where I come from. It's a nice piece."

"It is," Claytor said, to make conversation. "I don't know what it is . . ." After another silence fell among the three of them, Lavinia finally spoke up. "Well, I think it might be Rachmaninoff's Piano Concerto Number Two in C Minor."

And both men glanced at her in frank admiration when the announcer gave that very title after the piece ended. She had thought to herself, What are the odds of that ever happening again in a single lifetime? Lavinia didn't know much of anything about music. She had only been able to identify that particular piece because, after she had flunked out of Wellesley and was living at home in Charlottesville, an earnest and dreary beau had made it his mission to improve her mind, in part by playing and explaining that particular Rachmaninoff concerto over and over. She could tell Claytor was proud of her intellectualism, which, in turn, pleased and emboldened her, even though she knew her reputation was counterfeit. But, after all, who knows why anyone gets married?

Lavinia brought her attention back to the matter at hand. "It was Sidney Bechet's band playing that first night I met your father, Mary. And the crowd . . . Well, that's not important. After your daddy died, though, you see, he couldn't sit on the bench with us anymore."

Whenever her mother began to introduce the subject of her father, Mary's attention lapsed; she had never connected any part of the story to herself. But just now her mother's voice was suddenly dramatic and surprised, as if she had just found out something new, and Mary sharpened her wits and listened carefully to what her mother was saying.

"And then! What happened then . . . with your daddy gone . . . All of a sudden the park became cold and lonely! Dark clouds came up. . . . They were like a wall around us, Mary. And the wind! Sheets of newspapers were blowing around, empty cigarette packs, gum wrappers . . . grit from the sidewalks blew all over the place. It seemed to us that a terrible storm was coming in!" She could sense Mary's attention re-engage, and Lavinia found herself caught up in the metaphor she had constructed. She had fallen into the spirit of her own invention. She straightened up and put out her cigarette.

"Mary, you and I were all by ourselves on the bench! And then — just in the nick of time — Claytor came along. Before that storm swept us away right out into the ocean! And we liked him. Pretty soon he came by our bench almost every day. Finally he asked if he could sit down, too. If we would make room for him. And you and Claytor and I have been so comfortable together on our bench. There's plenty of room, and the weather's always nice. The gardens are in bloom again. . . . Everything is fine. But now I'll tell you what's happened! Now, well! Claytor and I've noticed a stranger wandering all alone in the park . . . a *little* stranger. And, you and Claytor and I are all so comfortable, the three of us, but we do have some extra room. And you're getting big enough that sometimes you think it might be nice to look around the park . . . to play with children from other benches." Lavinia looked at Mary to see if she agreed, but Mary's expression was impassive.

"Oh, Mary," she pleaded, "that little stranger is so lonely. He doesn't know anything about the park. Claytor and I think it would be the right thing to do to bring him to live with us on our bench. To live with the three of us. And he or she will turn out to be someone we love and take care of. All of us will love him," she said.

"Sometimes, though, he might be hungry," Lavinia hurried on when she noticed that Mary's attention had started to wander. "Or he might have an earache, you know, and he might cry. He'll need to be burped. I'll have to spend an awful lot of time with him. Take care of him and change his diapers and feed him. And sometimes you might feel mad — that you have to give up some of your room on the bench for the baby. And it's perfectly natural to feel that way, Mary. You might come home after play-ing somewhere else and think that there wasn't really any room for you. That might make you sad and angry. But there will always be room on our bench for you, and room for the baby, too! But you'll probably feel a little . . . *crowded* by the newcomer . . ."

Lavinia smiled encouragingly at Mary, who was study-ing her mother's earnest expression. Mary had been paying rapt attention, but finally her eyes drooped closed. Her head fell back limply against the seat, and she fell fast asleep in self-defense. She hadn't known they were going to live on a bench. She didn't even know how to imagine it.

When Claytor and his wife and her daughter, Mary Alcorn, finally arrived, Dwight and Trudy and Betts were right at hand. Agnes was trapped chatting with various neighbors and friends. Guests had begun assembling at Scofields after the Washburn Fourth of July parade, which had stepped off at eleven o'clock and been over about a half hour later.

As soon as Claytor's car pulled up, Dwight bounded down the steps with Betts right behind him. Trudy moved with more restraint since she was too pregnant to rush anywhere. It was they who absorbed that initial spike of joyousness Claytor felt for a moment, when nostalgia and reality intersected. He had a great hug for Betts and Trudy, an elated handshake and a clap on the back for Dwight, and a quick grin and a kiss on the cheek for his mother by the time she reached him. In just the time it had taken Agnes to maneuver her way though the guests and cross the yard, Claytor and Dwight were already in the middle of a conversation.

Agnes hadn't been able to get to Claytor's wedding during the war, and when Claytor turned back to talk to Dwight after only that quick acknowledgment of her, Agnes determinedly moved between them. "This is Mary Alcorn, isn't it?" she asked. "And, of course, Lavinia?" Claytor turned back to his mother in surprise, embraced her, too, and then pulled away, beaming.

"I've been on the road too long! I think the heat's finally addled my brain. Here they are! Here are my girls!" Lavinia held out her hand while Claytor urged Mary forward a bit. "And here's the apple of my eye! Here she is at last. This is Mary Alcorn," he said.

"I'm so glad to have you here," Agnes said, taking Lavinia's hand and then turning her attention to Lavinia's daughter. "And I've heard so many wonderful things about you, Mary Alcorn! Why, Claytor," Agnes said, "she looks just like a little Scofield! Blond hair! And such brown eyes. I'm very glad to meet you!" But the little girl was leaning against Claytor's knees, scarcely even awake. Agnes turned back to Lavinia, who was much prettier than Agnes had imagined. Petite and with huge green eyes.

"That's an awfully long trip for a little girl! For all of you. And all these strangers! You know, I should have suggested you postpone your trip by one day. But so many people wanted to see you, Claytor. And especially to meet Lavinia and Mary. And lots of people haven't even had a chance to see Trudy and Dwight and little Amelia Anne. Howard's home! And a friend of Dwight's. Sam Holloway," she added.

"I hadn't thought how tired you might be, though. I hope it won't be too much! Lily and Trudy and Betts have everything under control. Howard got fireworks from somewhere . . ." Agnes caught her breath and slowed down. "Well. I'm so glad to see you," she said inclusively and then turned to Lavinia. "Mary Alcorn really was born on the fifteenth, wasn't she?" Agnes asked, with a note in her voice that surprised Lavinia, as if for some reason Agnes might have doubted it. "Yes, she was. March of nineteen forty-three," Lavinia said.

"The ides," Agnes said. "March fifteenth was Claytor's great-uncle Leo's birthday, too. And, you know Claytor's father and aunt . . . Warren and Lily Butler — well, she was a Scofield. And Lily's husband, too, Robert Butler, were all born on the fifteenth of September. Well, of course, I'm sure you've heard more than you want to about that. I certainly did! But I do wish Uncle Leo could have seen Mary Alcorn. He wouldn't even have been surprised that he and she were born on the same day once he got a look at her."

Agnes saw that Lavinia looked blank. "Didn't Claytor tell you that his great-uncle Leo always claimed that every Scofield was born on the ides of the month? Goodness knows I heard about it before I'd even met the Scofields! I heard about that all my life. It was quite an event, I suppose. Warren and Lily and Robert born on the same day. Uncle Leo was right, you see. Most of the Scofields do seem to be born on the ides — different months, of course."

"Well," Lavinia agreed softly, nodding her head, which made her thick hair swing forward. "Claytor was born on the ides."

Betts and Dwight spoke up simultaneously, as did Agnes.

"Claytor wasn't —"

"No, he just missed —"

"Well, no," Agnes said. "Claytor is the only one who wasn't . . ." Agnes interjected. "He was born on April thirteenth. He only missed by two days. All the others, though. But the ides of March! That's when Mary Alcorn was born! *Macbeth,* isn't it? Didn't Uncle Leo always say it was *Macbeth?*" she repeated, raising her voice a little to be heard. "Those witches? Or maybe *Julius Caesar.*" Agnes was so nervous under Lavinia's impassive attention that her mouth had gone dry, and she ran her tongue across her upper lip.

She was horrified to find herself gushing on like this. Blithering, she always thought, when Bernice Dameron went on and on, determinedly explaining all the tedious particulars of some story or other while she and Agnes stood together if they were on duty at recess or when they were eating a quiet lunch by themselves in the cloakroom.

There was something about Claytor's wife that disconcerted Agnes. She couldn't think what it might be, but at once she felt dowdy and unsophisticated in her daughter-in-law's company. The Scofields always all talked at once, their voices tumbling over one another with opinions, ideas, enthusiasms, or disagreements. But Lavinia listened to Agnes with the keenest attention and without any change of expression as Agnes chattered on. Agnes was painfully aware, though, that nothing she was saying deserved such earnest consideration, and as a result she became more and more anxious to fill any silence.

"But, Mrs. Scofield —," Lavinia began.

"Oh, please. Just 'Agnes' is fine. Unless it makes you uncomfortable. Warren's mother — Claytor's grandmother — always asked me to call her 'Mother.' I had the hardest time — I never could do it, and so I was always trying to tell her something without having to call her anything at all . . ." And Agnes finally ran down as though she had been a tightly wound music box. She just stopped speaking.

Lavinia nodded that she understood. She glanced around the group of Scofields who had gathered to greet her and Claytor. "But, you know," she said mildly, "those birthdays. Warren Scofield and Lily Butler? And Robert Butler? They were all three born on September fifteenth?"

"Isn't it odd?" Agnes said. "One of those coincidences that happens that just doesn't seem possible."

"It is a coincidence," Lavinia agreed. "All of them born on the same day. But the ides of September is on the thirteenth of the month." She didn't speak with an air of insistence, as though the point was particularly important. In fact, she seemed only languidly interested, peering out at them from under her dark bangs with such intense green eyes, emanating a smoky, careless interest. No one wanted to disagree with or correct her, since they had only just met her and wanted her to feel included.

Howard had arrived, though, and had been standing at the edge of the conversation, intrigued. "Is that so? Hah! Is that right?" He thought Lavinia was stunningly exotic among the rest of them. He was entranced with this new sister-in-law — so clearly a foreigner among them. "What about that! Now what about the rest of us? I'm November fifteenth," he said. "I'm the baby. Nineteen twenty-six. And I'll tell you what! Dwight's never forgiven me for being born on his eighth birthday. He'd been so excited about that birthday that I still hear plenty about it. Betts is February fifteenth. She's three years older. Well, almost. She was born in nineteen twenty-four. All of us thinking we were born on the ides of the month except Claytor. Feeling that it was too bad that he couldn't hang on until the fifteenth."

"Your birthday is on November fifteenth, too?"

Howard nodded, smiling down at her. "And it's so close to Christmas that I get terrible presents. Dwight makes out a lot better, even though Christmas is coming. I've finally just put it down to the curse of the last born."

"Lavinia, don't believe any of this," Dwight said lightly. "It's just because I'm ancient . . ."

"Oh, no!" Howard said. "Dwight has seniority, and he's hard to buy for. Everyone in the family spends months mulling it over and finally decides on whatever it is they think he'd like. And then there they are, in Phillips Department Store, wondering what they've forgotten. 'Oh, no,' they say. 'I forgot Howie! I'll just pick up some little thing.' . . . Last year Betts sent me a screwdriver with interchangeable parts."

"Howard! I thought you'd need —," Betts began, but Howard was cheerful, never having worried much about his place in the family, and Lavinia was already speaking.

"The ides of November," Lavinia was saying to him, "is the thirteenth, you know. In fact, the only months when the ides do fall on the fifteenth are March, May, July, and October. In all the other months it's the thirteenth. Mary was born on the ides of March. I always hope it won't be bad luck. *Beware the ides of March!*" But Lavinia was just flicking over that notion; all the Scofields could tell that she wasn't really interested but was only making polite conversation in her own soft-voweled, unhurried way. "So only Claytor," Lavinia went on, speaking to Howard primarily but then addressing Trudy, "and your daughter . . . Amy? . . . were actually born on the ides. Isn't it funny how notions like that spring up in families? In my house, it —"

"Amelia," Trudy corrected. "Amelia Anne."

"I'll be damned!" Howard interjected. "Now that's amazing. Great God! We've spent our whole lives talking about the ides of the month and the Scofields. I'd started hating to have my birthday come along. And not one of us thought to find out when the ides were. Uncle George and Uncle Leo were . . . But all the other birthdays . . . So! Only Claytor was born on the ides. We always teased him about being the only one of us who wasn't!"

Finally Agnes gathered her wits. "Well, in any case, it certainly is all so interesting, I think," she said, trying to dismiss the whole issue — which she found oddly unnerving — by brushing it aside. "You'll have to ask Uncle George to explain it. I'm sure I've probably got it confused." And Agnes spoke at the same moment Betts and Dwight — and even Claytor — dismissed Lavinia's idea out of hand; it was clear to them that Lavinia simply hadn't understood what their mother was saying. Of course their birthdays were on the ides of the month; it was part of being a Scofield.

"I know you must be exhausted," Agnes proposed, "and you haven't met all these people who've come to see you. You must want a chance to freshen up. Dwight and Trudy and Betts have planned a picnic, and Howard's found fireworks . . ."

Lavinia didn't realize that Agnes was directing this at her, and she stood next to Claytor with a dreamy, distracted expression, which held Agnes in place while her new daughter-in-law shook a cigarette out of a pack from her purse. Claytor offered her a light right there in public, in the front yard in the middle of the afternoon. Lavinia noticed Agnes's surprise. "Oh, Mrs. Scofield. I know women almost never smoke these," she said, "but it's hard to find any other brand at the PX." She held up a pack of Camels and was careful to exhale away from Agnes, but in the still heat, the smoke lingered in the air. Claytor took one for himself and lit it, cupping his hand around the flame of his lighter.

Agnes finally nodded, and Betts grinned. "Now, I know you two must want to get your things out of the car," Agnes said. "Claytor, I've got your room all made up for you and Lavinia. I thought Mary Alcorn could be next to you in the sewing room. I've set it up as a nursery. Dwight and Trudy and little Amelia Anne are next door. You'd better go introduce Lavinia to all these people, Claytor. I've got to get the ham in the oven . . ." Agnes was suddenly aware that she was tired; she saw their friends the Drummonds making their way across the square, and she didn't have any energy to spare for them.

Claytor and Lavinia moved aside, turning to find other friends of the family approaching, and Dwight and Trudy and Howard were still there. Reunions and introductions and conversation went on while Agnes made her way across the yard. She was surprised at the sort of woman Claytor had married. Lavinia was very pretty. Maybe she was beautiful. She was certainly glamorous, Agnes thought, in a movie-star way. Prettier than anyone had told Agnes. But there was something . . . Well, Agnes hardly knew her, and Lavinia had just arrived after three days of traveling. But there was a way Lavinia suddenly became part of a conversation she hadn't even seemed to be listening to. And, when she suddenly spoke up, her manner and expression were impassive, oddly detached, so that it was impossible to discern what tack she was taking, what her interest might be. It was difficult to know how to respond in a way that would be agreeable to her.

And it did surprise Agnes, too, that Lavinia didn't seem to be anything at all like a Scofield.

Agnes put the ham in the oven and hesitated at the door on her way back to her guests. Finally she turned and slipped up the back stairs to her own room. She took off her flowered voile dress, which she had thought would be cool, but which stuck in transparent patches to her back and shoulders. She lay down on the counterpane in her white slip — just for a minute, she said to herself. The shades were drawn against the heat, and the electric fan oscillated slowly and stirred the heavy air a little. There was no escaping the vague dreariness that had settled over her spirits, and she concentrated on the intermittent relief of the moving air as the fan swung its head back and forth.

The house was quiet upstairs, and she fell into a sudden, profound sleep from which she came into consciousness with no memory of dreaming and no sense of lapsed time. And then she realized she had been awakened by Will, who had slipped into bed behind her as she lay on her side. She realized with alarm that he had undressed, was embracing her, gently cupping her breasts, and his chin was resting against the top of her head.

"Will! Will!" She raised herself on one elbow and whispered furiously, "What are you doing? The whole family — the whole neighborhood — practically the whole town is out in the yard, Will! You get dressed! You go on! I'll be down in a minute."

"Not a soul even saw me drive in, Agnes. I parked out back and brought the corn and tomatoes in. The beans, too. Put them in the kitchen. Everyone's out front. No one's even in the house. I didn't see you outside so I came to look for you."

"What are you thinking?" She was whispering still, but Will lazily encompassed her, curling his large frame around her and carefully sliding the straps of her slip over her arms and down to her waist. "Why, I'm just enjoying my front yard," he said softly, and Agnes was puzzled, but she also felt loose all over, as if her joints were melting.

"Will, this isn't a good idea . . ."

"Ah, Agnes. Well, that's just your opinion," he spoke lazily and with a round, ripe note in his voice that was peculiar and unlike him. "I have a good friend with me who wouldn't agree a bit," he said, speaking dreamily into her ear. "See here," he said, pressing himself against her, so that she felt his erection. "Private Peters at your service, ma'am! Why, he's standing at attention. This old soldier is ready for a parade!"

Agnes lay perfectly still for a moment, wondering if her idea of what Will was saying could possibly be correct.

"In fact," Will went on, "he'd be real pleased to shake your hand . . ." Will reached for Agnes's hand and closed her fingers around his penis. Agnes lurched forward and turned over, placing her hand firmly over Will's mouth, and he took that gesture to be an indication that there was no need for any more talk between them.

Eventually they lay together sated and sweaty, but chilled, too, when the slow air moved over them. Agnes pulled her slip on over her head and drew the sheet and the light bedspread up to cover them, and then — even in that appalled instant of realizing where she was and what had just happened — she drifted off again into a sticky sleep.

Mary Alcorn was still drugged with travel, and in her drowsy state she had an impression of brightness everywhere. Sun glinted on the leaves of the tall trees and was refracted by the broad fronts of the houses along the curve of the drive. Sunlight gleamed around her as the assembled adults exclaimed their greetings with an upward timbre of enthusiasm, an airy lilt of pleasure. She couldn't sort out what they were saying; their greetings and endearments and conversation flickered through the air as they stooped and bent over her with their bright hair. She couldn't accommodate so much that was new to her all at once, and she fell out of any state of curiosity or even attention. She retreated to a mindless kind of waking sleep.

She stayed where she was, entrenched against the brace of Claytor's knees, until finally he disengaged himself distractedly and moved away to take Lavinia's arm and introduce her to friends and family whom she had not yet met. One of those very tall people who had gathered in the yard crouched down beside Mary and took her hand.

"I've heard so much about you, sweetie, and I'm so glad you're here. But I know you must be exhausted. All you have to do is move to be miserable in this heat. I'm so glad to meet you at last! I'm your Aunt Betts."

Mary was transfixed by the intense brown glance with which Betts regarded her; Mary was aware of the heavy sweep of Betts's yellow hair as it fell forward around her shoulders. "Well!" Betts said, straightening up, still grasping Mary's hand. "I can see you're as tired and hot as you can be. You can visit with all these grown-ups later on. Everyone is dying to meet you, but you probably need some time to catch your breath. It's awful, though, isn't it? When people sort of study you and you have to be so polite and friendly? And all you want is for everyone not to look at you. People ought to wait a little while! You come along with me and we'll see if we can find Amelia Anne. She's your Uncle Dwight and Aunt Trudy's little girl. She's been waiting for you all day. Too excited even to eat any lunch. She was upstairs taking a nap on the sleeping porch the last time I saw her. She's going to be awfully glad you're finally here."

Mary didn't want to leave the vicinity of her parents in this strange place, but she didn't have the unconsidered courage most children possess. It didn't even occur to her to say no, or to cry, or to call out for her mother; she had been almost entirely in the company of grown-ups during her life, and she had no idea of any way to refuse her aunt. Betts crossed the stepping stones, still holding Mary's hand, and Mary trailed with apprehension across the yard and up the stairs of the tall white house, wondering where they were going and where her parents were.

Just inside the door, Betts stooped again, encircling Mary Alcorn's shoulders lightly. "We'll go upstairs and find Amelia Anne. But someone might have taken her home, because I don't see Bobbin anywhere. He's her dog, and he just about never leaves her side. We can find Amelia Anne and Bobbin later, but maybe you'd like to have a cool bath first? It would make you feel so nice and fresh. You can use some of my Shalimar bath soap. And the dusting powder, too. It smells wonderful, Mary Alcorn. You'll smell like a dream! I never let anyone use my Shalimar. It costs the world. But after the long trip you've had . . . Well! It'll be just the thing. Shalimar is my signature scent!"

Mary was sure that she didn't want to take a bath in this unfamiliar house under Aunt Betts's supervision. She liked Aunt Betts, but the idea of taking a bath in this strange place made her mute with dread. Somewhere from the back of the house, though, the phone rang, and her aunt Betts stood up. "Ah! I've got to answer that, sweetie. It's been ringing off the hook! Everyone in town is wondering if Claytor's home yet. In this town! Oh, you bet! They're dying to size up the new Scofields. Well, half of them thought they were going to be the one who married Claytor. Go ahead on upstairs and see if Amelia Anne is here, if you want to. I'll be up in just a minute."

Mary stood just where she was for a little bit, after Aunt Betts hurried off down the hall, until finally it seemed to her that she'd been standing there for a long time. Her aunt had told her to go upstairs if she wanted to, and when Mary had stayed where she was a while longer, and her aunt continued not to reappear, Mary approached the staircase as she'd been directed to. She moved slowly, lingering at the foot of the stairs and leaning her head back to take in her surroundings.

On fair days, Agnes Scofield's house held at its center a core of pale light, which fell from the window of the second-story landing. On a day as bright as this one, though, the blazing sunlight filtered through the old glass and streamed fiercely through the upper window, angling across the floor and striking the balustrades of the stair railing, so that dark, precise blades of shadow were cast in an upward progression against the wall. The day outside was flat with heat; only in that hallway at the very heart of the building did the air stir at all, rising and falling in a gentle cycle as the temperature increased.

For a moment or two Mary was reassured. She observed the whole of the two-story space, and it was comforting to bask for a moment in the relative relief of this enclosed radiance as opposed to the overbright daylight outside. She leaned against a chair beside a tall clock in the lower hall, but its sonorous ticktock, ticktock suddenly struck her as ominous in the silent house, and a fluttery panic began in her stomach. She wished that Aunt Betts would come back. Mary was worried about how she would find her parents. She began to wonder if she would ever see them again.

The regular ticking of the clock produced a tension exactly like the feeling she had when she waited for her mother to count to twenty while Mary scrambled to find a hiding place when they played hide and seek. All at once she was beset with an anxiety that propelled her a few steps up the stairs, where she stopped in sudden alarm. She listened to the sounds of the house, and she heard no one speaking, only the clock and the creaks and sighs particular to that building but unidentifiable to Mary. She proceeded gradually, as equally alarmed at the thought of turning back as she was of going forward.

When she turned at the middle landing and faced the flight of five stairs more, she stopped still. The space ahead was shadowed beyond the light of the window in the upper hall, and she was scared. But when she turned to see where she had been, the tall clock still loomed, and the umbrellas spiked in all directions from their copper stand.

Beyond the light from the window, however, she could see down a short hall to another door, and she continued up the staircase and then moved slowly toward that doorway. She had forgotten why her aunt had suggested she go upstairs, had forgotten, in fact, much of anything about Aunt Betts except that she existed and had led her into the house and then disappeared. Mary was simply where she was, and she didn't ponder any reason for it. When she reached the door of the room, she cautiously turned the glass doorknob, pushed it open just enough to slip through, and studied the room's interior for some time. Nothing moved at all, except a fan that rustled the corner of a drawn shade every time it turned in that direction.

She entered the room by moving along its perimeter, keeping the wall at her back so nothing could come up behind her. When she reached the vanity bench across from the bed, she stayed very quiet, because she saw there were people lying on the bed. People who were not moving at all. The face of the person nearest to where Mary was standing was turned away, and Mary was frozen there, terrified and curious. She had never seen anyone lying so still, and she leaned against the vanity bench, keeping watch. There was no choice to be made as far as she knew. She would remain until someone found her.

Agnes came awake slowly, with a headache and a fuzzy feeling that inevitably stayed with her if she fell asleep during the daytime. She had never liked naps. They weren't at all refreshing but left her feeling faintly sick. She didn't open her eyes but just lay still in the hopes that the fact of Will lying next to her would resolve itself. She was horrified at the risk she'd taken. What had she been thinking? How had she become a woman who abandons guests in her own house and has sex with a man who names his own penis? Who had nicknames for her breasts? She wished more than anything that in just a moment she would discover she had dreamed they had made love in the afternoon with the house full of Agnes's children and even her grandchildren. What had come over her? She tried to imagine who might be in the house just now, if anyone. Will would have to leave from the side door off the sitting room, which no one ever used.

Her headache faded into just a heavy feeling behind her eyes as she began to concentrate on the strategy of protecting herself from being found out in her own irresponsible behavior. Finally she forced herself to open her eyes, and she sat up and swiveled in the direction of her vanity, intending to wrench her hair into a state of respectability.

Agnes was so unnerved to find herself observed, however, that she cried out — just a brief elongated vowel of surprise — and next to her in the dim bedroom Will, too, gasped a startled "Ahhh" and slid farther down beneath the sheet. But Mary Alcorn was the most surprised. At first her face was blank with shock, then her mouth dropped open and her eyes went round, but she made no sound at all. Before Agnes could say a word, Mary Alcorn ran out of the room, gaining momentum as she reached the hall and finally emitting a high, tiny squeak that became fuller as she clattered down the stairs.

Agnes hurried after her, but Mary Alcorn was at the front door by the time Agnes recovered and reached the landing, where she stopped and realized she was standing barefooted and wearing nothing but her nylon slip. By the time the little girl had wrestled with the latch of the front door, she was hopping from one foot to another in terror and emitting frantic little bleats of fear.

"Mary Alcorn? Mary Alcorn? Honey! It's just me! Sweetheart . . ."

But by then Mary had managed to pull the big door open enough so that she slid through, and she sustained a sirenlike sound of alarm as she ran across the grass toward the group of people still gathered on the lawn. The Drummonds' grandchildren were playing some loud game, and the adults weren't distressed by Mary Alcorn's sudden shriek once they glanced around and saw that no one was imperiled. But Mary ran full-throttle toward her father, who was turned away from her, and finally she threw her arms around his knees, too winded to make another sound. He automatically bent to scoop her up while he was still talking, and he braced her beneath her knees in the crook of his arm. He turned his head to smile at her, and she looked straight into a face that was not Claytor's. It was not her father! She was too appalled even to exclaim, because this man moved like her father, bent toward her in exactly the same way her father did, and his eyes and his hair were exactly like her father's. Mary understood then that something had shifted in the world, and she went limp, simply dropping her head against the man's shoulder.

And, as it happened, Dwight Claytor was more than happy to shoulder the temporary burden of Phillip Alcorn's little daughter. The Alcorns were cousins of his on his mother's — Catherine Claytor's — side, and he and Phillip had found themselves stationed together briefly in Texas. In fact, it was Dwight who had urged Claytor to look up Lavinia after Phillip had been killed in a car accident on the base.

Claytor smiled and reached out to take Mary Alcorn, whom he had noticed racing toward them apparently rejuvenated, full of energy. Claytor wrapped Mary Alcorn in both arms, and she didn't resist. "Good Lord, Dwight! Scofields is brimming with babies," he said, gesturing with a tip of his head toward Trudy and Lavinia, both obviously pregnant, who were standing together talking. "We've got to be careful. We're like a bunch of rabbits! Pretty soon there'll be a Scofield under every bush." Dwight nodded and smiled. The atmosphere within the Scofield compound on that hot, hot day was heavy with fecundity. Claytor carried Mary Alcorn off toward the house so he could give her a bath before dinner, now that she seemed to have recovered from their long trip.

Chapter Eight

JUST IN THAT SHORT BIT OF TIME she stood watching Mary Alcorn's back receding down the stairs, watched her struggle frantically with the heavy door and make her escape, Agnes's notion of where she fit in the world swung around full circle. As she turned back toward her bedroom, passing through the shaft of sunlight falling through the high window, the new status of her own life clarified itself: She was the custodian of her children's frame of reference; she was the keeper of the house; she alone was the authority on the nature of her children's childhood. The idea her children had of who they were was partly in her hands. She neither desired nor shied away from that role; she merely recognized it.

What on earth was she doing, then, in light of her matriarchy, carrying on with Will Dameron? He simply didn't belong anywhere in the context of the definition of Warren and Agnes Scofield's family. He was still in bed, half sitting, with his arms crossed behind his head and a rueful smile aimed in her direction. Agnes sat down on the vanity bench and peered at herself in the mirror, beginning the task of working a comb through the tangle of her hair. She didn't have a thing to say, and Will's smile faded. He swung his legs over the side of the bed and began to get dressed.

"You'll have to wait till I'm outside before you leave, Will. And then please go out the side door in the sitting room," she said. "No one ever uses that door, and it only opens onto that little path beside the hedge."

"You know there wasn't anything going on to scare that little girl," Will said, and Agnes nodded her head and made a hum of agreement around the hairpins she held between her teeth, but she didn't turn around and address Will. She concentrated on her hair, which was still damp at the roots with sweat. She was merciless in straightening and clamping it at the back of her neck, but her bangs were still not long enough to be held back, and they settled over the front of her head and her forehead in a curly pouf. Once more, as she regarded herself, she resolved never, never again to allow anyone else to cut her hair. She could always do a better job herself, despite Lily's opinion, and it was Lily's hairdresser who had left Agnes feeling that she looked like a clipped poodle. When she had said so to Lily, Lily hadn't even disagreed.

"Oh, my goodness," Lily had said, moving around Agnes to see the cut from all sides. "Well, it was only that I thought it would be easier for you. . . . And, really, Agnes, your hair grows so fast . . ."

When Agnes was satisfied that she had done the best she could, she turned around on the bench and gazed at Will, who had pulled on his pants but was bare-chested. She suppressed her impatience at the inefficiency of the way Will always got dressed, although she had so often wanted to tell him to — for goodness sake — put his shirt on first. Dwight and Claytor and Howard, at least when they were little boys, and Warren as long as she'd known him, had all followed exactly the same illogical procedure, but today she found it maddeningly unforgivable.

When Lily had first read Freud and explained to Agnes the notion of penis envy, Agnes had just laughed. As close as Lily had been to Robert and Warren, she hadn't grown up with brothers, hadn't had sons, and had never been aware of the anxiety that overtakes a little boy at about age three or four when he suddenly becomes conscious of the external vulnerability of his own genitalia. Agnes had assumed that her brothers — whether they ever considered it or not — would have envied the elegant efficiency of her own discreet interior arrangement. Perhaps, then, a naked man would feel more secure getting his pants on before worrying about the rest of himself, before even remembering that he would have to tuck his shirt in.

"I really want you to leave, Will. I mean, I want you to go home. I don't know what I've been thinking."

"Ah, God, Agnes. That's ridiculous. Why don't we just get married?"

"I'd never marry you, Will. It wouldn't really work out. I've thought about it, and we've been over all this before. And, really, Will, I don't want to hurt your feelings, but this afternoon I'd be so much more comfortable if you'd go home."

"I don't see why you're so mad. All right. This afternoon was my fault, and it was a bad idea. I'm sorry. I am sorry. But you're acting like it's the end of the world. Like you never want to see me again. You've blown this all out of proportion, and you're making a mistake."

"I never do want to see you again, but I just hadn't realized it," Agnes said. She glanced up at Will and realized how unkind she sounded. "Oh, I don't mean I never want to *see* you again. Of course we'll see each other all the time. But all this . . . this is just over, Will."

Will himself was suddenly angry. "All right. I'll go. I'll certainly go. But I'm not going to hide out up here and sneak away. Explain it any way you want to, Agnes, if anyone sees me. I don't think you understand how much I care about you. How much you care about me. I don't think you're in any state of mind right now to make this kind of decision." But by then he was dressed, and he didn't storm out of the room; he simply walked down the stairs, out the kitchen door and drove out Coshocton Road, past his old house and up the long drive to the handsome old farmhouse that had been built by Agnes's grandfather. A few people had noticed Will leave. In fact, Betts had been in the kitchen when he passed through, but no one thought twice about it among all the comings and goings of so many people in and out of the house.

There was a certain spot in Agnes's bedroom, between the bed and the tall desk with its glass-doored bookcase, where, in the summer, the light from the bay window fell a certain way, and where — early in the morning, or if she'd napped in the afternoon — she often found herself standing stock-still, looking out at the yard as if she were watching scenes from novels through the window panes. It was a trancelike state from which she would emerge slowly, reorienting herself to the real world after a momentary lapse in which all but the most basic self-consciousness fell away. In the moment itself she had no thoughts at all. She thought of these small fugues as being slippery wisps of time, empty of context, that now and then enshrouded her, reducing her to her essential self — entirely unaware of time or place. She was only alive; she was no one's daughter, no one's wife, no one's sister, no one's mother, although even those non-connections were merely a way she could understand or describe the sensation after the fact.

She had been subject to these short-lived spells as far back as she could remember; they weren't alarming to her anymore, but as she came back into the world, everything had a flattened look; even light and air seemed to exist as flat parallelograms. Everything she saw seemed only to be images moving across a wavering screen. For just a little while people and objects were familiar to her but lacked dimension.

Warren had been fascinated. "It must be like just being born," he said. "Maybe it's a memory of being born. Or maybe of before you were born. Sorting out how you became aware. Of when you first started to compare one thing with another. I am this; I am not that. I've never had a feeling like that. I've had the feeling of walking into a place I know I've never seen before and being convinced that it's familiar. I'll discover that I have an intense memory of a place I know for a fact I've never been. Even the smell, the colors. Déjà vu. I've had that happen twice that I remember, but never any state as . . . unlimited as what you're describing."

The afternoon of this Fourth of July 1947, however, when she realized she had momentarily been caught up in just such a spell, she came back to the moment with her hand still clutching the spring-loaded window shade that she had coaxed upward. She looked out at the people shifting about in the yard below, and it was exactly like looking at a glossy page of an expensive book depicting people enjoying themselves on a summer day. It seemed to her that the scene must have come from something she'd read — not seen before but deeply known to her. Maybe that poem of Robert's about Sweetwater. Children under trees. And adults as well, floating over the grass, the shirts and dresses and pants far more discernable in the ebbing light than the features of the people who wore them. Or she could be witnessing a bit of life that had already happened in this very place, with Dwight and Claytor and Betts playing out under the towering, trembling catalpa trees. Trudy and Howard as well. Only rushing inside now and then to get a glass of water.

Warren had often taken Dwight and Claytor along to his office on a Saturday morning when they were three or four years old to pick up the mail or on some other errand, and the little boys would telephone her from the offices of Scofields & Company, although Warren dialed the number.

"May I speak to Mrs. Scofield, please," came a shy voice when she answered the ring.

"Yes. This is she," Agnes would answer in her telephone voice.

"This is me, Mama."

"Oh? I hope you're well today. But I'm very sorry to tell you that I think you must have the wrong number. I don't believe I know anyone by the name of 'Me.'"

There would be a moment of excited laughter and solemn conferences on the other end. "No, Mama. This is your son. Claytor Scofield."

"Oh, well! Hello, Claytor. How nice to hear from you. How old are you now? Let me see. . . . Yes, you must be thirty-five years old by now. Are you married? Are you calling me from far away? Are you phoning me from California? You sound so far away. Is the weather nice where you live?"

"I'm not married. No! Mama! I'm not thirty-five! I'm not in California!" And then Dwight might take the phone.

"How are you, Mama? This is Dwight Claytor. We aren't in California."

"Oh, no? Well, you do sound awfully far away. Are you in Kissimmee, Florida? Or Joliet, Illinois? Are you calling me from Kalamazoo, Michigan? Or maybe Damariscotta, Maine? Oh, I know! I bet you're calling from Natchitoches, Louisiana."

"Nooo! Mama! Why are you saying that? We aren't anywhere! We're here, Mama. How are you today?"

"Well, I tell you, it's surprising that you should ask me that just now, Dwight. Because I'm really not feeling a bit well. I'm awfully weak and shaky."

That would be met with baffled silence, and then Agnes would carry on. "I was just going to call your father to see if he could stop and buy some ice cream. And maybe some chocolate syrup. Maybe even half of one of the small cakes from the bakery if they've got cake today. I think that would be just the thing to put me back on my feet. But I don't know where your father is. I'm afraid he must be lost somewhere. I had thought that maybe some cake and ice cream —"

"— and whip cream!" Dwight would interject.

"Oh, yes. That would be exactly what I need. But I don't know where your father's got to, so I guess I'll see if castor oil is any help. I feel very strange."

"No! Mama! Don't take castor oil! It's horrible. It never makes you feel better. I know where Daddy is."

"But Dwight, you've never had castor oil. It might be just the pick-me-up I need."

He was quiet for a moment, considering the truth of this. "Don't take castor oil, Mama. It smells horrible. I know where Daddy is . . ."

"I'm so glad to hear that. Castor oil does smell bad. I'd much rather have ice cream."

"— right here! He's right here."

Warren, though, had been there so short a time in their lives. So short a time in her own life. She stood looking out the window and realized that by now she had been without Warren longer than she had been with him, but that bit of her life was more vivid to her than when she recounted something that happened the day before yesterday. She thought that was probably because within the twelve years of her marriage to Warren, she had unknowingly been at the very heart of the slow swirl of her lifetime, awash in sensations that she had never had before. New babies. Unimagined and indescribable passions and joy and fear and despair. For those years she had been at an emotional extreme on every front; she had been fervent in every direction, and in retrospect she found the idea of her younger self exhilarating. She had often been filled with conflicting passions.

Nothing in her life then had been bleached of color; every new experience was a bluntly shocking slash of red or yellow, a glistening blue — always primary colors, whereas now she thought of her existence as continuing in a far more subtle palette and done in watercolors. Often lovely, but never as intense. That notion neither pleased nor distressed her; it struck her as the way an ordinary life played out, and there was something to be said for both stages.

She did sometimes miss the unusual sense of being important, busy at the center of the universe that, for a while, had been the houses of Scofields in Washburn, Ohio. She had been the most important person in Warren's life; he had often told her so, but she had never doubted it, anyway. It was the only time she had believed herself entirely secure in someone else's affection. And, of course, he had certainly been the most important person in her life. She didn't think that was a coincidence that happened very often. Lily and Robert, for instance, each loved the other. There was no mistaking that, but neither one was in need of any assurance that he or she was loved. She and Warren had fallen into that rare coincidence of being exactly the person the other needed. She knew that it was she whom Warren had considered the protagonist of his life — other than himself, of course. That's what he had been for her and what he would always remain in whatever versions of their childhoods her children told themselves. But she also fell sometimes into a brooding bitterness whenever she came hard up against the fact that ultimately she and Warren had each failed the other.

It was now and then enraging to Agnes to know that — with the exception of Lily and Robert — all the people of Washburn were certain that what they had first considered an unlikely alliance between Agnes Claytor and Warren Scofield had turned out to be the perfect match. An ideal marriage against which other unions were measured. Sometimes Agnes longed to say to the children, at least, that their father was no saint. That no one had any idea . . . but then she would be overtaken by a sense of Warren, of his huge and occasional unhappiness that she couldn't appease, and she was silent out of loyalty. Besides, the whole household had also been swept up in the long spells of Warren's remarkable ability to enjoy every moment of some days, his enthusiasms and euphoria.

Over the years, whenever Agnes began brooding, those times when she fell into states of mild self-pity and wondered if, knowing at nineteen what she knew now, she would still have married Warren — well, she never even bothered to carry on the thought. Considering the idea that she might not have married Warren was as impossible and irrelevant as trying to imagine God or as getting a grip on the idea of the universe. The moment you thought you had succeeded, you failed.

She had considered his death so often that she knew exactly what had happened, although she never revealed what she believed to anyone else. Warren had been in a terrible way before that trip to Pennsylvania, and so had Leo Scofield, ever since his wife, Audra, had died the previous summer. "Just after the catalpas bloomed," Leo said repeatedly. He had planted those trees as saplings the week before Lily was born, in 1888, to line either side of the entrance from the street to the garden. But Leo had thought he was planting tulip trees, which flowered beautifully.

"Audra hated those damned catalpas! They were pretty for about a week in late spring, but then they began to stink to high heaven and dropped pollen all over anyone who came in through the garden. Wouldn't you think I could have made the time to take them out? To *have* them taken out? Audra wanted dogwoods in their place, and I always thought, well, next year . . ."

Agnes should never have let the two of them leave early that morning, with Warren driving Uncle Leo's big black car. But it was the first time Warren had been determined to leave the house in nearly two and a half weeks, and she had been sick of his bleak mood. Tired of walking on eggs whenever she was around him. In the aftermath of his death, however, Agnes had considered the incident with nearly obsessive intensity, had thought it out in such detail that it took on the quality of narrative. She might as well have been in the car with them. She knew exactly what had happened: a shroud of hopelessness had enveloped Warren just as Uncle Leo said to him — across the distance of the front seat of the big Packard — that there was never a time that he wanted to go home again, now that Audra wouldn't be there to greet him. Warren had been unable to respond, because he himself was fighting his way out from under the debilitating idea of eventual and permanent sorrow.

Agnes knew that Leo's articulated loneliness had hovered between them in the car for a moment or two, had then seized Warren in an instant when he needed only that bit of proof to complete a state of such desolation that it finally captured him after stalking him all his life. Agnes always winced — and the impulse to call out a warning caught in her throat — each time she envisioned Warren easing his hands off the steering wheel, letting that big car drift off the road like a slow, ponderous sailing ship, the tires whispering over the sere grass, and for one long, blank, hollow moment no other sound at all in the world as that big automobile went sailing out of control. Nothing but the brittle grass shattering under the tires until the car veered toward a sturdy tree at the edge of the drop, producing no more than a heavy thud of sturdy metal giving way a little bit, preventing the machine from disappearing into the brush-filled gorge.

Finally Agnes blocked this familiar story and refused to allow her imagination to carry her further. She wrenched her thoughts back into the world of 1947 and the party assembling in the yard below. When she looked at her watch, she realized how late it was, and she turned away from the window and made an effort to shake herself out of her fuzzy-headed disorientation. She began to search for something cooler to wear than the gauzy voile. She took a crisp cotton shirtwaist from the closet and began briskly to tick off a list of what still needed seeing to before she could set out supper. She could smell the ham, and Mrs. Drummond was bringing a turkey. . . . The ham could go at one end of the table, the turkey at the other end, and the fried chicken in the middle. She buttoned her dress as she made her way toward the stairs.

She wanted to check on Mary Alcorn, who had been so terrified. Agnes realized with relief, though, that the little girl had only been frightened because she had somehow gotten herself lost in the house and didn't know yet exactly who Agnes was. Mary Alcorn hadn't expected to come upon a person in the quiet room, and Agnes was certain that the little girl hadn't even taken into account that anyone else was in the same bed. And Agnes deplored her own thankfulness at the fact that even if Mary Alcorn had noticed Will, she wouldn't know that was unusual; she wasn't familiar enough with all these people to have any idea who belonged with whom.

Agnes was deeply embarrassed, with that dreadful sense of personal mortification that made her blush even though she was all by herself. How had she become a person who was able to give herself over entirely to lust despite everything? Despite the fact of her children's return, and even though this was the first day they had all been in the same place since before the war? What in the world was she doing in the late afternoon of this Fourth of July — which had turned into the reunion she had antici- pated for so long — spending any time at all entangled in bedsheets, having sex with a man her family thought of as an old and trusted friend. Even if she had been in love with Will . . . Even if they had been planning to get married . . . There were no circumstances in which her behavior was excusable.

Agnes hurried down the back stairs just as Betts dashed in through the screen door, hurried through the kitchen into the hall, and put the phone back on the hook.

"Oh, good," Betts said. "There you are. No one's anywhere, Mama! Mr. Drummond called to speak to his wife, and I'd just seen her in the front yard. But when I went to call her to the phone, I ended up going across the square to her house. Mr. Drummond was still in the front hall, holding the phone, because he'd gotten worried that the turkey was getting overdone. But Mrs. Drummond had gone home and was in the kitchen checking on the turkey! He didn't know she was in the house, because she'd gone around the back way. I can't find Howard. I don't know where Amelia Anne has gotten off to. I thought she was taking a nap on the sleeping porch. Oh, and I feel just awful! I left Claytor's little stepdaughter waiting for me at the foot of the stairs and forgot all about her. I just saw her tearing across the yard, so I guess she's all right. Maybe Trudy has Amelia —"

"I didn't mean to leave all this to you, Betts. I'm sorry —"

"There's no reason for you to be sorry, Mama. After all, now that we're all home, I guess I'm as responsible for being the hostess as you are. I need a chance to freshen up, too, though. I'm going to run upstairs and change clothes, but I'll be back in just a second."

The table was set up on the long, screened side porch, and Dwight and Claytor came inside, still involved in an earnest discussion, glancing quick smiles at their mother. "I've gotten used to a really good edge," Claytor was saying. "I take all the knives into the hospital once a week —"

"I'll get just as good an edge with the steel," Dwight interrupted. "It was one of the first things Daddy taught us. Do you remember that? As soon as we got tall enough."

One of the Drummond sons-in-law was crossing the square, carrying one of his mother-in-law's elaborate silver platters, on which sat the turkey, partially draped with a linen towel. The ham sat at the other end of the table, resplendent with pineapple rings and maraschino cherries. Someone had done a pretty job of tucking parsley and dill among the pieces of fried chicken arranged on one of Agnes's own silver platters, and Trudy and Lily went back and forth retrieving dishes of green beans, potato salad, cole slaw, fruit salad, and plates of biscuits. Each dish was divided between two separate serving platters so that the guests could help themselves from either end of the table without jostling or crowding one another and before the food got too warm, in the case of the jellied fruit salad, or too cold, in the case of the ham and the turkey.

Gradually people began to drift toward the porch in clusters, continuing their conversations as they stood a moment, assessing the table before serving themselves. Agnes joined the company on the porch, where Trudy had taken charge of the occasion and where Lavinia moved around the outskirts of the group, proffering the platter of fried chicken, which had proved hard to reach at the center of the table. Agnes came up beside her to relieve her of the chore. "That's a good idea," Agnes said. "I should have put a platter at each end, but I didn't think so many people would want chicken. You go on and visit, now, Lavinia," she had said. "You shouldn't have to be a hostess on your first day at Scofields."

"I'm glad to do it," Lavinia said, which was absolutely true. She felt shy among this group of people so well known to each other; it was a relief to have a job to do.

Howard had materialized right behind her, and he spoke up just to make conversation. "It's got to be hard to remember who we all are," he said kindly. "Sometimes I think it's hard even for Mama. All four of us look exactly like our father. I don't remember him. I never knew him in any way I can remember. But you can see the resemblance from any picture of him. The others got the good parts! I just got the height! I was interested in an awfully pretty girl when I was stationed in Missouri, and she always said I made her think of Ichabod Crane." Lavinia didn't know the Scofields well enough yet to realize that one of their greatest charms was a genuine and good-humored self-deprecation.

Lavinia had no choice but to give the large platter of chicken to Agnes, and she folded her hands on top of her stomach, hoping to stop the baby from kicking while she appraised Howard. "You know, that's not true," she finally pronounced. "Your whole family is good-looking. Which is always lucky, I think, because it would be so hard on the one who wasn't good-looking. My first husband's family was the same way except for one younger sister who was just sort of ordinary. Not homely or anything, but just someone you wouldn't notice one way or another. She's nice enough . . ."

Lavinia dragged herself back into the moment. "But, Howard," she said, "I think you're probably the most interesting looking of all of you. Your face — your features, really. That slight droop of your eyelid and the way your mouth is a little crooked. You don't have a cookie-cutter face," she said, and Howard couldn't think of any reply at all. "But all four of you look like your father?" Lavinia asked, and Howard nodded. "I don't see how that could be," she went on. "Now Dwight and Claytor! Those two do look alike! Mary Alcorn scared herself to death when she mistook Dwight for Claytor."

"Well, that's what we've been told all out lives by every living soul in Washburn," Howard said. "People in town used to call Dwight and Claytor the 'Scofield twins,' although it must just be something about their manner. When you look at them up close, their faces aren't really all that much alike. At least I never thought so. It's just something about the eyes and the coloring, I think."

"But anyone who saw all of you together couldn't possibly mistake the fact that you're all your mother's children," Lavinia insisted.

"Really? Do you think so?" Howard asked, and everyone in the vicinity — all of whom had picked up a word or two — paused to hear what Lavinia was saying. George Scofield was particularly intrigued and held his empty plate by his side as he leaned in closer to her.

"Oh, of course they would!" she said. "Why, your faces . . . Anyone can see it. And your eyes . . . Why, you know, you're all exactly like beautiful cows. Your cheekbones. All of you look like your mother. I don't know what your father looked like, though, except what Claytor's told me." Lavinia was picturing the lush eyelashes and the hollow-cheeked faces of the cows they had passed on the long drive across the country. The cows who leaned with bovine delicacy — which Lavinia had never before taken into account — to dip their caramel heads into the long, sweet grass on the other side of whatever sort of fence contained them. She was remembering how they lifted their eyes to gaze at her from under their lashes as the car passed, and how she had thought it was odd that she had never noticed how elegant these common creatures were.

Agnes didn't hear much of anything Lavinia was saying, but, in spite of herself, she experienced a surge of pleasure at having the children told that they looked like her. She had grown weary of the endless remarks about how much the children resembled their father, and it hurt her feelings that her children were delighted to be told that they resembled no one so much as they resembled Warren.

"I always notice that people who grow up together don't really know what the others look like," Lavinia went on. "I mean, they might tell you that . . . Well, in my family everyone is always saying that our French ancestry is impossible to miss. But I don't really think any of us look French. I don't know enough people to know if the French even have a particular look." Lavinia spoke in a musing tone of deliberation, so that it was hard to know if she was making a statement or asking a question. "And I've always thought that somewhere along the line, one of my forefathers — or my foremothers, for all I know — had a wandering eye for one of the house servants, or maybe the cook. I think my family just preferred to think of itself as French. I guess the French are thought of as . . . oh . . . as olive-skinned. Like Joseph Cotten. The actor? He's from an old Virginia family, too. Horse country. Orange, Virginia. Right around there, anyway. His family was there before the Revolutionary War. Which explains his looks, of course."

The nine or ten people within range were dumbfounded, but Lavinia finally got to the point she intended to make. "So, since your father was tall with light hair, it's just natural that you all assume he's the one you took after. And you probably all do look like your father. But you all have your mother's huge, round eyes — just the same color brown, too — and her high cheekbones. Your expressions are so much alike. . . . I've noticed that that happens in families, too. Do you think it's because people automatically take on the expressions they see around them? I think it must be inherited, because no matter how long people are friends, I've never noticed that they take on each other's expression."

Howard had assumed the responsibility of filling a plate for Lavinia, who fascinated him, and he and Betts guided her away from the porch and settled her at a table next to Trudy. Howard had to hurry off to help Sam Holloway organize the fireworks.

Dwight was in charge of the corn, but he refused to cook it until everyone had served themselves and settled on the grass or at tables set out on the lawn. He wound his way through the crowd of neighbors and friends and his own family, dispensing buttered corn on the cob. "Three minutes!" he declared as he made the rounds. "It's got to be boiled in half milk, half water." He was cooking it in batches, because Trudy and Betts had shucked seventy-five ears of Will's fresh-picked corn.

Claytor and Lavinia's little girl, Mary Alcorn, and Dwight and Trudy's daughter, Amelia Anne, were busily digging under the trees with teaspoons, their heads bent together, with Bobbin lying no more than three feet from them, alert to any threat to his small flock. One of the girls now and then earnestly explained to the other something about the elaborate tunnels and ravines they were exca-vating. Even one glance at Mary Alcorn and Amelia Anne made it clear that their acquaintance had immedi-ately been a profound connection. Now and then that happens with young children, but more often than not there's a long period of shy suspicion and negotiation.

Trudy looked up as Agnes settled between her and Lavinia at one of the cloth-covered card tables that Agnes had borrowed from the church along with plenty of fold-ing chairs. "Aunt Agnes, I'm afraid they have two of your silver spoons. But I'm keeping an eye on them. I'll be sure they aren't lost."

"But look how well they get along," Agnes said. "Isn't that a nice thing?"

"I think they're going to get sleepy all at once," Trudy commented, and Lavinia glanced at Trudy without indicating whether she agreed or not, but neither of them seemed unduly concerned.

"Howard's helping Sam Holloway with the fireworks," Lily said, as she pulled up a chair and joined them. "He says Sam won't start the show until the fireflies can't be seen except for their light."

"Howard's been the safest person with fireworks — Claytor and Dwight, too — since little Eddie Parsley blew off his hand that time," Trudy said. "When was that? Howard was out of grammar school, I think."

By now it was easy to see the glimmering of the fireflies as they rose in the woods at a distance, but up close they were still visible in their unglamorous brown insect bodies. Agnes excused herself and went to turn off all the lights in the house and on the porch, and also to make coffee and set out the cakes and pies and slice the melons. She was arranging things on the porch when the first brilliant explosion illuminated the sky, and she stood still for a few minutes as, one after another, the rockets and Catherine wheels and shooting stars followed each other into the air in a spectacular sequence. It turned out that Sam Holloway had spent one summer in New Orleans helping produce a nightly fireworks show at an amusement park, and he and Howard had gone off to buy some other types of rockets Sam suggested and that Howard hadn't known about.

It was the best show Agnes had ever seen, planned with care so that each sputtering, gleaming light rose higher than the one before, and the colors were extraordinary counterparts to each other, combining in arcs of unusual aqua and brilliant pinks as they showered umbrella-fashion back to earth. Sam Holloway was an unusual man, Agnes thought. Maybe he and Betts would be interested in each other. Who would have thought that a man like Sam Holloway would be an expert on fireworks shows? He seemed too worldly, too sophisticated somehow to be taking part in so universal and simple a diversion. But then, Agnes thought, you rarely ever find out all the things a person can do or that he cares about.

The morning of July fifth, all over town the people who had been at Scofields the night before discussed the picnic, the fireworks show — it had been at least twenty minutes long. And, of course, they discussed Claytor Scofield's wife and little stepdaughter. Lavinia Scofield was a puzzle. No one knew quite what to say about her; they were still surprised from the night before. She wasn't like any other person they had ever met. On the other hand, she had just arrived that afternoon and must have been terribly tired; perhaps it was too soon to know what she was like. But imagine telling the Scofields that they all looked like cows — beautiful or not. It was hard not to think of that as being rude on her part.

And so, on the morning following the Fourth of July celebration, all over Washburn, the Scofields' previous night's guests pondered Lavinia's meaning. But in the case of her ancestry, the subject was only alluded to obliquely. Could she possibly have meant that she suspected one of her forebears of miscegenation? Did she honestly mean to imply that she might have Negro blood in her family? And what was all that about Joseph Cotten?

"Do you think Claytor's wife looks French?" Mrs. Drummond asked her husband and her oldest daughter, who was home with her husband for a visit.

Even Lily was perplexed as she sat at breakfast with Robert, drinking her second cup of black coffee and smoking a cigarette. "What do you think Lavinia could have meant, Robert? Do you think she meant to insult everyone? That would be such a strange thing to do when you're a new member of the family."

Robert smiled and then gave a short laugh. "I don't think she meant to insult anyone at all. I think she meant it as a compliment. You mean when she said that Warren's children all looked like Agnes? That they looked like beautiful cows? I'll tell you, I looked around and saw that she was exactly right. Most people underestimate — have never noticed — the beauty of cows."

And Uncle George Scofield had awakened before dawn, hastily gotten dressed, and headed over to his Civil War museum, where he kept several boxes of diaries and scrapbooks he had collected over the years. He pored over photographs of Southern families taken before the Civil War, and a great deal suddenly became clear to him.

Across town, in her cramped apartment, which had been hastily eked out of the small upstairs of their landlady's house, Nancy Turner Fosberg was saying to her husband that she thought it was going to take some time to get used to Claytor Scofield's wife. Nancy and Betts had both had Washington romances — Nancy's not so passionate as Betts's — but Nancy had come home from Washington and almost immediately married Joe Fosberg, whom she had been in love with all the while she was in high school. "She's awfully pretty," Nancy said, "Lavinia Scofield is. Although she's so pregnant that it's hard to tell what she really looks like. But I never am sure what she's talking about. I suppose it's because of her being Southern and being French," she said to Joe. But he had slept late and was eating a quick breakfast; she was standing at the sink and didn't see him nod in hasty agreement, but she wasn't really expecting him to answer her, anyway. Like almost everyone else who had stayed too late at Scofields the night before, he was already late for work.

Part Three

Chapter Nine

CLAYTOR'S FAMILY STAYED ON with Agnes even after their daughter Julia was born early on the morning of September 13, 1947. All over the country, housing was scarce, and Claytor had very little income while he finished his residency in Cleveland. He shared a rented room with another student and came home to Washburn whenever he could, but it was a long trip by train, and especially unpleasant by bus. Betts and Howard, too, had taken up their lives again from home base.

Under the GI Bill, Howard had managed to work out an arrangement affording him tuition at Harcourt Lees College, and even the expense of books and student fees was covered, since he could live at home and waive the cost of room and board. Except at supper, Agnes rarely saw him when he wasn't just about to miss the bus to Harcourt Lees or rushing to catch a ride with Robert Butler.

In fact, Agnes's house teemed with people who were running late.

Betts took up where she'd left off at the Mid-Ohio Civil War Museum, just next door, although she only worked until Uncle George came in after lunch. Group tours were scheduled for the mornings, and George Scofield spent the afternoons reassessing his collection, evaluating its strengths and weaknesses, and generally just browsing about. With Dwight and Trudy and Amelia Anne at Lily and Robert Butler's, George enjoyed the peacefulness of settling into a comfortable chair in a room filled with the artifacts he had spent his life collecting. Betts was always there by eight-thirty and ready to open at nine, but she worked a second job at WBRN in the afternoons, making a dash to get to the radio station on time, begging a car or a ride from Agnes or Lily or anyone she could find at the moment.

Every Saturday morning, when Agnes sat down at the dining-room table to sort through her coupons and make out a shopping list, she studied the calendar she kept next to the telephone, where everyone in her household had been asked to record their comings and goings for the upcoming week. Now and then someone had penciled in something or other, but generally on Saturday morning Agnes would look at the squares of deceptively virginal days lined up neatly across the page and feel vanquished. She envisioned those days as opaque rectangles through which she would pass, closing the door of each evening firmly behind her while carrying leftover meat loaf or the rest of a baked ham along with her as she moved through the week.

The only day about which she was thoroughly sanguine was Thursday, when she and Lily played bridge, and Agnes unapologetically made her double-boiler dinner. A whole meal, using only the two interlocking pans! No one looked forward to it, including Agnes, but there it was, a complete dinner responsibly prepared. She had clipped the recipe from an advertisement for cream cheese:

The Savvy Career Woman's New England Boiled Dinner

1) Boil, covered, for one hour, in largest half of a double boiler, one head green cabbage, outer leaves removed.
2) Save cooking liquid. Remove cabbage and cut into segments. (One per serving. Cannot serve more than eight.)
3) Place segmented cabbage in smaller insert of double boiler.
4) Add one frankfurter per serving to cabbage broth.
5) Remove wrapping from one block Philadelphia Cream Cheese. Place cheese on cabbage segments, cover, and replace insert on top of double boiler. Return to stove.
6) Boil frankfurters for twenty minutes, or until cheese has melted. Serve frankfurters arranged over cabbage and cheese sauce.

One of those Thursdays Sam Holloway had given Betts a lift home from the radio station, and she invited him to come in and have supper. Agnes added another frankfurter to the pot, but when she brought the platter of cabbage and frankfurters to the table and passed the bread, Sam looked up at her after serving himself. "Good Lord, Agnes!" he said. "This . . . Why, you just can't serve this to a Cajun. To anyone from Louisiana. Or even Mississippi. You let me see what's out in the kitchen, and I'll turn this into something with a little spice. A nice gumbo. Or jambalaya if you have some rice. And if we get rid of the cabbage . . ." Sam was already up and collecting plates from Mary Alcorn and Lavinia.

"Oh, you're no more Cajun than I am! I'll grant you this isn't anyone's favorite meal," Agnes said, "but I'm leaving in half an hour for duplicate."

"I'll leave your plate then, and pray for your soul," Sam said. "But the rest of you folks come help me turn this into something edible! We need to get rid of this cabbage and add something. Maybe some tomatoes . . ."

Since the day he had arrived in Washburn, Sam and Agnes had been as relaxed around each other as though they had a shared history, but the fact that they knew almost nothing about each other — that they never had to backtrack in order to interpret or explain how they had come to be where they were — only strengthened their alliance.

"Mama, you'd think Sam Holloway was some long-lost cousin," Betts had said. "Or even a brother. He's here more than your own family." Agnes looked at her daughter curiously, because she sounded indignant, and Agnes had thought that at least a flirtation would spring up between Betts and Sam. In fact, Betts *had* developed a slight, unreciprocated crush on Sam. He apparently thought of her in the same way he thought of her brothers, and it annoyed her to think that he found her mother just as interesting as he found her.

Sam often dropped by on a weekend afternoon to sit on the porch and listen to the Cincinnati Reds or the Cleveland Indians. Sometimes Agnes set up dual radios if the teams were being broadcast simultaneously. Usually other people joined them — Howard and Dwight and Claytor were all Cleveland fans, as were Trudy and Betts, and Lavinia liked the game but was maddeningly loyal to whatever team happened to be the underdog. It proved impossible to make clear to her the concept of fan loyalty. The little girls were in and out, needing one thing or another, a glass of water, a Band-Aid. People came and went, and it was a pleasant way to spend an afternoon.

And since that evening of the Career Woman's Boiled Dinner, Sam arrived at the house with Betts every Thursday night with exotic groceries he had picked up when he was in Columbus, perhaps at a tiny German butcher shop, or at the small Italian or Asian markets where the owners barely spoke English and where he could buy fresh garlic, fresh or dried mushrooms, gingerroot, and coconut milk. He enlisted everyone's help in creating the meals he planned. He cooked garlicky Bolognese sauce with fresh sautéed mushrooms, and he threw together various kinds of curries and served them with a short-grained rice that smelled like popcorn. From nothing more than corn meal and water Sam produced a creamy-textured dish that he let Amelia Anne and Mary Alcorn take turns stirring before he spread it in a pan to bake.

Generally, by the time Lily and Agnes got home from bridge, everyone was still around the table swapping stories. Lily or Agnes would briefly report on the outcome of their evening at cards and accept a glass of sherry or one last cup of coffee before the group finally dispersed.

In the early months of 1948, George Scofield set up a succession of meetings with the trustees of the Civil War museum at his lawyer's office, which was in the Ohio National Bank building. George was eager to get the legal future of the museum fully clarified, and he had asked Betts to represent the rest of the family.

In late February, Betts hurried to meet her uncle at the bank building after she was finished with her dentist appointment, and just as she was rushing up the long flight of marble steps, she caught sight of a beautifully dressed man just ahead of her. He caught her eye because she hadn't seen a suit so well tailored or wool of that quality since she had lived in Washington. But these weren't clothes held over from before the war; the jacket was fashionably cut, and the man was wearing a handsome hat with the new rakish tilt and dimpled crown. She continued to watch him as he passed through the doors, but when she entered the lobby she realized, with an actual shiver of surprise, that the man she had been admiring was Will Dameron.

"Will!" she said. "Where have you been keeping yourself? You haven't been to the house in . . . oh . . . I don't even know. It seems like years. It's been so long that I swear I didn't even recognize you just now. I generally see you when you're not so decked out. You're looking like some big-time executive come to visit your country cousins."

"Ah, I have another meeting in Chicago. Tying up the loose ends of the board is turning out to take more time than getting it under way ever did. You look wonderful! It's funny you should say you didn't recognize me. Just the other day you were coming down the steps of the post office, and I thought, My God, who is that? I was across the street and I thought you must be some movie star in town for some reason or other. Dan Emmett days. A concert. Something." Will had turned to face her with a grave expression, tense with the desire to explain exactly what he meant, and Betts was surprised.

"Will —"

"I'm not even the kind of man who can tell one movie star from another, but I thought, well, I've seen her in some movie or in a magazine somewhere. You looked familiar, you see. And then I realized who you were. When did all this happen? I don't imagine you're going to find any shortage of suitors these days, with all our heroes coming home."

Betts was taken aback, because he wasn't teasing her, and he seemed to be waiting for her to answer him. "Well, what a nice thing for you to say to a girl! That'll put me on cloud nine for at least a week." She smiled at him to indicate that she knew he was exaggerating, but he was determined.

"No, I'm serious. When did it happen?" He looked at her with a perplexed frown, as if she were being obtuse, and Betts settled back a little on her heels and considered him carefully.

"I'm not sure what you're asking me."

"Oh . . . I was just . . . well, I guess I don't even *know* what I'm asking. When I saw you, it felt to me almost like you'd played a trick. . . . I remember faces, but I honestly didn't have any idea who you were for almost . . . oh . . . maybe for as much as three minutes." Betts laughed, and Will realized he was being far too serious — too earnest for the occasion — and he smiled an apology at her.

"I haven't played any trick," she said. "It's just me. I think I just got older, Will."

"I suppose so. Well, but we all did that. You just managed to do it better than anyone else. Say, I don't suppose you could spare the time to have lunch? Just over at the Monument. My train's not till three o'clock, but it would be a real pleasure to catch up on everything. How your family's doing. What you've been up to." Betts agreed right away and forgot all about the meeting with her uncle. She and Will were still chatting over coffee when he realized he just had time to get to the train station.

He paid the check and helped Betts on with her coat, and before they headed off on their separate ways outside, Betts had insisted that Will join the family for Thursday dinner. "You never know what there'll be to eat, but Sam almost always comes up with something good. Better than my mother's New England Boiled Dinner, but that's not so hard to do." He thanked her and was still smiling as he turned away, and Betts watched him with a kind of attention she had never paid to him before. She thought he didn't seem any older than he ever had and that he was a wonderful-looking man. Something in the way he moved — his lack of self-consciousness and assumption of authority — put her in mind of Hank Abernathy.

Thursday dinners at Agnes's became a fixed occasion, with the extended family and often various family friends at Agnes's house. Betts invited Will, and he, too, became a regular guest. Agnes was glad enough to see him; he was a pleasant man as long as she wasn't responsible for his being there. Robert had taken to bringing wine, although the choice at the state liquor store in Washburn was limited to red wine or white wine, both American and too sweet. Will sometimes brought back French and Italian wines when he made a trip to Washington or Cleveland. Agnes and Lily always drank coffee through dinner, as did Lavinia and Betts most of the time, but Trudy enjoyed a glass of wine, although she chilled even the red Californian wine to cut its syrupy sweetness.

One afternoon Sam arrived with all the items he said he needed to make a paella. "Pie-AY-yah," he explained after he spelled it. No one else had any idea what the dish entailed, which Sam said was a good thing, since the only seafood he had been able to buy was some shrimp that had been shipped fresh to a restaurant in Columbus whose owner he knew.

"Mary Alcorn! Amelia Anne! Look at this!" He rubbed a small, dry thread of something between his fingers and opened his hand out flat for them to see that it had turned his skin a brilliant yellow. "This is saffron. It always reminds me of being on the swim team in high school. It smells like chlorine. If you don't have saffron, though, there's no point in making paella."

Mary Alcorn had proved not to be the shy little girl she had seemed on the day of her arrival; she had only been cautious for a little over a week. Once she had sorted things out, she chattered all day long, full of questions. It was Amelia Anne who looked on serenely, much like her mother had done as a child, Agnes thought. Much like Trudy still did, really. Both little girls were well mannered, but Mary Alcorn lived in Agnes's house and asked endless questions about everything. She climbed up to kneel on a wooden stool so she could lean her elbows on the counter to watch Sam unpack all his treasures.

Sam was the only person who had ever allowed Mary Alcorn to taste vanilla extract, and he didn't know that in doing so he had gained her grave, five-year-old's respect. Her mother and Agnes had both discouraged her, and so had her father. "It just smells good, sweetie," Claytor said to her. "You wouldn't like it." But how could Mary Alcorn believe that? There wasn't anything that smelled better, and Sam unhesitatingly let her tip a little bit from the bottle into a spoon and looked on while she tested it on her tongue.

They had all been right, all those people who had told her it wouldn't taste good, but she did discover that it tasted like it smelled. "You know what?" she said to Sam. "I bet this is how Mama's perfume would taste." And the next time Sam was in the house, Mary Alcorn brought Amelia Anne over from next door, because Mary Alcorn hadn't been able to persuade Amelia Anne that vanilla extract was very bitter.

Everyone counted it as great good fortune that Dwight and Trudy and Amelia Anne, along with their own new baby, Martha, born only twelve days after Lavinia and Claytor's little daughter, lived right next door with Lily and Robert Butler and Uncle George Scofield. Mary Alcorn and Amelia Anne were together all day long and, for the most part, were happy in each other's company. Bobbin had moved next door as well, in spite of the fact that Lily didn't want a dog in the house. He was devoted to Amelia Anne and rarely left her side. But now that Amelia Anne and Mary Alcorn were five years old and spent the morning at St. James Episcopal Church's kindergarten program, Bobbin returned to Agnes's back door and stood gazing at her while she hastily put her lunch together. She just had time to get to her own class-room before the first bell rang.

She let him in, though, knowing that there were plenty of people in the house who could let him out again. Agnes had maintained a cheerful pretense of amusement in the face of the dog's treachery, but she sighed when she watched Bobbin circle round and round, then finally settle into his accustomed place under the kitchen table. "Oh, Pup! I miss you . . ." She had depended on the dog; she hadn't understood that before he deserted her. But she gathered her wits and forced herself to look at him with a cold eye. "But just so we're straight about this, Pup. I'm not taking you up when you're on the rebound. You're happy as a clam at Lily's. And, after all, you made your own bed. . . ." Then she stopped speaking aloud, because Betts or Howard might be up and about, or Lavinia might show up with the baby at any moment, and Agnes also stopped speaking because she felt the pressure of tears rising in her throat and thought to herself how ridiculous she was.

Agnes left Bobbin in the house so he wouldn't follow her to Jesser Grammar School. But all the while she walked along the alley, past the backyards of the houses on Church Street, she fought down an unreasonable melancholy. She did really love the dog; she had recognized it in surprise once again that very morning, but she was afraid she was losing the ability to love the people in her life. It seemed to her that the protective passion that had governed her existence for all the years the children were growing up had just evaporated into thin air. And, too, although she had never thought that she expected reciprocity for what was simple, instinctive maternal love, she continued to be surprised every time she saw a look of annoyance cross one of her children's faces when she said something — recounted a fond story, even, from their childhood — that implied a particularly intimate knowledge of their personalities.

Of course, even if the nature of her affection for her children had changed, she was still as bound to them as she had ever been. Whenever she picked up a hint of discontent or unhappiness from any one of those children, she herself was thrown into a low mood. Part of the difference between her feelings about her children when they were young as opposed to her affection for them now was that they had become more pinned down in the world, and she was more clearly aware of their quirks and weaknesses.

And it was increasingly clear to her, too, that they had always believed she had plenty of faults of her own; they counted against her many things that she had considered her strongest attributes. Perhaps she was only melancholy, she thought, because she had failed to imagine that her children's adulthoods would be a foreign country where she wasn't even fluent in the language. She was tired of exercising diplomacy, tired of always being caught up in a round of negotiations.

Sometimes she felt besieged by her children's opinions flying around the room, lodging in the corners, absolute and unwavering but not always in agreement with each other. Dwight and Claytor's irresolvable difference of opinion about bombing Hiroshima, for instance, and the anger it sometimes generated throughout her house and Lily's, too. Agnes had once interrupted yet another version of the same subject when Lavinia and Trudy and Howard began to take sides. "For goodness sakes, Dwight! Claytor! Why can't the two of you just agree to disagree?" Agnes said, but the conversation had become too passionate already, and no one paid any attention to her objection.

When the whole family was at Lily's one evening, though, Robert spoke up. "I'd say you two are in treacherous waters here. Why, some of the world's greatest thinkers — artists, poets, philosophers — have come to unshakable but opposing conclusions about the great arguments of their day. And yet they remained the other's staunchest ally. You boys are a step behind. You'll have to take it as a given that you each have a valid point. I'd say, in fact, that thoughtful disagreements are the single impetus for rational progress." That notion did catch Dwight's and Claytor's attention, because it put them on an appealing intellectual footing, as opposed to their mother's implication that they were little more than quarreling schoolboys. The conversation enlarged and turned to a discussion of politics in general.

In her own house, though, Agnes still treaded softly during moments of sudden discord or explosions of hilarity about something or other that seemed to her devoid of any trace of humor. She was isolated by the fact that she was, through no fault of her own, the authority in residence, the curator of long-established traditions. Her own children were often unwittingly rude in their offhand comments, and Agnes was fully aware that in part it was because it never occurred to them that a criticism of anything in the household — the old-fashionedness of the refrigerator, the faded wallpaper in the back parlor — was an indictment of her.

She had been very pleased with herself, for instance, during the rationing, when she had hit upon a tidy way to combine the end of a bottle of ketchup or honey with its replacement so that every bit was saved. Lily had been impressed, too, when she discovered Agnes using the cylinder of a tin can — from which the top and bottom had been removed — to encompass and hold stable a jar of newly opened honey on top of which a nearly empty jar of honey was inverted. Agnes stuffed newspaper into the empty spaces of the can in order to keep the bottles steady.

"By the end of the day," Agnes had explained to Lily, "the old jar will be empty. Though honey doesn't work in the winter. But all sorts of things . . . syrup, even some preserves. And I don't have to prop the bottles in a corner. They never slip apart, either, and dribble down the side." Agnes knew full well that there was nothing remarkable about what she'd engineered, but it was one of those instances when a tiny, unimportant, but happy revelation affords any housekeeper a smug moment of satisfaction. Agnes had taken up Lily's technique, for instance, of storing onions in a discarded, laddered stocking, each onion tied off before adding the next. In the basement of both their houses, knobby hosiery full of onions and potatoes hung from the beams like strings of beads.

But now and then one or another of her children would be driven to distraction by some perfectly ordinary habit of Agnes's. At dinner one night Betts had presented her mother with four bottles of ketchup — each tied with a white bow — with a flourish and a laugh. "Mother, I can't stand to see that bottle contraption set up on the kitchen table anymore. It's disgusting! With the old ketchup all crusty around the top! So this is the first installment of my gift of a lifetime supply of ketchup. I'll replenish it as need be if you just won't try to save the last drop!" Everyone at the table had laughed, and Agnes laughed, too, although she understood perfectly well —

even if Betts did not — that the whole idea was about more than saving ketchup.

Agnes even managed to annoy Howard for no reason that made sense to her. One afternoon when he had just come in after classes at Harcourt Lees, she asked him how far along he was in *Moby Dick,* which rested on top of the books and notebooks he had put down on the kitchen table.

"Mama, you ask me that every time I come in the door," he said, trying to make a joke of it. "Why do you care one way or another?"

"Why . . . oh, I don't care exactly, Howard. It's just that I liked that book so much myself, but none of my friends . . ." But Howard hadn't waited for her answer; he was bending into the refrigerator and asked her if she wanted a glass of iced tea.

"I'll pick some of that fresh mint by the back door," he added as a sort of apology in case he had sounded cross.

Agnes had been looking forward to hearing what Howard thought of that novel, though, which had mesmerized her when she had read it in her senior year, but which her friends had bemoaned being forced to read. Before Howard came in she had been sitting in the kitchen marking her students' workbooks, but when Lavinia and Mary Alcorn and the baby returned from a walk, and Lavinia and Howard fell into an animated discussion of that great white whale and what it symbolized, Agnes collected her stack of booklets and retreated to the desk upstairs in her bedroom.

Her own mother had been so different than Agnes believed herself to be that she had no yardstick with which to judge her own situation. She did believe that her children loved her in the way that her friend Lucille had loved her family and presumably loved them still. Even though they had often irritated or hurt her feelings, Lucille had extended to her parents and to her three sisters an unconsidered loyalty, a sort of devotion, that Agnes had observed all the years she and Lucille were growing up together.

But Agnes was beginning to understand that, at least for the time being, her children weren't much interested in what she thought or said, and, in fact, they didn't even seem to like her very much, although she didn't believe they were conscious of that dislike; she knew they didn't name it aloud. It was a situation she tried hard not to brood about, but they lived in such close proximity to one another that it was hard to ignore. And, too, Agnes found that she was even more disheartened when the children were overtly and patiently kind to her, as though she was so removed from the issues they cared about that she was slightly pitiable.

One Thursday evening Sam showed up with his usual bags of groceries and a cardboard box enclosing two straggly gray kittens just past their round cuteness and grown into a long-legged, stringy adolescence. "I thought maybe you could keep these, Agnes. Their mother disappeared. Probably hit by a car. Here they are! Just scraps of flotsam and jetsam left to drift by themselves in an unkind sea," he teased as he opened the box in which the two kittens cowered. Sam had discovered them outside Giamanco's Market in Columbus, where two boys had them in a laundry basket, selling them for twenty-five cents apiece. Sam had been a witness to Bobbin's desertion of Agnes about three days after he had arrived in Washburn. He thought it was probably because he had still been so much an outsider at the time that he recognized Agnes's false cheerfulness immediately and knew the poor dog had hurt her feelings.

"Oh, well, Sam . . . I don't know. With the baby in the house . . ."

"Nothing's better with babies than a cat," Sam said.

Although Agnes hadn't thought she wanted a cat, and especially not two cats, every night when Flotsam stealthily crept under the covers and settled himself firmly in the curve of Agnes's lower back, she was gratified despite herself. Jetsam was always neatly tucked on the end of the bed when she woke up, but she had no idea where he spent his time when she was asleep. During the days she surprised herself now and then by laughing out loud at the drama with which Flotsam and Jetsam invested their mock fights, or their battle against a roll of toilet paper or a simple empty paper bag. You don't expect anything at all from cats, she thought, whereas people and dogs can always let you down. She didn't want that ever to happen to her again; she would be more protective of her affections.

During the fall of 1948 and all through 1949, when veterans — by themselves or with new families in tow — returned in droves from far-flung places, Will Dameron discovered that he was relieved Agnes had been thinking clearly for both of them. He was fond of Agnes, but it seemed to him that their affair — or whatever it had been — had existed in some other world. A drearily sparse season of wartime, during which the two of them had huddled together for comfort. But now, with all the young families out and about all over the place, the notion of settling down with Agnes in a companionable second marriage for them both was so predictable that Will finally understood it was a stale idea, would have been, in fact, a tip of their hats to defeat.

He envied the energy — the heat generated by all the couples wrestling with their expectations, coming to grips with their new lives. He thought of his wife, Sally, often, and the few years they had been married, but he couldn't remember the feeling of their enthusiasm for rushing headlong into whatever their lives might be. Now and then he came across proof that they, too, had brimmed over with ambitions for themselves as a couple: half-filled scrapbooks, old letters exclaiming over what now seemed to be perfectly ordinary events, a list the two of them had put together sometime or other of all the places in the world they wanted to visit. In a chest of drawers in the attic, he turned up a meticulous notebook Sally had kept, detailing menus and plans for holidays and social events. She had noted the dress she had worn, the gift she and Will had given if the occasion had required one.

But Will simply could not recall the urgency they had felt about getting on with things. He developed a deep yearning to anticipate the future with curiosity once again, to look forward to finding out what would happen next. The next day, the next month, the next year.

*　　　*　　　*

Late morning of Christmas Eve 1949, Agnes was in the dining room polishing the silver, annoyed at herself for not having done it sooner, when the Lambert's Furniture truck pulled up in the semicircle of the front drive that served all three houses in the compound. The driver got out and was clearly trying to match the directions on his work sheet with one of the houses, which weren't numbered. Agnes hastily threw a coat on over her housedress and crossed the front yard to direct the driver to the parking area in back, and eventually she agreed to accept delivery of a big Du Mont television set tied with a red bow. The driver didn't know who had sent it, and Agnes was still uncertain if hers was the house for which it was intended. But she scurried upstairs to get dressed while the driver and his helper retrieved it from the truck.

By the time she was back downstairs, the two men had hefted the television, carried it straight through the front hall, and set it down next to the Christmas tree in the room Agnes had first known as Lillian Scofield's front parlor. Lillian had given pride of place to all the furnishings that filled the room, and the television sat in odd juxtaposition to the cherry hutch, the sternly upholstered horsehair sofas, and the inlaid piecrust tea tables, the tops of which folded down against their tri-footed bases and stood flat against a wall to be whipped out and opened whenever they might be needed, although they were notoriously unstable. The cabinet of the big Du Mont television was a dark, heavily carved wood box that looked Chinese, as did its squat latticework base with inward curving, chunky legs.

Agnes didn't know what to say. Her mother-in-law had once explained to her with timid pride that she had ordered the heavy brocade drapery material in that front parlor all the way from Paris via New York. In fact, when Agnes remembered the afternoon she and Warren's mother had gone through the house, while Dwight was asleep in his crib and Agnes was pregnant with Claytor, she realized that it had been a shy attempt on Mrs. Scofield's part to make Agnes feel included in the household.

Mrs. Scofield had meant those solemn bits of information about the silver service (never, never put a rubber band around sterling) and the crystal, the provenance of each cabinet or intricately carved table, to be an indication that she was ceding them to Agnes; that, other than Warren, here it was: the chief accomplishment of Lillian Scofield's life. Here her influence within her immediate family was manifest: this particular order she had imposed; here was the context in which her husband and son had registered the events of the world. At the time, though, Agnes had found the house tour of that long afternoon almost intolerably stultifying. Nevertheless, after Lillian Scofield's death in 1933, and even though the front parlor was Agnes's least favorite room, she had maintained it scrupulously. It disturbed her to see the television sitting in front of those carefully dressed windows, and she said so to the men from Lambert's Furniture.

"I wonder if it wouldn't be better to put it in the back parlor . . . not so formal. I'm not at all sure you've brought this to the right house, although maybe Lily . . . though I don't know why . . . This is far too much money to spend."

"Ma'am, if you want it moved, we'll have to come back after Christmas. We have three more stops to make, and one's a washing machine, so we have to meet the plumber." The driver looked over his delivery schedule. "All it says here is 'Scofields.' You say next door's the Butlers? And the other side's the war museum?"

"That's right," said Agnes, "but, you see, Mrs. Butler is really a Scofield. I think this must be a gift to her from her husband. I was Agnes *Claytor*. From out Newark Road?"

"If it turns out we got the wrong place, just call Mr. Lambert and he'll find the invoice. But, I'll tell you, as I always say to my wife, don't look a gift horse in the mouth. Why, this set! I've never seen one like it. It's the Manchu model." He grinned at her. "Maybe you have a secret admirer. Or maybe it's from Santa Claus!"

As it turned out, the television set was a gift from Will Dameron. Howard had called Lambert's to find out, and when he told his mother, his tone had been teasing and fond. "I don't know what's been going on around here, Mama. I can't think of anyone I care about enough that I'd give them a television!"

"Howard, don't be ridiculous," she said. But Agnes was baffled. Will had evolved into a family friend. He and Betts were teaching Amelia Anne and Mary Alcorn to ride, and Betts boarded her horse at his stables. Claytor hadn't wanted to ask any more of his grandfather, who had helped him through college, and he had finally asked Will for a loan that would carry him through his residency. But Agnes scarcely ever saw Will, except when he joined the family for Sam's Thursday dinners, and even then she and Lily left early to meet their bridge club.

Will arrived early for the Scofields' annual Christmas Eve dinner. He caught up with Agnes in the kitchen. She was dreading the conversation. "I wanted a chance to talk to you if you have a minute," he said, leaning against the door frame with his hands in his pockets, trying to stay out of the way.

"Yes, me, too. I mean, I wanted to have a word with you, too, Will. It was such a generous idea, but you know I can't accept a gift like that . . ."

"Oh. Oh, no, Agnes. I hope you won't give it a second thought! It's for the whole family. It's the least I could do. Why, you give me a fine dinner every week of the year. I had a case of the best bourbon I could find sent over to Sam's house. And a mixed case of wine. If you'd rather have that . . ."

Agnes smiled and Will went on. "People are beginning to think I'm awfully refined for a country farmer. You should see me in a huddle with the owner of Fine Wine and Spirits, down in Washington. He can hardly stand to see such an uncouth fellow make off with his best wines. He can hardly let me out the door." Will approximated a foreign accent. "'Remember, Mr. Dameron, the sweet wines — the Gewürztraminer — you don't drink that with your roast beef!' I generally check with Sam before I go, so I'm getting to know a little bit," he said. "Anyway, I thought the little girls would enjoy a television . . . Lavinia. And Claytor, too, when he's home. Howard. And you, too. But there's something else I was hoping to talk to you about. I know you're busy . . . I won't keep you long?" he pleaded.

Agnes nodded that his gift of the television was accepted, but she steeled herself in case simple generosity and gratitude hadn't been his only motive, as Howard had implied earlier in the afternoon. "Will, I've got all these people . . ."

"Just give me a second. I know this isn't the best time, but I've already spoken to Dwight. He was courteous, but I can't say he was overjoyed. I thought I should speak to him first since he's the oldest man of the family. But it's only proper . . ."

Agnes was astounded that Will had talked about his — and possibly her own — personal life to Dwight, but she held her tongue and hoped Will would get to the point. She reminded herself that he always approached any subject in a roundabout way, and she managed to wait attentively.

"I don't know . . . ," he continued. "I hope you won't think I ever meant to go behind your back. Well, the thing is, Agnes . . . well, I've finally asked Betts if she'd marry me. She's accepted. I'm hoping that you'll wish us well, too."

Agnes stepped backward and sat down at the table. "Will! Betts? Oh, Will! Is that really true? Does Betts know about this? Oh, what am I saying? How stupid! Of course Betts knows about this. Betts accepted, you said." She looked at Will appraisingly for a moment, wondering if he had misunderstood. "Betts knows that she said she'd marry you?"

"She does. She certainly does. In fact, she wanted to run off and elope. She wanted to surprise everyone," he laughed. "I didn't think that would be a good idea . . . but you know Betts when she's made up her mind. It was a struggle, I'll tell you, to get her to agree to a wedding."

Agnes bristled at Will's assumption that she would conspire with him about her daughter's nature. "I have to say, Will, you've managed to surprise me," she said. "I had no idea! I never imagined. I hadn't ever even thought . . . in fact, I thought Betts and Sam. I guess I hadn't ever thought of you as being my son-in-law, exactly," she said, with a wry note back in her voice.

"I know the difference in our ages —"

"Oh, no, no. That's the least of it —"

"Well, Agnes, I hope you're not worried. . . . I've never said a thing to anyone about you and me, you know. Back during the war. I don't want you to think I'm the sort of man who'd betray . . . Well. I suppose it's not *my* honor to betray. I wouldn't want you to think I was the kind of man who would betray your honor. Or embarrass you, or ever hurt your feelings. You were awfully strict about just being friends, and I never even thought . . . I had no idea I'd fall in love with Betts! And never that she'd feel the same way."

"No, no. I'm not . . . I'm just surprised. Honestly, Will, I'm not worried that my honor is at risk." She paused for a moment, looking around the kitchen, reminding herself that she had things still to get done before the rest of the guests arrived, and Will said nothing at all, as if he were waiting for a verdict.

"It's just a surprise," she said. "Betts is always off on some tangent. I didn't know she was serious about anybody. I did think Sam Holloway . . . But maybe this will all work out. Maybe it's exactly what should happen. . . . Oh, Will, I have sixteen people coming to dinner, whether or not this is the best idea or the worst idea in the world. I can't think straight right now."

But after all the guests had gone, Agnes found Betts getting ready for bed while Lavinia and Claytor were still putting Mary Alcorn's gifts from Santa Claus under the tree, and Howard was out somewhere. Agnes's level-headedness had evaporated; she was exhausted and discouraging.

"Why didn't you let me know what you were thinking? I wish you'd had the courtesy to say something, Betts! It's ridiculous to have to find it out from Will. And all this time I thought you and Sam —" She was whispering furiously, and Betts followed suit, but the more desperate each one became to make her point, the more strained was the suppressed volume beneath the rustle of her words.

"Oh, Mama!" Betts shook her head at the wrongheadedness of her mother's ideas. "You must see that if Sam's interested in anybody, it's got to be you! But I don't think Sam's ever going to get over that girl. Carol? Claire? She was English? Killed in the war?" But Agnes couldn't fill in the blank, and Betts went on. "No one could have been as perfect as Sam thinks she was, but really that's neither here nor there. I'm not in love with Sam, anyway. I like him a lot. But I'm in love with Will. We have so many plans! So many things we want to do . . ."

"Betts! Just think about it for a little while! At least a few months. You can't . . . Will is a nice man, but he's not the right person for you. Betts, Will is my age!"

"I knew that's what you'd say! I knew Dwight would say the same thing. Now do you see why I hate to have my family involved in my life? Everyone feels they have the right to give me advice! But if *I* don't care about our age difference, then it just isn't anybody else's business!"

Betts suddenly felt the release of tension across her shoulders; it was a relief, she realized, not to keep this secret. She reminded herself that her mother had known Will her whole life, and it was unlikely in those circumstances that she would ever see him as he was now. Prominent not only in the community but depended upon even by the government. He was an authority on the newest developments in agriculture, often traveling to Washington to speak to one committee or another.

"I should have said something, Mama. I just hate it, though, when everyone knows my business. I just hate it when everyone thinks they can say the rudest things to me and disguise it as advice!"

"Betts! I'm not trying to disguise anything! I've known Will all my life, and he just isn't the right person for you. He's a man who . . . Why, he's perfectly nice. He's an attractive man. But he's a man who —"

"Who *what,* Mama? I thought Will and I should just go get married. I didn't see any need to get anyone's approval. In fact, if Will didn't have such an old-fashioned idea about what's proper . . . I really wanted to just go get married and not bother with all this. I know this family . . . Dwight and Claytor . . . even Howard! None of you would have been anything but polite if we'd just come in the door already married. You don't worry about insulting *me,* but God knows you wouldn't ever have been rude to anyone outside the family. Not one of you would have said to Will's face that you didn't approve!"

"Betts, it's . . . I don't approve or disapprove except that he's just not the right person for you." Agnes stopped herself for a few seconds to consider what she was saying, to consider what she might say. Just briefly — just in a flash of a thought — Agnes questioned her own possible motives for discouraging the marriage. But, no, she concluded, she certainly wasn't jealous, and her own involvement with Will seemed to have been so long ago and under such different circumstances that for all intents and purposes it hadn't happened in the real world. Agnes was certain that nothing but good intentions were at the heart of her objection.

"Betts, really! He's the sort of man, oh, you know . . . the sort of man who says . . ." She realized Betts's patience was about to give way, and Agnes finally just plunged ahead. "He's the sort of man who's always telling you what sort of man he is! He'll say, 'I'm the sort of man who doesn't approve of that language,' or 'I'm the sort of man who doesn't like seeing a woman smoke cigarettes.' He's not as sophisticated as you are, Betts! You'd get bored. . . . He's not as *smart* as you are!"

"Mother! I never would have guessed you'd be such a snob! Will's smart as a whip! He's just . . . It's just that he's straightforward. It's just that he's a very smart man from Ohio. He doesn't care about impressing other people. Being clever at anyone else's expense. You can't imagine how provincial people are! People from New York! Or Boston . . . or even Charleston, South Carolina. People who come from Los Angeles. You'd think anyone from Ohio was a lumbering, blond oaf of some kind with a blade of grass between his teeth. Will doesn't pretend any-thing. I've had enough of mysterious, I'll tell you. More than enough of romantic men. . . . I got sick to death of what passes for sophistication when I was in Washington!"

Agnes stood up from where she'd been sitting on the bed and started rummaging through Betts's closet, finally reaching up and taking down Betts's train case and extracting a pack of Lucky Strikes and a book of matches.

"Mother! I knew —," Betts began, but Agnes waved her off and lit a cigarette, handing the pack and the matches to Betts.

"Oh, you're right, Betts. And it's certainly not for any-one else to decide. I'm sorry," she said, sitting down again and leaning against the headboard, exhaling a long sigh of wispy smoke. "Of course, you understand that there isn't a man any mother thinks is good enough for her daugh-ter." But that sounded absurd coming from her as soon as the words left her mouth. Agnes knew that no one would ever think of her as that sort of woman, a sentimental mother. "Will's seemed like part of the family for years. Now we can make it official. I do think he's a nice man, Betts, but you can't blame me for being surprised. I've known him since I was born. . . . It's impossible to imag-ine your daughter marrying a man who . . . Well. Who you know so well! I was in school with Sally Trenholm, you know. She was one of my best friends, and it's hard to think of my daughter . . . But I do think that Will is the sort of man you could trust with your life."

Chapter Ten

SAM HOLLOWAY FIRST MET Dwight Claytor in 1944, at Deopham Green when they discovered they had mutual acquaintances, but they had become friends over a long, boozy conversation at the Dorchester Hotel in London, where they had been surprised to run into each other. The weather over Europe was bad and expected to remain too cloudy for bombing runs for six or seven days, and each of their crews had been given a three-day pass. Dwight and Sam had headed separately to London.

Sam was staying at the Dorchester, and Dwight had been waiting at the bar for an old friend who never showed up. Dwight didn't know where he was sleeping that night, since he had had such short notice to make arrangements and every hotel was filled to the gills. Sam insisted he take the other bedroom of the suite that had been put at his disposal by Douglas Boatwright, who owned the radio station and both of the newspapers in

Baton Rouge and had been Sam's boss at WJBO. Mr. Boatwright was in London serving as the head of the Department of Censorship, although he was often away for one thing or another.

"He left word with the Dorchester," Sam explained to Dwight, "that whenever I was in town, I was to have the use of his suite. I couldn't see any reason not to take advantage of it. So, the first chance I get, I call up the hotel, called from the base, and I say, 'This is Sergeant Holloway, and I'll be coming to London on such and such a day.' I explain that Mr. Boatwright has offered me the use of his suite. But the fellow I was speaking to seemed uncertain about that. Handed the telephone to someone higher up. So I begin to explain all over again, and by now I'm feeling like a fool. Wondering if Mr. Boatwright had forgotten to notify the hotel and if the manager thought I was some sort of cocky American flyboy. I'm trying to explain, but the manager interrupts me and says that of course they were delighted Mr. Boatwright had made his suite available, and so forth . . ."

Sam paused for a moment and smiled. "So finally there I am, in the lobby, introducing myself, and the door-man seems glad to see me. Tells me he'll have my things delivered to the suite. Hopes I'll enjoy my stay with them. All that sort of thing. And then he says, 'Please notify me if you require any assistance, Lieutenant Holloway.'

"I thought it was odd that he called me 'lieutenant.' The way they pronounce it: *lefttenant*. Maybe I had misunderstood or he was confused . . . but, you know, I didn't want to embarrass him. And I was in a hurry, too.

"But the next morning when I go out — when I say good morning to him — he says, 'Good morning, Lieutenant Holloway. I hope you were comfortable last night.' So this time I think I need to straighten this out. And I say I was very comfortable, thank you. But I tell him that there's some sort of misunderstanding. 'It's Sergeant Holloway, I'm afraid,' I say.

"'Oh, no sir. I'm certain you're mistaken about that. The Dorchester, you see, doesn't take enlisted men.' At first I didn't understand what he was telling me. But then I had to laugh. And I go on my way and don't complain again about getting a promotion." Dwight and Sam had moved to a table, and Dwight was delighted to have discovered a good storyteller. Someone he enjoyed listening to.

He and Sam sat up for hours, trading stories and absurdities. Dwight told Sam about a diplomatic mission he had been on to the Ukraine after the split between Stalin and Hitler. It had been a hare-brained scheme from the start, Dwight had always thought. And he went on to recount the tale of the whole squadron being stranded in the Ukraine with their planes shot up and being unable to avoid their Russian hosts' efforts to entertain them by playing balalaikas and insisting that the Americans join them in what seemed to be hours of rigorous dancing.

"We didn't know if we were stuck there for the duration," Dwight said. "And every day we would ask if this was the day someone was going to come get us, and every day they would say, 'Uncle Joe say no.'"

Sam Holloway had spent much of 1943 in Salt Lake City, Utah, training with the other nine men assigned to the same B-17 flight crew. They practiced bombing runs and night flights, and in the spring of 1944, they flew to Goose Bay, Labrador, then to Iceland, and from Iceland to Ireland, where they left their plane and were ferried across to England.

Eventually they were stationed in East Anglia at Deopham Green and told not to worry, that their first flight would be little more than a milk run. Sam thought they would probably be flying an easy mission to acclimate the crew, perhaps just across the channel.

But their first mission, it turned out, was Berlin. They flew in formation in a great, dark cloud of B-17s in broad daylight, and at least sixty of those heavy, lumbering bombers were shot down that day, each with a crew of ten. Sometimes Sam saw chutes open, and sometimes not, and so many planes went down on either side of him that Sam thought he wasn't likely to live through the day, much less the war. In fact, he never understood why his crew had survived that first mission or even how he himself had survived hour after hour of unremitting and horrified disbelief all alone, kneeling in the tail of the plane, connected to the rest of the crew by intercom, able to breathe because of his oxygen mask, and kept from freezing only by plugging in the underlayer of his flight suit. He had done all this before, time and again, but it had always seemed to him melodramatic, cumbersome, and in some way slightly ridiculous. For the first time, on that mission and under fire, however, his connections seemed not cumbersome, not melodramatic, but wretchedly tenuous and vulnerable.

At first he had been overwhelmed with empathetic horror as a plane skewed out of formation: my God my God my God they're all going to die! But soon, even on that first run, he shut down his imagination. By the time he flew his third mission, he had fallen into a calm detachment and even a sort of fascination as one after another of those B-17s went down. He looked on as an observer of an ill-thought-out game; he couldn't have withstood it if he had looked on from the point of view of a participant. And he shut away his certainty that there wasn't enough luck in the world to allow him to survive. Those Flying Fortresses flew at such high altitude most of the time that, even when he was firing at enemy planes, he remained curiously indifferent. Throughout the war he never saw a person killed; he only saw planes go down.

In the end, he only remembered all the details of his first mission of the required thirty-two; the others ran together if he made any effort to distinguish one from another. Only that first flight and, naturally, his last flight. Every man in the Corps remembered his last flight, certain that having gotten that far, he wouldn't survive it. But by the time of Sam's final flight, the Luftwaffe had pretty well been destroyed and their oil supplies wiped out. Sam's last flight — his thirty-second and final flight — was a mission to drop supplies to the French Resistance fighters in Savoie, near Switzerland. The weather was perfect; the air had such clarity that it seemed to Sam to have substance and depth, appearing to thicken in the distance to a pure, gelid, translucent blue. And the sunlight was all-encompassing and apparently without a source, as though it would not come and go with the hours; it illuminated every object, every vista, equally.

The chutes that were dropped from the squadron of B-17s were color-coded: red, for instance, for medical supplies, yellow for food, green for ammunition, and other colors for other things. There was something playful about the blossoming parachutes floating to earth, their cargo swinging gently from side to side, with the Alps in the background and cloudless skies above Lake Geneva. It was as though they had happened upon a new and perfect amusement park ride. A wondrous thing, a diversion that would more than meet the expectations of any eager child, unlike the disappointing tedium of a pretty carousel or the terrifying sway of the flag-flying Ferris wheel. And, although the plane itself vibrated with the noise of its engines, the aspect of the big gray airplanes casting shadows over the valley and the hundreds of parachutes drifting through the air was one of silence. They were flying at relatively low altitude, unhampered by oxygen masks and untethered to a power source, and below them the Resistance fighters waved their arms in acknowledgment, signaling V for victory.

Sam looked out at the panorama as it unfolded and was unable to keep his guard up against the seduction of relief. He had been puzzled, had put his hand to his face and discovered a wash of tears, although he hadn't been aware he was crying. In fact, he wasn't crying in any sense of the idea he had ever had; it was more as if he were simply overwhelmed at having to accommodate once again the idea of after. After the war. He had driven it from his mind, and suddenly there it was again, the prospect of his life going forward.

At that moment Sam was conscious — for the first time in his life — of what it was like to be happy. Of course, he often had been happy, but he had been literally careless and had taken it for granted in the same way that, before the depression, he had discarded pennies, leaving them in a dish on his bureau, because they were inconvenient to carry. Years later he realized that the only thing of value he had come away with from the war — other than his life — was the occasional ability to be guiltlessly and unapologetically glad. It wasn't a complicated sentiment; it was merely an exuberant acknowledgment of being responsible only for life as he was living it in the moment. Every now and then he was able to recognize that there was nothing he could do about the miseries of the world; and in that instant of liberation, his self-ness was triumphant and overwhelming.

And even though gladness — joy, perhaps — wasn't a complicated emotion, it was rare. When he boarded the bus from Columbus, Ohio, to Washburn, in June of 1947 and gazed out the window at the rolling hills planted with corn, which he recognized, and other sweeping, cultivated fields of crops he couldn't identify, he began to feel the tension of pleasurable anticipation, though he couldn't think why. Sam had taken advantage of seeing the countryside wherever he happened to find himself when he was in the Army Air Corps. For four days in Tehran and several more in Cairo, for instance, he had been interested in everything and gone out to see whatever he had time to investigate, whereas his crewmates remained uninterested and stayed behind, playing endless card games and keeping out of the sun.

He had gone to some trouble to see the pyramids and had attempted to summon a sense of awe, although it wasn't until after he had survived his tour that he was able to think back on them with wonder. He had surely tramped over half of Ireland and much of Scotland, as well. And he'd spent lots of time in London. Certainly he hadn't expected to be affected one way or another by the countryside of the state of Ohio.

But when the bus pulled into the little station in Washburn, across from the square, which was shady and dark green on a very hot, bright day, Sam was unexpectedly overtaken by a welling up of euphoria, very nearly exactly the feeling he had experienced on that final mission looking out at the bright parachutes floating to earth on a beautiful day. Although he had jotted down Dwight's address and had been told how to get there, he headed off in another direction for a brief stroll along the limestone sidewalks and across the old brick streets. He passed nicely groomed houses and two churches that stood in handsome opposition to each other, catty-cornered across an intersection that was also deeply shaded by fine old trees that appeared to have stood forever on each of the four corners where High Street and Vine intersected.

He had expected to walk off his unreasonable joy, to stretch his legs and tamp down this odd fervor, but, in fact, his sense of well-being only intensified. The town of

Washburn affected Sam with the same surge of light-heartedness he had experienced on that final run. Here was everything, Sam thought, but all of it in moderation. The countryside was rolling, though not mountainous, and there were fine old houses, though not particularly grand ones, and small bungalows, but no signs of real poverty. It seemed to Sam a place in which one's life could be ordered to the shape of his true nature, as opposed to living in an extreme atmosphere, like New Orleans, or New York, or San Francisco, or even Natchez, Mississippi, where it was too easy to surrender one's character to the prevailing climate of the place. When, eventually, he returned to the bus station to retrieve his duffel, Dwight and his wife, Trudy, were waiting for him, and the three of them walked together across the square to Scofields.

Although Sam had officially been hired only as the program director of WBRN, he worked at the radio station in nearly every capacity. He did a show at five in the afternoon in which he summarized the local news from the townships in Marshal County, and eventually news from other counties, as well. He gave a brief account of the national news that came in on the wire, read the weather predictions, and announced upcoming events. He had a knack for divulging information in a kind of lazy chatter that made even the worst news sound manageable and the least interesting information seem worth knowing. He was good at stimulating local interest in an upcoming play or a concert. He talked about the program or the plot a little bit, seeming to have a surprised but simultaneously low-key interest in the occasion. And he did gain listeners, although the network programs were the station's bread and butter.

The salary he made at the station he put away in the bank each week, because his main employment was as a sales representative for Lustron Homes, whose headquarters were in Columbus. The Lustron Corporation mass-produced porcelain-coated stainless-steel homes that could be assembled with a wrench in less than two weeks by a modestly accomplished homeowner. The idea had seemed brilliant to Sam in the abstract.

In the spring of 1948, the day Sam's own house was delivered on two huge Lustron trucks, he had already explained enough about it on the radio that a sizable crowd gathered in front of and in the yards next to the small lot Sam had bought on Birch Street. By the time his house was fully assembled, he had sold three other models. He wrote to Carl Strandlund that the houses sold themselves.

The fact was, though, that Sam didn't like living in his efficient, pale yellow porcelain-enameled house with the turquoise-blue shutters, the whole of which only needed hosing down once a year or so, never requiring repainting. But whenever a driving rain hit that steel exterior, he felt as though he inhabited a tin can at which someone was shooting a BB gun. The house was quirky but not charming, with odd shelves and cabinets built into the design, ample storage everywhere in efficient but peculiar places, and clean-lined, lean furnishings provided by Lustron at Sam's request and at a discount. It was remarkably neat and well organized, but, to Sam's way of thinking, it was not especially appealing.

"You know what, Sam," Betts said to him one evening, looking around the living room from her seat on the built-in couch beneath the big front window, "this is a house that you can't imagine getting old in. It's like a place you go to wait for something else. Like a train station or the bus station. Do you know what I mean? This is a house you only stay in until you leave."

Sam stayed on there, though, and oversaw the construction of the other Lustron houses he had sold in Washburn, but within less than a year, he resigned from the company, which was running into all sorts of unexpected problems with production in any case. He concentrated on his job at WBRN, which was steadily adding advertisers. Sam had come up with an idea for a weekly on-air talent competition with a live audience, and it had become surprisingly popular, although some of the various acts didn't translate very well over the radio and required Sam to think fast in order to describe what was going on to the listeners at home.

Will Dameron was intrigued by those Lustron homes. He didn't like them, but he liked the idea of them. Eventually Will traded a hilly, forty-seven-acre tract of land adjacent to the Green Lake Golf Course for a partnership with Sam; the two of them were convinced that prefabricated homes had a promising future if they were carefully planned. Sam had found a company outside Boston, in Framingham, that thought along the same lines, and he persuaded Cardinal Homes to put up a few houses on spec, entirely under his supervision. The Cardinal Corporation would retain all but ten percent of any profit in exchange for their initial investment. If the speculation was successful, Sam and Will would have sole rights to operate the franchise in the twelve counties surrounding Washburn, as well as in the city of Columbus.

"For a while I thought about staying with Lustron, since the buyer can get government subsidies," Sam explained to Will. "But, I don't know. I don't really like living in one. Those houses . . . There's no way you can ever feel moved in. You can just wipe off or wash away any sign you've ever been in the place. Inside and out. I thought I'd like that. The easy upkeep, I mean. But, I don't know. . . . Carl Strandlund's saying they'll be able to produce four hundred houses a day. But I was thinking what it would be like. Lustron's thinking they'll be able to sell them for somewhere around nine thousand dollars. But I think it'll have to be more if they're going to make any profit. You see, what happens," Sam said, "is that they crate the entire house right at the plant. Load it on flatbeds in reverse order of assembly. That part's fine. The idea's good. But the cost . . . each house weighs close to twenty tons. Now, Cardinal ships on flatbeds, too, but the product isn't so heavy. The strength comes from traditional framing at the site. And they're bigger. Can be about as big as you want. A lot more variety."

Sam spent all his spare time poring over the various possible floor plans. "The thing is," he told Will, "not to have every house look like the one next to it. Different layouts, different uses of materials. It's awful to see what they're doing out on Long Island. And they're building on slab to save costs, but I don't want to do that. Cardinal includes the cost of a cellar, since their houses are designed with cold weather in mind. In the Northeast. But we get plenty of cold weather in Ohio. I've always thought there's a way to do this right. People want to own their own houses. But why would they want a house that looked like every other house on the block?"

The two men had agreed, though, that before any construction began, it only made sense to get the utilities in place, the water, gas, and electric services set up in one fell swoop, because they were planning for growth. Here was the real risk they were taking, and both of them knew it. The time-consuming chore and expense of obtaining permits and variances, of installing the gas, water, sewer, power, and phone lines, was unsatisfying and frustrating and done at their expense. There were endless problems, just as Sam and Will had known there would be, and they often reminded themselves or each other that this was the part of their investment that allowed them to foresee long-term benefits.

As the big yellow shovels and earthmoving equipment began crawling over the acreage — turning the soil and throwing up high walls of dirt on either side of the furrows they dug — both Sam and Will were discouraged at the sight. This part of the project wasn't a bit exhilarating. The tidy streets they envisioned looked like trammeled cattle runs. The foundations were dug, but the forms hadn't been set in place yet to pour cement, and the basements and winding channels filled with rain and then became muddy trenches, as though an army had just departed. Will and Sam were glad, though, that the water drained away so quickly; they had done perc tests, but, said Will, "the proof of the pudding is in the pie."

Later that evening Sam telephoned Will. "That can't be right," Sam said as soon as Will picked up the phone. "Why would the proof of the pudding be in the pie? Do people around here make pies out of pudding? Is, say, a custard pie considered a pudding? At least the custard part? I've never heard of that." But Will said he had no idea; it was just a saying his mother and grandmother had used all his life, and that he only meant that they didn't have to worry about drainage. But Sam knew all that; he was simply nervous as building progressed, and he wanted to nail down every detail. It was quite clear to him that, although Dr. and Mrs. DeHaven from WBRN and Dwight and Claytor and Robert Butler drove out now and then to look around at the site and made encouragingly hopeful predictions, not one of them — or anyone else in Washburn, for that matter — believed people would want to live so far out of town and up on a windy, muddy hill.

Since Will and Betts had announced their engagement at Christmas, Will had taken to coming by Scofields late on a Sunday afternoon and, if Betts was available, inviting her — and anyone else who happened to be around — to join him at the Monument Restaurant. "Just for a bite to eat," he always said cautiously, as if there were other things going on at the restaurant of which they would not be expected to partake. It was touching to Betts in its courtliness, the invitation's careful courtesy — not asking for any other sort of obligation, only supper, and including everyone in the family. Generally Lavinia begged off, and Howard and Agnes as well, knowing, of course, that Will and Betts must want time to themselves.

One Sunday, though, Betts and Agnes had spent the day looking over patterns and fabrics for Betts's wedding and honeymoon wardrobe. The wedding itself would be the middle of May, at St. James, and with only the immediate family present. All the Scofields' friends and family would be invited to the reception, though, which would be at Lily and Robert's house, where Agnes and Lily planned to have tables set up in the garden. When Agnes began to decline Will's invitation, Betts urged her to join them. "Oh, no, Mother. Please come with us! I want you to explain to Will what I'm wearing."

"I don't think that's a good idea, Betts. Don't you think it should be a surprise?" Agnes asked, still reluctant to join them.

"But it won't be a surprise he'll like. Will, you're old-fashioned about these things," she said fondly, pretending to rebuke him. She turned back to her mother. "Mama, if you bring along the patterns . . ."

The three of them crossed the square together, chatting. As they reached the curb, Agnes wasn't aware that she leaned toward Will slightly, and that he automatically cupped her elbow in his large hand as she stepped down, just as a matter of habit. But for Betts it was a moment exactly like the revelation in Mrs. Frazier's fourth-grade class when, one by one, students took turns looking through a powerful microscope Mrs. Frazier had borrowed from her husband's lab in the Harcourt Lees biology building.

Mrs. Frazier instructed the children to consider a small, shallow, seemingly unremarkable dish of water, and Betts had waited her turn to peer through the microscope, simply glad of the break in the routine of the school day. But, as it turned out, she was astounded when she finally got a glimpse of the water through the microscope. She had taken a place once more at the end of the line in order to have another chance to see if it might be some trick or illusion. She was a natural-born skeptic, and Mrs. Frazier was gratified at her interest and showed her how to adjust and focus the lens for herself. Betts watched the busy, turbulent life within that shallow bowl for a long time. And the recognition that shot through Betts like an electric shock — when she caught site of Will's hand gently guiding her mother's elbow — was exactly like the discovery that in what appeared to be nothing more than crystal clear liquid many things were undisclosed.

Just in witnessing Will's small, unconscious gesture and her mother's equally oblivious expectation of it, Betts understood on a visceral level that between her mother and Will there was a deeper connection than merely that of old acquaintances or good friends. She didn't realize she had drawn in her breath in a small but audible gasp, and her mother and Will turned to look at her quizzically. "Oh! No, no," she said. "I just remembered something. . . . It's not important. . . ."

Betts had learned to shut down her imagination during her near obsession with being in love with Hank

Abernathy — if his wallet fell open when he was paying a bill at a restaurant, for instance, and she almost saw the picture of his wife and two daughters. Or in his apartment lobby, when she glanced away while he collected his mail, which generally contained at least one pale blue envelope addressed in black ink and with a California postmark. So on that bleak February afternoon — with the remaining snow pitted and gritty with sand and dirt where it had been cleared from the paths that crisscrossed the square — as she and Will and her mother approached the Monument Restaurant, Betts managed not to consider anything very carefully, although it was a hard-pitched battle against her rising consternation.

What on earth had her mother been thinking? Had she been in love with Will? Had he been in love with her? But that was ridiculous; her mother didn't seem to think much of Will one way or another, which, in fact, had often made Betts defensive on his behalf. And besides, her mother was fifty years old! Betts couldn't throw off the idea of the implicit betrayal of her father. The emotional betrayal; any other sort of infidelity on her mother's part was truly beyond Betts's imagination.

Once they were seated, Betts managed to close her mind's eye; she refused to know anything more than whatever appeared to be true at that moment. She even reprimanded herself for thinking such things about her mother. In fact, when their dinners were served, Betts became unusually proprietary about her mother's welfare, making sure Agnes had the salt or pepper and checking that the waitress kept her mother's coffee hot. At the deepest level of Betts's orientation of herself to the world, she defined Agnes first and foremost as her own and Dwight and Claytor and Howard's mother, and then as Warren Scofield's wife. Betts wasn't able yet to concede her mother's widowhood.

These days Betts had often sought out her mother, surprised by her sophistication about fashion, her knowingness about the way people lived now. Agnes seemed simply to assume that Betts knew all about sex from experience. Nor did Agnes appear to be in the least surprised that Nancy Turner had gotten married because she was pregnant. Agnes didn't even seem distressed by it, since Nancy and Joe Fosberg were happy enough and clearly adored their new baby. Most of all Betts had been surprised by her mother's humor and their agreement about all sorts of things they had never agreed upon before the war. And, too, Betts was basking in her mother's affectionate and wholehearted attention. It would have been simply foolish of Betts to do anything other than put out of her head the tiny, fleeting vignette of her mother's elbow cupped in Will's large hand.

As for Agnes, she was infatuated with her daughter once more, just as she had unexpectedly been smitten the first year or so of Betts's life. Once again the two of them were involved in a conspiracy aimed at insuring Betts's pleasure, just as they had been when Betts, and Howard, too, were infants. The whole scheme induced in Agnes a no-holds-barred indulgence of that child's desires. It was very nearly erotic to allow herself to luxuriate in a guilt-free generosity of spirit. By the time Betts was born,

Agnes knew that a child couldn't be spoiled by affection, could be fed at any time of the day or night, if she was hungry, without becoming a tyrant, should be comforted when she was in distress, and that whatever a doctor, or mother-in-law, or a well-meaning friend might suggest, there simply wasn't any wrong way to love her children.

By then, Agnes also knew that it was simply a coincidence if you happened to love whatever children you ended up with. Even better if you liked them, as well. She had been too young and too self-conscious, too caught up in Dwight's and Claytor's well-being — and how their well-being reflected on her — to savor their infancy. Certainly she had loved them, too, with a kind of devotion that she kept under wraps, that had seemed unreasonable even to her, and that was discouraged by the mood of the day.

These days, when she caught herself imagining Betts's delight at one thing or another, Agnes understood that she had fallen into a state too intense to sustain. She was convinced, for instance, that if she made for Betts the most beautiful coral-colored silk robe — managing to gather the sleeves sweepingly into the tight cuffs — then nothing else would be needed to insure her daughter's happiness in the world. It was what she believed for the time being as opposed to what she knew. Every time she fingered the glorious fabric, she believed once again that it could be the answer to any problem whatsoever; she didn't yet have to abandon her magic thinking.

Agnes and Betts were caught up in what amounted to a sort of last waltz — a honeymoon, even — before either one turned her attention elsewhere. At first Agnes was reminded of the unexpected attachment she and her own mother had fallen into not long before Agnes herself got married. The beautiful clothes her mother had arranged to have Aunt Cettie make. But poor Catherine; she had been incapable of contentment, and it had taken Agnes a long time to forgive her. Catherine Claytor either flew through the hours of each day in a state of elation or dragged herself through the tedious minutes with listless indifference. In fact, frequently Agnes found herself caught up in a memory of her mother and frozen in place with her jaw clenched and her hands closed into fists. After a while Agnes didn't let her mind wander with much particularity over memories of herself and her mother.

It was reassuring, though, to imagine Betts's life unfolding in small contentments as well as in the fever pitch of her frequent, spontaneous but short-lived, spells of joy. For her whole life Betts had seemed to Agnes to be a person who thrived best in extreme situations and floundered when stuck in the ordinary passage of time. Betts was mystified, for instance, by the realization that there were people who delighted in living under the tension of happy anticipation. By the time she was no more than three or four years old, she had declared her dread of such a state of being; she put her hands over her ears and hummed aloud when her brothers — as early as September — began to name the gifts they hoped to get for Christmas.

"Stop it! I can't stand it! I can't stand it! I can't stand to wait for Christmas so long!" It had amused Agnes at the time, when Betts was a little girl who clearly knew herself so well, and it amused her still. But she had also felt sorry for Betts a little bit even then and wished her daughter would allow herself the same greedy, gleeful hopefulness the boys enjoyed. In Agnes's experience, that was always the best part of any major occasion; no celebration ever lives up to the act of anticipating its pleasure.

In the case of her wedding, though, Betts relished the anticipation; she was deeply intrigued and entertained by the official, solemn nature of the preparations for her marriage. She was filled with goodwill toward everyone, and also with gratitude. She repeatedly thanked her mother for offering to make her trousseau; it was an undertaking that Betts couldn't fathom taking on. The monotony of repetition; the frustration of getting a seam wrong and taking it out again with care. And Agnes never tried to explain to anyone who didn't like to sew the marvelous transformation of a piece of fabric — often beautiful in itself — into what seemed to her an architectural construction that approached fine art. When she was by herself in the sewing room, she would hold up a blouse she had finished and regard the subtlety of the bound buttonholes, or the drape of the yoke, and she would experience a brief, euphoric surge of pure creative satisfaction.

In early March, though, Betts came down with what seemed at first to be a mild cold, but which turned into a serious case of bronchitis. Even when Agnes gave her tea with honey and propped her up against a wedge of pillows Betts couldn't stop coughing. Agnes's *own* mother had been suspicious of her children's ailments, as though their illnesses might be an indictment of her, or a way to elicit unreasonable attention. But Agnes's youngest brother and her mother, too, had died of influenza, and

Agnes took exactly the opposite attitude toward any affliction that descended upon her own children. As they grew out of childhood, she nearly drove them crazy, and even now she was overanxious. "Mama!" Betts said, "you make me think there are vultures circling outside my window! I'm fine. I just need to sleep."

Agnes wanted to call their doctor, but Betts begged her not to. "I think if Dr. Caldwell came, it might kill me, Mama. I think it might drive me right over the edge." When her fever rose, though, and her rib cage ached unless she kept her breathing shallow, Betts became frightened herself. And the afternoon she came out of a short spell of sleep and knew that if she moved at all, she would hurt all over — the afternoon when she lay perfectly still and yet the atmosphere of the day bore down on her painfully — that moment of consciousness terrified Betts. She suddenly understood that she would die, but she didn't have enough strength even to call for her mother or Howard or Lavinia.

Agnes found her a little later, lying rigidly in bed with a shaft of sunlight falling over her face and shoulders through the narrow space where the curtains didn't meet. Betts's eyes were closed, but tears ran down her face. "I feel so bad," she said to her mother in no more than a whisper, although the sound of her own voice was enormous to Betts, echoing and bouncing painfully against the chamber of her skull. Agnes was filled with dread at the sight of Betts so unglorious and gray, so limp against the pillows that she seemed to be slowly deflating.

Dr. Caldwell came to the house and was clearly concerned. He shook his head in a private communication with himself as he read the thermometer. "There's not much to do," he said. He gave Betts codeine syrup that subdued her cough, although he cautioned her not to use it during the day. The cough, itself, he explained, had a purpose. "There's not much you can do for bronchitis," he said, "except relieve the symptoms to some degree. I've found that my patients think we can cure just about anything now. And right away, too," he added.

"In fact, most people, when they get sick, they simply fail to appreciate God's design," he said to Betts, settling back in the chair beside her bed to get comfortable. "I used to hear preachers and such talk about the 'intricacy of God's design' when I was young . . . oh, when I was studying medicine. I thought they were making excuses. But over all the years I've practiced, I've thought about it a great deal. I do think that the relief of pain . . . making my patients as comfortable as I can . . . I think that's a reasonable pursuit. Why shouldn't we consider those gifts we've developed to *be* God's design? But I've never believed in fighting a fever, you know. The body is a subtle creation. I've always thought that for almost every illness the symptoms are generally a means of healing. . . ." And as he talked on, Betts drifted off to her first sound sleep in more than four days.

In the days following that first visit, though, when her cough nearly exhausted her and she felt no better at all, Betts took a teaspoon of the codeine syrup day or night. And one night Agnes took a teaspoon herself, desperate to get some sleep of her own. None of her regular methods of seducing herself into sleep were at all effective with

Betts so sick right across the hall, because Betts had never been bedridden by an illness in her life. Not even by chicken pox, not even measles. Perhaps for one day, or a half day, she would stay in bed not feeling well, but she had been far more resilient than her brothers.

Sometimes it had nearly driven Agnes to despair when she and the other children were all sick and needing sleep except Betts, who required her mother's attention although Agnes could hardly stay awake. There had been days when Agnes had felt so miserable that she had been reduced to silently weeping while forcing herself to stay awake in order to keep an eye on Betts, who was playing contentedly. But now that Betts was so sick that she slept almost all the time, Agnes was wretchedly alert. She only realized that she had fallen into sleep when she was jolted awake by the sensation of falling. It seemed reasonable to Agnes that she had brought this terrible luck down upon her daughter by having now and then resented Betts's energetic healthiness when she was just a little girl.

Dr. Caldwell came every day for a week, and Will was in and out inquiring about her. Betts refused to let him come upstairs. "Mama, I haven't even washed my hair!" But he kept the house full of flowers and fresh fruit. During the next week, when Betts started to improve, Dr. Caldwell came every other day, and Betts pulled herself together and allowed Will to sit with her in the evenings. By the middle of April, Dr. Caldwell believed she was well enough to be up and about as long as she came to his office once a week so he could listen to her lungs and check her progress.

Agnes was elated; when she had come upon Betts at the point when she was so ill that she didn't even realize she was only whispering — that she could scarcely be understood — Agnes had honestly entertained the idea that Betts might not survive. It had brought her brother Edson right into the room. Just as Agnes had come upon him only a day or so before he died. She had been thoroughly alarmed by Betts's gray pallor and the striking difference in her when she lacked animation — as opposed to the natural state of drama that radiated from and energized Betts, that made her lovely and magnetic and that Agnes understood, now, in fact, to be an essential quality of her daughter's personality. What Agnes had often considered Betts's overwrought sense of drama, out-of-proportion enthusiasm, turned out to be the foundation of Betts's nature.

Betts was well enough for Agnes to do the final fittings of the clothes for her trousseau, and with the wedding no more than three weeks away, Agnes was filled with the urgency of things to get finished, including the cream-colored linen suit Betts would wear instead of a standard veil and gown. The Sunday back in February when she and Betts had shown Will the sketches while they sat over coffee at the Monument Restaurant, Betts had laughed at the idea of a traditional white satin gown when Will seemed disappointed that she wasn't planning to wear one.

"For goodness sakes! There's nothing more likely to make a girl look like she's being served up for human sacrifice," Betts told him, and Agnes had silently agreed with her. Besides, that sort of romantic, draping gown — not to mention any kind of gossamerlike veil — would undermine what was the strength of Betts's beauty. Her good looks were glamorous as opposed to sweet, and nothing set her off better than a beautifully made suit and a wide-brimmed, face-framing hat. That was one of the few useful things Betts had discovered during the time she worked in Washington.

While Betts was sick, Agnes hadn't been able to sew a stitch of Betts's trousseau without feeling that she would be tempting fate, and she had steered clear of the sewing room entirely. But now that there was so little time before the wedding, Agnes was busy every minute. She knew she was going to be in a hurry until the moment Betts was standing at the altar, and she was delighted to be flying around with the inevitability of life going on.

On the last Saturday morning in April, Agnes gave up counting on the arrival from New York of the beautiful buttons she and Betts had selected for the linen suit; she would have to see what was available locally. She also needed a darker thread for the linen, buckram for inter-lining, and softer wool for the shoulder padding — which had turned out far too stiff and boxy.

The stores were surprisingly crowded, even for a Saturday, and as Agnes made her way from the post office to Phillips Department Store, she spotted Dr. Caldwell in the next block, heading her way. It went without saying — although, of course, she had said it — that she was extremely grateful to him, but she didn't have time to stop and tell him so again. Besides, he was a tedious man, humorless, and given to long explanations and conversations of one kind or another. He was tall with bright white hair and a long, pinched face — like an exclamation point that didn't agree with itself, Dwight had once said — and Dr. Caldwell generally seemed oblivious to his surroundings. Agnes saw him before he saw her. In fact, as Agnes withdrew a list from her purse and made a show of studying it as she moved along the sidewalk, Dr. Caldwell stepped off a curb and crossed against the light, although luckily no car was coming. But clearly he was preoccupied, and Agnes was hoping she could slip right by him.

Just as they passed each other, though, Dr. Caldwell wheeled around and said her name, and Agnes had no choice but to pause and greet him. She never looked forward to seeing him, even when she was well, but she was indebted to him, and she did respect him, and, in any case, she certainly would never be rude to him.

His manner was quite serious, however, when he bent to shake her hand, and he said to her that he had become more than a little worried about Betts. That he had been meaning to get in touch with Agnes, so wasn't it fortunate that he had happened to run into her this morning. Agnes felt her heart sink when he said that. Why would he be worried about Betts? Doctors didn't seem to realize the terror that accompanies parenthood, and yet who knew better than they what easy prey any parent's child was to, say, an ear infection that overnight turns into meningitis? Or a simple insect bite that suddenly causes a child to break out in hives and gasp for breath as his throat swells closed?

"About Betts? But, why's that? It's just wonderful, really, to see her back to being her old self again," she said. "She's so much better. It's like night and day. It seems to me — oh, the whole family is amazed! You simply seem to have worked a miracle!" Even as she shaped the words she was speaking, Agnes realized she was attempting to flatter this man into reinterpreting whatever it was that worried him about her daughter.

"Oh, yes. Certainly she's better. She's perfectly well right now. But bronchitis . . . It's not a thing to take lightly," he said to Agnes. "I'm afraid to say that your daughter . . . well, I don't think she's taking me seriously. Frankly, I don't think she's a very serious girl," he added with an air of annoyance. Agnes almost replied, but she remembered that she was in a hurry and that it wouldn't serve any purpose to argue with this man about Betts's character.

"If your daughter keeps smoking, Mrs. Scofield, she's likely to have one case of bronchitis after another. And it can turn into pneumonia in no time at all."

Agnes regarded him for a moment, amazed at how much she resented this man who was only trying to be helpful. "Well, Dr. Caldwell, I hope you've made that clear to Betts herself and haven't been waiting just to tell me. My daughter is a grown woman who's about to get married. I hope you've warned her —"

"Oh, my! I should say so! Certainly I've told her that myself! I've told that to each and every patient time and again. All my patients. Other doctors' patients. My wife and my two daughters and my stepson. It doesn't do a thing. I no longer bother trying to explain it —"

"Oh, well then! Maybe if you did explain it . . ." Agnes tried to suppress her exasperation. "Tell her exactly what might happen. How sick she could get. About pneumonia . . . and whatever else —"

"I'll tell you," he said, "all the time I've been in medical practice, I've tried to *learn* from my patients. It was one of those pieces of advice that every instructor, every doctor — Well! I thought the idea was that since I was young, I'd learn . . . Oh! . . . Wisdom from just ordinary folks. That's what that advice did mean. But what I *have* learned from my patients is that human beings aren't logical creatures. They have the ability to act on their knowledge and save themselves a great deal of unhappiness. Misery. But will they do it? Even if it's quite a simple thing?"

He wasn't making any attempt to curb his own exasperation, and Agnes snapped back at him instinctively. "Goodness! Have your patients made you that cynical? I believe you're too pessimistic. I suppose it comes with the territory. But I expect a few people make every —," Agnes said, but Dr. Caldwell held his hand up imperiously and continued.

"People won't stop smoking for an abstract idea, Mrs. Scofield. They will not be motivated to give up alcohol either if the reward is too far down the road. Your daughter won't stop smoking if the only reason is because she might get sick. . . . Now, if I said to her, 'Miss Scofield, your right arm is going to shrink to half the length of your left arm if you don't stop smoking!' well, that's about vanity, you see," he explained to Agnes. "Now, that might stop her. But to say to her that she's likely to get bronchitis again and maybe pneumonia . . ."

"Oh, yes! Oh, I see." Agnes was eager to agree with this man about something so she could be on her way. "I see what you mean. Tell her that, then! Betts loves to play golf. Tennis. She'd hate to have her right arm get shorter. Well, even though she's left-handed. . . ." Agnes had managed only to pause midstride, having come to a stop after she had passed him by. She had remained turned slightly away from him, and now she was able to smile and thank him for his concern as she edged away, holding up her list as an explanation. "The buttons haven't come for the wedding dress. . . . I'm on a search. . . ." And she was off.

Dr. Caldwell stood in the center of the sidewalk like a tall boulder in a fairly shallow stream as people made their way around him on either side. He was taken aback a bit, and he looked after Agnes Scofield as she dashed through the Saturday crowd. She was a tidy, voluptuous little woman with the most remarkable hair. . . . Finally he remembered he was on his way home and that he was already late.

Agnes spent more time than she intended searching though the sewing department at Phillips Department Store, with no luck at all except to find the buckram. Phillips carried basic sewing supplies, but since they didn't have anything else she needed, and since the store was crowded, she decided to buy the buckram elsewhere. By the time she entered Neate's Fabrics and Notions, that unnerving conversation with Dr. Caldwell had slipped her mind entirely.

Chapter Eleven

WASHBURN, OHIO, was officially incorporated in 1800, and in December of 1949, the *Washburn Observer* ran an editorial asking point-blank if there would or would not be a sesquicentennial celebration. One way or another, Dwight Claytor, who was the newly elected president of the Washburn Historic Preservation Society, became the de facto director of the event, and he was wearied by the project within a few weeks. Eventually, in late February of 1950, after many separate and, finally, joint meetings with the two garden clubs, the Knights of the Eagle, the Knights of Fithian, the Masons and their sister lodge — which was planning the dedication of its newly built Home for the Elderly Women of the Eastern Star — as well as the Marshal County Chamber of Commerce, Dwight was able to announce that Washburn's sesquicentennial celebration would extend to all of Marshal County and would also encompass Washburn's Dan Emmett Days celebration, which hadn't been observed since 1939.

Dwight had called upon every ounce of his patience and his burgeoning skill at diplomacy in order to extract an agreement from all concerned that the events would commence on Saturday, July first, encompassing the Fourth of July, and would come to a close at the Sesquicentennial Ball Saturday, July fifteenth. What had finally tipped the balance in a disagreement between the Chamber of Commerce and the Knights of the Eagle was Dwight's reminding all concerned that the downtown merchants would have their stores stocked with back-to-school inventory and that the festivities were bound to bring a great many people to town. "I didn't want the Eagles to be unhappy," he said to Trudy, "but they really didn't have a leg to stand on, since they don't have a marching band. Now, the Knights of Fithian are another matter —"

"Dwight! You sound like . . . oh, I don't know. Some small-town businessman engaged in boosterism. Like you're a man in a bad suit with a big smile. How did you end up being in charge of all this?" Trudy wasn't particularly interested in any of the local events; she had thrived in New York City, even though she had found her job tedious, and even though it meant trading off child care. After the war, though, she had been perfectly willing to come home to Scofields with Dwight, who had offers from several law firms elsewhere but who clearly, and increasingly as the war went on, had longed to be back in Washburn.

"It seems like heaven to me at the moment," he had written to her from his base at Deopham Green:

The clean streets and all the well-kept houses. I miss what I think of as the common-senseness of it all, the predictable problems of any small town. It seems to me now that that's a reasonable goal to aim for. I always thought that Leo Scofield was admired in part because he understood that the lives of people are ordinary wherever they live. He believed that being responsible within a community is probably the greatest good that most men can do. I think your father believes the same thing, only he's chosen the community of letters. I've seen acts of courage and sacrifice here, but war brings out the most ruthless instincts of survival, too. I have met a few men who have become good friends, but in general I think that the war brings out the worst in people.

You would be amazed to see London. I took a walk around the city to see what had happened, and I was ill at ease the whole time, which probably seems like a natural reaction. But I couldn't figure out what was bothering me besides the obvious, the destruction and waste. Then I realized that somehow the day was too bright. *What I could see was sad and private and seemed to me to be too exposed. Children's toys, not even damaged. That wasn't really the worst, because I had heard people talk about being especially upset by the randomness of the damage. Like when I saw a lamp with a fringed shade standing upright in the middle of fallen bricks and dust. On that same street there was a woman's ball gown hanging in a closet that was the only remaining structure in a house that had been turned to rubble. I kept wondering, why just that gown? Where were her other clothes? The light was so bright that it almost made me angry. I wanted to protect the privacy of whoever had been living in those houses. I could see too much, if that makes any sense. Then I realized that the trees had been blasted away. They were simply gone. I don't know why that hit me so hard. Maybe there had never been trees on that street. Trees will grow again anyway, of course, but more than anything, it made me want to be back sitting in Monument Square under the shade of those big oaks.*

Trudy had been touched by that sentiment and had thought it perfectly understandable, although she hadn't known that Dwight had written that letter after returning from a mission during which his plane was so badly shot up and low on fuel that the pilot had considered landing in Sweden. The crew had jettisoned guns, ammunition, anything they could to lessen the weight, and the plane made it just across the channel to Kent. Communications were so bad that, by the time they finally managed to make their way back north to Deopham Green, every man on the crew found that any of his possessions that might be of use to someone else had been pilfered from his tent, although none of them took it personally. Photographs and letters, and even old and tattered magazines, had been scrupulously left behind. Their wing commander was only two days away from notifying the families of Dwight's flight crew that the men were missing in action.

For Trudy's part, though, during the time Dwight was overseas, politics had become an abiding passion — endlessly fascinating as she began to grapple with the big ideas and issues of the day. Her father had arranged for her to meet various literary friends of his, poets and writers who lived in the city, and she had fallen in with a group of those friends' children and students and assorted young writers and artists. And she, too, was caught up in their passionate progressivism. That very February morning that the Washburn newspaper announced the plans for the sesquicentennial, Trudy had a letter from a friend in the morning mail, reporting that the case of *Dennis et al. v. United States* was pretty certainly headed to the Supreme Court. As they sat at breakfast, she had tried to read the letter aloud to Dwight, but Amelia Anne had interrupted off and on, and little Martha, too, was agitated and cranky, and finally Trudy handed the letter to Dwight so he could read it for himself.

He skimmed over it and then returned to its first page and read it again, shaking his head. "Ah, God," he said. "This is a shame. Well, it's hysteria," he added, handing the letter back to her. But in light of his reaction to such serious news, Trudy was baffled by Dwight's having thrown himself full force into the insignificant details of planning so trivial an event as the sesquicentennial celebration of Washburn, Ohio.

Having weathered the scare of Betts's illness, Agnes had become increasingly enthusiastic about Betts and Will's upcoming marriage. They had seemed exactly like a happily married couple when Will sat with Betts in the evenings when she didn't even feel well enough to chat. Will sat with the paper, now and then reading an interesting item aloud to Betts. There was no mistaking the remarkable compatibility of the two. And now that Betts was up and about, Agnes threw herself wholeheartedly into the preparations for the wedding itself.

As the middle of May grew closer, however, Betts had become indifferent to it all, had become uninterested and hard to pin down about any decision concerning the choices of buttons or trims. "Really, Mama . . . it doesn't matter. Whatever you think looks best."

Agnes, herself, was entranced by the exotic fabrics now available to her, and sometimes she would unfold a length of cloth she had splurged on and lay its transparent paper pattern on top, so that she could envision the garment it would become. She was having far too good a time creating Betts's wardrobe to be particularly bothered by what she imagined was the inevitable listlessness that followed an illness.

Betts was preoccupied with her health. She tilted the mirror of her vanity to various angles and spent hours at a time studying her reflection. She had thought Dr. Caldwell was an old fool when he warned her of the consequences of smoking, and when she phoned Claytor, he said he hadn't heard of anything like that. But Betts had been so worried about hearing a grave answer that she hadn't been as forthright about her anxiety as she might have been. She had phoned Claytor, in fact, on the pretext of inquiring about a doctor to recommend to Will, who hadn't been impressed with Dr. Caldwell.

"And you know, Claytor," she said over the phone,

"I'm not fond of him at all! Do you know that he told me one of my arms was shorter than the other? Because of smoking!"

"Everybody's arms are different lengths, Betts," Claytor had told her. "Who knows why? But I tell you, I think Frank Pierce is probably a good man to see. Will should give him a call. Is there something particular Will's worried about?"

"No, no. Just . . . well, really, just someone in case we need a doctor." Betts hadn't told him that Dr. Caldwell had said she was suffering from progressive atrophy. It was plain enough to Betts when she looked in the mirror that her right arm had become a scant bit shorter than her left. At least a half inch shorter, she thought. Maybe even an inch.

And even though it was smoking that was at the root of the affliction, whenever Betts considered her situation, she ended up scrabbling through her purse, searching for her Luckys and a book of matches. She had rarely in her life needed a cigarette more. She was as unnerved as when she was living in Washington and seeing Hank Abernathy and one month thought for sure that she was pregnant. Was it, in fact, immoral, she brooded, not to tell Will about this disease?

She hadn't said a word about any of this to her family. It seemed to her only fair that if she told anyone at all, it should be Will. But what, if anything, should she tell him? She might well be misjudging him. He had a powerful sense of integrity, after all. She sat on the end of her bed near the open window, able at last to think clearly as she smoked a cigarette, and she considered the possibility

that telling Will about her predicament might be inter-
preted by him as an insult to his honor. Insulting to imply
that he might reject her for something so removed from
the reason he had fallen in love with her. He would probably be hurt that she had imagined such a thing. On the
other hand, she and Will had talked about having children. Was it possible that hers was an affliction passed
down through generations?

She tried and tried not to smoke; it irritated her throat
and often brought on a fit of coughing. But even the day
she left Dr. Caldwell's office after he broke the news to
her that cigarettes and coffee were causing slight atrophy
of her right arm — that if she kept smoking, the effect
could be that her right arm would appear shortened and
she might very well lose some of its strength — she had
stopped at a bench on the hospital lawn and had a cigarette, taking a long, shaky drag to calm herself down. And
since then, whenever her condition came to mind, the
only comfort she could find was having what she swore to
herself was just one last cigarette.

The day before her wedding, Betts was in a fragile
state of mind off and on all day. Lavinia came upon her at
the window of the staircase landing and stopped for a
moment. Betts had her back to the stairwell, bracing her
hands on the windowsill and leaning forward to gaze out
at the yard below, and Lavinia peered over her shoulder
to see what had caught her attention. Then she realized
Betts was near tears.

"I know just how you're feeling," Lavinia said. "I
remember . . . It suddenly seemed to me that I was pinning myself down for the rest of my life just before I

married Phillip Alcorn. It wasn't so bad with Claytor. I already knew. You just can't take it too seriously. I mean, you might stay madly in love the rest of your life. How can anyone know that, though? But it's not the end of the world one way or another. Well, because you never know what might happen. You could always get a divorce these days, or Will might die. . . . Don't think of yourself as trapped," she advised. Lavinia wasn't ever likely to give someone a spontaneous hug, but she did pat Betts lightly on the shoulder and then hurried on her way to spare Betts any further embarrassment.

That day, too, Agnes finally corralled Betts into the sewing room to make any last-minute alterations and to pin up the hem of Betts's linen suit. Agnes thought it boded well that it was an unusually pleasant day, moderate in every aspect, and she said so as she helped Betts step up and stand on the old, sturdy farm table her own mother had used as a pedestal where someone could turn slowly so that a pinned-up hem could be checked at eye level and adjusted to be sure it was even all the way around.

All at once the memory of Warren attempting to pin the hem of a dress she was fitting on herself came back to Agnes. The weather had been equally unobtrusive, and the two of them had at first become silly, as Warren had tickled her ankles and the backs of her knees, and then had run his hands under her skirt all the way to her waist. Eventually they had ended up together on the same sagging sofa that still sat against the wall, making love. They had spent the whole afternoon, until the light had faded, simply enjoying themselves. Agnes couldn't remember where the children had been, or her mother- and father-in-law, but she had always thought it was that afternoon that Betts was conceived.

"You know, Betts, I've never told anyone this. . . . Well, here you are! Right where you started," but Betts only murmured listlessly; she wasn't paying attention but only standing still in the manner of a well-behaved schoolgirl.

"Ah. The suit looks beautiful on you," Agnes said. "Here . . . turn a quarter-way round," she directed, and Betts obliged, but her peculiar sullenness was beginning to annoy Agnes. It cast a gloomy spell over the pleasant day. Betts had been moping about for days, and it was one thing to have second thoughts, if that was what was going on. If that was the case, then Betts should just say so and be done with it. It was quite another thing, Agnes thought, to put a damper on the mood of everyone in the house.

"I made the prettiest blue dress for myself in this room," Agnes chatted on. "Pale, pale blue with a darker blue pattern embroidered on the bodice. Like Queen Anne's Lace. Well, delicate. Embroidered around the hem, too." But Betts didn't respond. "Your father always said it looked like someone had aimed a blueberry pie at me. But, really, he liked that dress, too. I'd gotten so tired of dropped waists that I used one of my mother's patterns. It was your father who pinned up that hem for me, but it never was quite straight." Agnes glanced up at her daughter's face, but it was as inexpressive as if Betts were no more than a dress form.

"But I tell you what, Betts," said Agnes, her voice over-animated with bouncy cheerfulness. "This has certainly always been a lucky place for you." Finally Betts looked down at her mother as though she were surprised to hear her voice. "You can step down now," Agnes said. "I've got the hem basted. This is literally where you started off, you know. When your father was pinning the hem of that blueberry-pie dress. We certainly did get distracted. Why, I'd bet my life that was the exact time that you became more than a glimmer in your father's eye. On that very sofa —"

"Mother! My God, Mama. Parents don't tell their children . . . That's not the sort of thing you should ever say to me! Why did you tell me that?" But Agnes only shook her head, a little bit amused by Betts's priggishness. Betts appeared to be truly shocked, to be appalled, and she struggled to get out of the jacket of the suit, getting tangled in her hurry.

"Oh, wait, Betts," Agnes said. "Just let me get a quick measure of the sleeves. . . ."

And, at that, Betts went rigid, stepping away from her mother, crossing her arms corpse-fashion over her chest.

"Oh, God. I have to talk to Will. I can't go through with this. It's just wrong. It's not fair."

"Betts? I'm so *sorry,* Betts. Has something happened? What — Well, sit down a minute, Betts. You look like you might faint. Sit down! These things happen all the time. Maybe you just need some time to think."

"Oh, *God,* Mama," Betts said, "it's not right. I can't get married in my condition."

"What? What do you mean? I don't know what's wrong. I don't understand. This isn't . . . Have you changed your mind? About Will? Oh, Betts," Agnes said, her voice going soft with somberness. "You aren't pregnant, are you? But that's no reason —"

"*Mama!* No! Of course I'm not pregnant! I think Will's wonderful! I'd love to be married to Will!"

"Well, Betts . . . What's the matter? You're sure? It isn't that you're wondering if you'll be happy? I mean if you get married. You still *want* to have the wedding?"

"But I just can't," Betts said. "I can't. It would just be selfish, Mama! And it would be like playing some kind of trick. . . . I can't do that. I've got this condition I haven't said anything about. My right arm. Progressive atrophy. I haven't told anyone. I haven't told *him* — How could I ever do that? Marry him without —"

"Oh, my Lord, Betts. Oh, my Lord!"

"Well, I know. The whole thing is upsetting. But I don't *do* much with my right —"

"But it's not true! It isn't true, Betts. Everyone's arms are different lengths!"

"That's what I said to myself, and that's what Claytor said —"

"No, Betts! You don't understand what I'm telling you," Agnes interrupted. "Betts, it really isn't true! Dr. Caldwell . . . I saw him on the street. He stopped me on the street. He was worried about your bronchitis. About your smoking. He . . . oh, he thought you wouldn't listen!"

"You knew about my arm?" Betts asked.

"Yes! Of course! Well, no! I told him . . . He thought you wouldn't take him seriously. Something like that. I was in such a hurry. It's not true! But I never thought . . . I didn't know . . . Betts, there's not anything at all wrong with you!"

Betts's expression was tense, and her voice flat. "Dr. Caldwell told you that my arm was getting shorter, and you didn't —"

"No! Of course not. He was only going to tell you that your arm would get shorter if you kept smoking. . . . Oh, he had some bee in his bonnet about vanity! I wasn't paying much attention. I was trying to find buttons. . . . He thought that if you believed smoking was —"

"Dr. Caldwell told you that he was going to tell me a lie about some terrible thing happening to me, and you thought that was all right because it might stop me from *smoking?*"

Agnes looked up at Betts, whose expression was hawklike with her eyebrows raised in arched wings and her eyes brilliant and focused. All sorts of ways to explain the situation flew through Agnes's mind, but she realized that in many ways Betts had it right.

"Oh, not exactly, Betts," she said. "I never even remembered it till now —"

Betts stood up and moved stiffly toward the door. "I just can't believe you'd let him tell me something like that. And then . . . My God! To tell me about having sex with my own *father!* I don't know why you'd do that! And I have no idea why . . . I know you can't stand it that I'm marrying Will. I don't know why. I don't know what happened —"

"Don't say another word!" Agnes said, in a tone so authoritative that it stopped Betts in midsentence and surprised Agnes herself. "Not another thing! You really have no idea about my life. Don't say anything else! Don't say something that you can never take back!"

Betts shed the linen skirt of her suit as quickly as she could and let it drop to the floor. "I can't be around you right now, Mama. I don't care what I wear to get married in, but I can't stay here in this room with you even for another minute!"

Agnes stood dumbfounded for a few moments, and then she gathered up the skirt, spread it carefully on the ironing board, and sank down on the sofa, exhausted and so sorry. She was full of regret. Was it her vanity, Agnes wondered, or even some sort of spite, a misguided declaration of her own existence, that had prompted her to conjure up for Betts the actuality of her own mother's sexuality? Had she really thought that she and her own daughter could ever be on such equal footing? That the two of them could ever discuss anything so intimate and powerful?

Betts Scofield and Will Dameron were married the next day, Saturday, May thirteenth, 1950. Betts made a beautiful bride in the linen suit and the sweeping wide-brimmed hat. The weather had turned gray and unseasonably cool, and they weren't able to use the Butlers' garden for the reception as they had planned, but Lily and Agnes and Bernice Dameron hastily cobbled together an indoor seating arrangement with the caterers from the Eola Arms.

After the cake was cut, Betts and Will made their departure with kisses for everyone and a shower of rice. Will had practically lifted Agnes off her feet with an ecstatic embrace, but Betts had managed to reach Agnes only in time to give her mother a perfunctory peck on the cheek. They hadn't spoken since the day before, although Agnes hadn't intended for that to happen. She had left the freshly pressed suit hanging on the banister right outside Betts's bedroom door, and she assumed Betts would come show her how she looked before they went downstairs. But Betts had gotten dressed and left without a sound, going with the Butlers to the church, leaving Agnes to follow along with Claytor and Lavinia and Mary Alcorn.

The reception moved along at just the right pace, so that when Betts made her exit, Lily suggested that if the girls were awake, perhaps all of the Scofields', the Damerons', and the Claytors' assembled families and friends would like to meet little Martha Claytor and Julia Scofield, who had not attended the small ceremony. Sounds of agreement and enthusiasm went around the room, because some of the guests were truly eager to see the newest additions to the family, and others would never have been so rude as to say that admiring children who aren't one's own is an exhausting business.

Lily settled Trudy and Lavinia on a sofa with Martha and Julia, and various guests made their way over to sit for a moment and congratulate the mothers and compliment their children. Claytor and Lavinia Scofield's daughter, Julia Agnes Scofield, had been born early on the morning of September 13, 1947, and Dwight and Trudy Claytor's daughter, Martha Lillian Claytor, was born on the afternoon of September 25, only twelve days later. In fact, for two days Trudy and Lavinia had shared a room at the hospital before Lavinia was allowed to go home. But that was less a coincidence than it seemed on the face of it; Trudy next shared the room with Sygny Peck, from Trudy's class at Linus Gilchrest, who had just delivered her second child. Everyone in the world was having babies.

Agnes's closest friend, Lucille Drummond Hendry, was visiting Washburn for Betts's wedding, staying at the Drummonds' house across the square, and she was finally able to make her way over to Trudy and Lavinia and the two little girls, who had both been stricken dumb with shyness. Martha buried her head in Trudy's lap under direct scrutiny. Lucille smiled broadly at Lavinia especially, since she hadn't yet met Claytor's wife, and introduced herself. "My family didn't move to Washburn until I was ... oh ... I guess I was about fourteen. It was just before Lily Scofield and Robert Butler got married. That wedding! The rose arbor ... Well, I'm sure you've heard about it from everyone. But here are these two little girls! I remember when I got the news. When Agnes telephoned about these babies. I had to laugh," she said.

"All of you people are born in batches," Lucille teased both Trudy and Lavinia. "How on earth will we ever keep everyone straight? All born under a full moon or something," she exclaimed delightedly, although she was struggling against nearly overwhelming remembrance and grief at having to endure one more celebration in the lives of her sisters' or her friends' children. Lucille hadn't recovered from her daughter's death during the war, although she went for days at a time, now, without thinking of it. Or, at least, without brooding over it, but only taking it into account as she went about an ordinary day. She smiled the smile of a sweet, still faintly pretty, rather daffy aunt, which was a role she had assumed unthinkingly so that her sisters and her friends wouldn't pity her, and so that she could conceal what she knew was occasional and unreasonable bitterness.

"Well, not exactly," Trudy said, smiling up at her. "Not under a full moon. We're all supposed to be born on the ides of the month."

"Oh, yes. I knew it was something . . . Lavinia, you must be surprised to have it all be true. I sent a telegram to my sister when Agnes called me with the news. Celia telephoned me from California. She said you could have knocked her over with a feather. All the Scofield coincidences! That Claytor's wife — and Dwight's, too — had had their babies on the same day! She asked me to send her very warmest —"

"Martha and Julia were only born in the same month," Trudy interrupted once again. "Not the same day. But it's nice for each of them to have a cousin the same age."

"I was surprised!" Lavinia said, and Mrs. Hendry leaned forward so she could hear her more clearly. "I was surprised," Lavinia repeated, raising her voice a little, "that Julia was born on the ides of the month. My other daughter, Mary Alcorn, from my first marriage. She was born on the ides, too."

"I'm so sorry, dear. I can't quite hear you. Who was it you said was born?"

"Oh, I was only saying that both my daughters were born on the ides of the month," Lavinia said loudly so that Mrs. Hendry could hear, but it was at a moment when a lull in the conversation had fallen, and everyone either turned to look directly at Lavinia or furtively glanced her way. "I hadn't heard about the Scofields and the ides. . . .

And, of course, it turns out that almost none of them were born on the ides. . . ." Mrs. Hendry nodded at her and smiled, having no idea what Lavinia was saying now that she had lowered her voice once more.

After the general flurry of seeing the bridal couple off, greeting friends, and meeting new spouses and the two new children, conversation became a little quieter and eventually turned into a discussion of all the various complications that had already cropped up in regard to the sesquicentennial celebration. The two garden clubs were very seriously jockeying for position as to which one would select the queen. Thomas P. Stamp had already been persuaded to be the queen's escort in the guise of Daniel Decatur Emmett, and he was letting his beard grow out.

"Well, though," Dwight said, "the children will love it. Amelia Anne and Mary Alcorn are old enough to have a great time. You remember, Claytor? I think we must have been about ten years old, and we thought we would die having to listen to the speeches — right out there in the square," he said, gesturing toward the front windows to illustrate what he was saying, "on a platform set up under the Dan Emmett statue. Before we could go out to Hiawatha Park —"

Trudy suddenly interrupted him in a sharp voice, abruptly and with clear irritation. "That's not Dan Emmett, Dwight! You never pay attention to a single thing I say. . . . Oh," she said, turning to Lavinia, "when you're married to a Scofield, Lavinia! Well, don't ever, ever imagine you'll get him to admit he's wrong about anything in his life!" She tried to lighten this last bit into sounding like no more than fond exasperation, but she didn't succeed, and the room was uncomfortably quiet. There was no way to imagine that Dwight and Trudy had had a happy morning.

All of a sudden Lavinia spoke up softly, with her mystifying but characteristic air of indifference, of seeming not to have been paying attention to the conversation that was already under way. "I don't have any idea who Dan Emmett is," she said, as though the thought had just occurred to her, which, in fact, was the case. "I'd never heard of him until I came here. I keep forgetting to ask someone to tell me who he is. Who he was. Did he found Washburn? Something like that?"

And everyone answered at once.

"Oh, Lavinia —"

"But I thought you came from the South —"

"It was your side that made him famous —"

"My side of what?" Lavinia asked, genuinely curious.

It was Dwight who answered her, and it seemed to be the case that everyone in the room had assumed he would take charge and straighten this out. "Daniel Decatur Emmett. That's probably the name you know him by. His older brother, Lafayette, read law under Columbus Delano. He left Washburn. Well, in fact, he eventually became a State Supreme Court Justice in Minnesota."

Lavinia gazed at Dwight solemnly but didn't make any remark.

"Well, and Dan Emmett was a vaudeville star," Dwight continued. "He performed all over the country. Toured for a while with Bill Gibson. . . . Dan Emmett wrote 'Dixie.'"

But Lavinia continued to watch him lazily, not realizing that he thought he had fully answered her question.

"The song 'Dixie,'" Dwight said. And when Lavinia still looked on at him expectantly, he said, "I'm sure you know that song!

> Wish I was in the land of cotton
> Old times there are not forgotten . . ."

"Oh! Well, of course, I know that song," Lavinia said, nodding. "But why would someone from Ohio write 'Dixie'? I don't understand exactly why a statue of Daniel Emmett would be in Washburn —"

"Oh, *God!*" Trudy snapped. "There's *no statue,* Lavinia! That statue is of a Union soldier! Facing south!"

Lavinia turned to look at her, and for the first time since she had arrived at Scofields, a stricken look of hurt feelings crossed her face and disturbed her usual impassive expression. Lavinia and Trudy had become fairly good friends, and it baffled Lavinia that Trudy spoke to her with such obvious irritation.

"Well, that's what Lavinia means, Trudy," Howard said, unexpectedly championing Lavinia before Claytor even thought to speak up. It looked to Howard as though Lavinia might cry, and his voice took on a languid, jocular note in an effort to ease the conversation into a more temperate zone, although he couldn't for the life of him think why anyone cared one way or another about Daniel Emmett. "I have to say I've always wondered about that myself. Washburn fought for the Union. Why do we celebrate Dan Emmett Days? I'm always happy to celebrate anything, but it seems strange. . . ."

The three hostesses, though, Agnes and Lily and Bernice Dameron, interrupted with trays of coffee and sugar and cream, and the day's festivities came slowly to a halt. People began to collect their wraps and take their leave. But no one who had been there was comfortable about that afternoon. When they thought of it in the next few days, they finally concluded that Lavinia Scofield was an unwittingly disturbing presence. After all, imagine not having any idea who Dan Emmett was. The state of Ohio had even placed official historical markers on Highway 4 — at both the entry and exit for Washburn — that declared that Daniel Decatur Emmett, author of "Dixie," had been born and had died there. Also, Lavinia had been so determined to let people know that both her daughters were born on the ides of the month!

And, too, although no one liked to admit it, it had been impossible not to notice that Trudy and Dwight's younger daughter, Martha, was a far prettier child than Claytor and Lavinia's little girl, Julia. In fact, most of the Scofields' friends thought — even though at a distance the two older girls looked so much alike they were often mistaken for twins — that, up close, Lavinia's older girl, Mary Alcorn, wasn't nearly as pretty as her cousin, Amelia Anne Claytor, who was a true Scofield.

Ostensibly the town of Washburn would be in a perpetual state of celebration from the weekend before the Fourth of July through Saturday, July fifteenth. In the exhaustion she fell into after the wedding, Agnes didn't think she could bear it. One afternoon, when Lily and she were sitting in Agnes's back parlor discussing the arrangements for the town's Fourth of July picnic, which was traditionally held on the grounds of Scofields, Agnes said sharply, out of the blue, "Why are we always celebrating these sesquicentennials? Every year is a hundred and fifty years after something." Lily looked up from the notes she was making and nodded her agreement with Agnes about the impending commemoration and all the fuss it would cause.

But Agnes began to brood privately about the upcoming occasion, and she realized that there had not been one single celebration in her life that she had enjoyed. Especially Betts's wedding, which was the most recent. She hadn't even enjoyed her own wedding. But then, as Lily often said, weddings were ridiculously overwrought in any case. But any celebration, it seemed to Agnes, required endless diplomacy. They were filled with emotions that got out of hand. They were laden with an imperative, forced glee that generally led to disappointment. Even birthdays. Especially birthdays in her household.

Claytor's eighth birthday party, for instance, had been one of the worst occasions she could remember. As always on one of their birthdays, Claytor and Dwight had been edgy through the morning. Dwight teasingly reminded Claytor that real Scofields were born on the ides of the month — on the fifteenth, not the thirteenth — and Claytor, so determined always to have Dwight's approval, never countered by reminding Dwight that Dwight wasn't a real Scofield, no matter when he was born.

Every year when those boys were young, they had gone through this, and it upset Agnes and took her aback each time. Dwight and Claytor had the happiest friendship she had ever seen between two children living in the same house. Except on either of their birthdays. Each year she was convinced that it would go smoothly, since the previous year she had taken each boy aside and given him an earnest little lecture on never, ever, purposely hurting people by saying things that caused them pain and — in Claytor's case — on not allowing oneself to be hurt by words that were only meant jokingly and with affection.

But when Claytor turned eight years old, the boys masked this inevitable twice-yearly tension by racing around the house in a hectic, overly excited, high-pitched game they had fallen into while waiting for the party to unfold. And on that particular birthday, while Agnes was in the kitchen frosting the cake, Claytor rushed around the corner of the back sitting room and didn't see the footstool that sat at an angle to Agnes's usual chair. He went stumbling over it, was unable to regain his balance, and cut his forehead as he fell against the marble mantelpiece.

The sudden spurt of blood terrified him and Agnes, too. Warren swept him up and pressed a handkerchief against the wound, handing him over to Agnes, who settled Claytor on the stairs with his head tipped back to stop the bleeding while she went to get iodine and gauze and tape. Warren stood looking at his son, who was shaken and pale, with blood saturating the handkerchief and seeping in a trickle down his cheek. It was hard to tell if Claytor had also hurt his eye, and Warren was as anxious as Agnes.

He glanced at Dwight for a moment, who was frozen in place and equally pale and appalled. Warren made a slow, dramatic turn, appraising all the rooms of the house that were visible from the front hall and from the stairs where Claytor sat. Warren announced loudly and absolutely that they would have to put a stop to all this.

"We just can't have this sort of thing going on!" Both Claytor and Dwight were filled with apprehension; neither could stand to fall under the weight of Warren's disapproval. "I mean it! This behavior has got to stop this minute! This day! And this year. I've put up with it for too long. We've all put up with it for too long!" Warren stepped into the parlor and snatched up the little wooden stool he had made years earlier for his mother, when he was hanging around the Scofields & Company shop and Tut Zeller set him to work and showed him how to do a bit of carpentry.

Warren held it up to illustrate what he was saying. "How dare this puny, splintery piece of wood leap up and attack my own dear heart! My own son. On the very day of the celebration of his birth. We can't have it! We can't have all the furniture getting ideas! Ambushing us in our own home. Why, the next thing you know, that fancy dining-room table'll just walk right over to me on its prissy legs and give me a kick in the shins!" Claytor's color began to return, and Dwight laughed with relief, hoping that perhaps this accident wouldn't turn out to be his fault.

"The piano bench will get it into its head that it can be wherever it wants. It'll just go wheeling itself away when someone gets ready to sit down — boom! Your mother could end up sitting flat on the floor while the bench goes whizzing around wherever it likes!"

Warren wrenched apart the two side supports of the little bench, so that the stool was almost flattened and certainly no longer of any use, and he flung open the door and tossed that ruined piece of furniture far out into the yard. "Why, that footstool just began to take itself too seriously. Tried to get the upper hand. The upper foot! But it won't be stepping out anymore!" He turned in a circle once more, addressing the furniture. "Don't think for one minute that you can get away with this . . . this mutiny! Why, you," he said, glaring at the sofa, "I know just exactly what you're thinking. Don't forget for a minute that you'd have to squeeze yourself through this door, and if we find you trying . . . Well! . . . You'd make a fine blaze, and the fireplace is right behind you!"

The two boys were delighted, but Betts was so young that, although she was intrigued, she was also frightened. And Agnes was almost ill with apprehension. Warren was giving the boys a way out of their predicament, but she noticed in her husband's words the exact moment his voice inflated with unreasonable and zealous gusto. She had learned that these ebullient swings of mood often left Warren depleted in a way she couldn't fathom but that frightened and eventually infuriated her. It was as if his spirit became unavailable to him, locked away from his own ability to temper it — and that he had been allotted a finite amount. When he overspent it, he paid the debt in long, bleak days and weeks with no reserve to tide him over.

On his eighth birthday, Claytor ended up with eight stitches to close the gash on his forehead, and Warren made much of that coincidence. "That's your lucky number from now on," he said to his son. In fact, Claytor still had a scar over his eyebrow, like a thin silver thread that was only visible if the light hit his face at a certain angle.

Agnes fell out of that gloomy memory straight into the immediacy of self-pity. She was still upset that Betts had believed that her mother would conspire against her. Agnes had so often been taken by surprise whenever one of her children's grudges against her came to light. Most of all she was amazed that they vividly recalled moments that she didn't believe had ever happened. In fact, just the morning after Betts's wedding, Claytor had started breakfast before anyone else was up, but when he heard Julia suddenly begin that desperate sort of crying that signifies furious exhaustion, and then when Mary Alcorn's voice floated downstairs in high-pitched indignation, he turned the gas off under the skillet of eggs he was scrambling and went to give Lavinia a hand.

He entered the kitchen once more with Mary Alcorn in tow just as Agnes was irritably scraping the eggs into the garbage. "That's just a waste. You can't start eggs, Claytor, unless you're certain you won't be interrupted," she said briskly, clearly annoyed. She was in a terrible mood, and the crying set her teeth on edge. She would have given almost anything to have breakfast by herself.

But Claytor laughed. "Mother, you never change! It's one of the few absolutes in my world these days. You remember when I brought home my long-division practice test from Miss Cotton's class? I'd been sitting at the table working on it for about an hour — terrible! I was terrible at math. Not even good at simple arithmetic. And you took one look at my answer sheet and tore it into little bits. 'It's no use going on with something you've gotten wrong from the beginning,' you said. I'll never forget it. I sat down and started all over again. You were right. I was just getting more and more confused. Wronger and wronger," he said in Mary Alcorn's direction, smiling.

"Oh! Claytor! That's not true! I would never have done anything like that in my life! How can you even imagine that happened? Why, it's not . . . You couldn't . . . It's something you dreamed. I wouldn't have been so mean." Agnes was crushed. "Claytor, I was just going to start over with these eggs because they were scorched. They would have had that taste eggs get. Like burnt foam. That smell . . . I wouldn't for the world have torn up your schoolwork."

"Well, I turned out to be a whiz at long division," he said. Mary Alcorn was pressing him to let her make toast in the pop-up toaster, and Agnes didn't say anything more about it, but she didn't believe that incident had ever happened. It hurt her feelings and mystified her that her children latched on to these ideas of her as a generally inept — often unkind — parent, as though she had bungled the whole business of being responsible for their lives, even though here they were, still thriving. Surely they understood the awful despair she had felt on behalf of any one of them when she couldn't alleviate some misfortune that befell them.

Of course, Agnes did remember that she had sometimes been unfairly angry at the children, had often been frantic and desperate herself. She hadn't been perfect in any way. But surely that was balanced out by how genuinely she had loved — did love — those children. Certainly by now it was clear to her children that any misdirected anger she had ever displayed toward them was one of the very things that plagued her with regret. Why, Dwight and Claytor had children of their own; at one time or another, Agnes had heard each of them lash out unfairly at one or the other of those little girls, and of course Amelia Anne and Mary Alcorn would grow up knowing their fathers had always only wished them well.

The thing that Agnes failed to grasp, however, was that what might have seemed like nothing at all to her — an inadvisable cross word, a brief spell of unsuppressed anger — had often pierced the armor of one of her children at a particularly vulnerable moment. Agnes didn't remember that anyone's memories of childhood are exactly like the first appearance of dandelions each spring. Agnes was always delighted to glance out the window and see the grass studded with the overnight emergence of the brilliant gold asterisks embedded in the lawn. But year after year, she failed to temper that initial gladness with the knowledge that those cheerful yellow buttons strewn across all of Scofields would grow tall and leggy, would become unappealing whiskery white globes that drifted off in the slightest breeze, leaving their thin, watery-pink stems tall and naked against the grass. They were simple weeds, after all, and it was impossible to know if or where any of their feathery seeds would take root.

Chapter Twelve

*I*N EARLY JUNE, Robert was to take part in a
symposium at The Johns Hopkins University in Balti-
more: André Gide, Richard Blackmur, Benedetto Croce,
and a few others, including Robert's great friends Red
Warren and Allen Tate, had agreed to participate in a discussion of the nature of criticism. Robert planned to go
from there to Bloomington, Indiana, where he would be
involved in discussing the future of the Harcourt Lees
School of English. The three-year grant from the Rocke-
feller Foundation had expired, and Robert had been
entertaining an invitation from Indiana University not
only to relocate the School of English but also to accept a
tempting offer himself, which would allow him far more
time for his own work.

Lily decided not to go with him. The Tates had visited
right after Christmas, and she felt no obligation to see
them so soon again, and she certainly didn't want to influence Robert's decision about the job at Indiana. She didn't

know anything about Bloomington, Indiana, and she thought the best thing she could do was to have no opinion about it one way or another. Besides, Lily had been thinking that the month of June might be the perfect time to open the house in Maine, which the Scofield family had rented for years and finally bought from Lily's great friend Marjorie Hockett. Marjorie and Lily had remained close friends since they first met at Mount Holyoke, and Marjorie had held on to — and still summered in — her parents' handsome old house in Port Clyde, Maine. Lily was very much in the mood for a dose of Marjorie's vinegary charm. "Agnes and I could go up for a few weeks," she said to Robert. "Jesser Grammar closes mid-May this year because of the new cafeteria construction, so the timing would be perfect," she added.

"I think the whole wedding business took the wind right out of Agnes's sails. Betts being so sick. And then the rush to get everything done at the last minute," Lily went on. "And with little Julia at that cranky stage. . . . Why, you know, we could take Amelia Anne and Mary Alcorn. That would be nice for them. Nice for their mothers. Don't you think it would give Agnes some time to recover before all this business coming up in July?" And Lily added that with both of them — and with some busy-work for the little girls — along with whoever they could hire in Port Clyde to help them, she and Agnes could probably get the house opened up and sorted out before they came home for the increasingly elaborate Fourth of July and sesquicentennial celebrations.

When she broached the idea to Agnes, Lily said that since Robert wouldn't be with them, there was no need to make plans carved in stone. "And you don't even need to worry about what to pack. Just throw any old thing into a suitcase. Well, you remember how it is in Maine. Or at least the part of Maine around Port Clyde. There's no place less fancy, and we'll probably be cleaning house, anyway," Lily added.

"Robert can't stand for any part of a trip to be spontaneous, but that's the way I think is the most fun to travel. We can just take our time and not feel pressed one way or another. We can stop whenever we want. With the little girls along, that's the best plan, anyway. We can play it by ear."

But neither Lily nor Agnes had expected the trip to stretch out over eight days, traveling on the third day no more than two hours from where they had been the night before and spending two nights in Portland when Amelia Anne got sick. They got a late start from Scofields the last Sunday morning of May, with the little girls in the backseat of the Butlers' 1939 Buick. That was their second mistake, Lily declared, three hours later, when she stood on the side of the road to flag down a ride to the nearest gas station because the radiator had overheated. "But I don't suppose we really had any choice. Oh, we could have gone by train. But we'll have to have a car while we're at the farmhouse."

And it was nothing more than their own lack of common sense, Lily said later — or maybe just outright softhearted cowardliness — that had led to their first big mistake. Before they had managed even to clear the shallow driveway in front of Scofields, Amelia Anne had begged them to stop the car; she declared tearfully that she couldn't go to Maine after all. She was distraught when Bobbin began howling from the foyer of the house the moment he became aware that her straw sun hat, her beach towel, and, most particularly, her suitcase — with which he had been unfamiliar — signified Amelia Anne's departure. And it was clear that something about the rushed morning, the hasty preparations, tipped Bobbin off to the certainty that Amelia Anne wasn't coming back soon.

The poor dog was nearly beside himself. He stood on his hind legs with his front paws braced against the decoratively carved molding and was just able to see the car from the lowest pane of lights framing the front door. He threw his head back, rolling his eyes up so that only the whites showed, and he made a sound of such desperate and heartbroken supplication that it was very nearly bloodcurdling. No one at Scofields had ever heard anything like it before. Both Agnes and Lily decided there was nothing for it but to take him along, and that delayed their departure at least another hour while Trudy and Amelia Anne found and collected Bobbin's leash, a bowl, and other paraphernalia.

They set out once again and made it as far as rounding Monument Square when Mary Alcorn considered the fact that Bobbin was coming along but poor Flotsam and Jetsam were left behind. "They won't even come out from under the bed unless it's me or Grandmother," she protested, and privately Agnes had worried over the same thing herself. She knew they certainly wouldn't starve to death, but she was afraid they might simply disappear after several days without her or Mary Alcorn in the house. Collecting the cats set them back another forty-five minutes at least.

Agnes and Lily had intended to stop at hotels or motels along the way, but by necessity they narrowed their evening destination to any place they might come upon that would accept a dog. They planned to leave the cats at large in the car overnight with a dishpan of sand Agnes had rigged up and a bowl of water. En route, the cats were restricted to a large, closed cardboard box with a series of holes cut through the sides, and they rode unhappily between Agnes and Lily in the front seat. Bobbin insisted on sitting next to a window with his head outside and his ears blowing straight back, so Amelia Anne and Mary Alcorn arranged a system of trading off the other window seat whenever they stopped.

The first afternoon, however, they discovered that there were very few places to stay that accepted dogs, and none at all that would permit cats, even though Agnes and Lily explained time and again that the cats would spend the night in the car. "That's what they all say!" the elderly owner told them when they stopped with the intention of staying at his alarmingly modest Guest Home. Lily gave him a dollar and simply informed him that she was going to use his phone. Agnes and the girls and all the animals stayed where they were, and the owner remained beside the car, leaning against the hood with his arms crossed, whistling through his teeth while gazing off in the direction of a cluster of tall, rusted rubbish cans. But no one in the car was fooled for a minute; it was clear that he was there to stop them in case they made a break for the house themselves. Lily simply let herself in the front door and presumably found the telephone.

Lily had been anticipating the peaceful anonymity of staying at hotels, declining several invitations from old friends who knew from her letters that she was coming their way. She hadn't wanted to expend the effort involved in being a guest, but Lily and Agnes, the little girls, and all three pets ended up staying with friends of Lily's every night of their trip. They were made much of that first evening by Lily's old friend from Mount Holyoke, Anna Cook Elliot, who lived in a handsome house in Erie, Pennsylvania, which had an enclosed porch where she insisted Agnes set up the sandbox and release the cats. "I'd be glad to let them have the run of the house," she told Agnes, "but I don't know how Gato might behave." She gestured toward an orange Persian cat who gazed steadily at Flotsam and Jetsam through the glass door with a squashed, malevolent expression that was probably beyond his control, but also with his ears — such as they were — lying flat back against his head.

Agnes didn't think she had ever in her life seen Lily in such a state of delightfulness. Clark Elliot, Anna's husband, had known Lily almost as long as Anna had; he had been at Oxford with Robert and was a great admirer of Robert's poetry and criticism. And Agnes herself relaxed when she realized that these two people were genuinely delighted to see Lily, even with her entourage. In fact, Lily turned the evening into an inclusive, celebratory occasion, and in the morning the Elliots tried to persuade Lily and Agnes to delay their trip for a few days. "I'm certain Roselle Alcorn's husband is originally from Natchez, Agnes. Oh, she's wonderful . . . she's just wonderfully eccentric! And you'll like him, too. I'd bet anything you're somehow related. Lily, just give me some time to put together a little gathering. . . . Oh, and for the little girls, there are children right next door . . ."

But Lily demurred, although they did stay for a leisurely breakfast, and Anna Elliot saw them off after arranging for them to stay with a mutual friend in Rochester, which was a comfortable day's drive farther along. And so it went, day after day; they made the trip in short hops from one acquaintance to another. By the time they reached Maine, Agnes — and especially Lily — each felt that throughout those seven nights, she had socialized with more concentration than she had ever brought steadily to bear over so long a stretch of time in her whole life.

"I feel like we've been passed along the underground railroad," Lily said to Agnes in the front seat. And she turned to tell Mary Alcorn and Amelia Anne how proud of them she had been. "You two must have been practicing all these weeks," she teased them, "so that everyone would know that there never were two nicer girls!" But the children, and Bobbin, too, were limp with fatigue. Bobbin had no more interest at all in looking out the window; he had relocated to the floor, which he had to himself, since the girls' feet only dangled over the edge of the backseat. Even the cats had given up their complaints two days into the journey.

Mary Alcorn and Amelia Anne had instinctively taken their cue from Lily and realized that the key to finding shelter was to win over their hosts with impeccable and unobtrusive good behavior. Watching Lily exude an odd, nearly frantic variation of charm, however, put the girls on the alert, although clearly Lily's friends had no idea that Lily's behavior was extraordinary. The little girls caught on at once and were both quick studies, and even Bobbin seemed to understand the situation. If he couldn't make friends with whatever ensconced pet he encountered, he stayed out of the way.

They left Maddy Forholtz's tall Victorian house in Portland, Maine, after breakfast on the morning of the second night they had spent with her, since she insisted they stay when Amelia Anne had eaten breakfast the day before and had promptly thrown up. Maddy had been three years behind Lily at Mount Holyoke, and they hadn't known each other very well at all, but Maddy had expressed delighted enthusiasm at having her company when Esther Merriam had telephoned from Boston and explained the travelers' plight. Lily and Maddy wouldn't have recognized each other, but they had a genuinely wonderful time sitting up late talking, because they were spared the necessity of discussing their days at college. Lily had been a senior the year Maddy arrived, and the two had no school experiences in common.

"Wasn't it nice," she said to Agnes in the car as they drove north, "that Maddy's husband was dead? It was so much more fun. . . . Oh, well! Of course, not so nice for Maddy. I never knew him," she said defensively. "I never knew Maddy for that matter. . . ." But Agnes understood precisely what Lily meant and agreed with her; she didn't even bother to reply. Almost six hours later they finally passed through Tenants Harbor, Maine, and Agnes spotted the big farmhouse as it came into view just as they rounded the curve into Martinsville. The house sat reassuringly on a hill and backed onto a meadow that stretched more than two hundred yards to the sea. The windows stood open and the muslin curtains billowed inward with the breeze. The enormous, ancient lilacs around the house were on the downward cusp of their blooming, the flowers hanging as heavily as grapes; the scent reached them before they turned into the drive, and even from the car, they could see the glittering blue-green spangle of the ocean.

"Thank goodness," Lily said as she pulled up in front of the sagging, attached barn. "Marjorie's been here already. I told her not to bother, but I'm glad she didn't pay any attention to me."

It was about three in the afternoon when they arrived, and they unloaded everything onto the lawn so that Lily could go on to Port Clyde and buy something for dinner and for the next morning's breakfast before the store closed for the evening. "Oh, I hadn't thought about its being Sunday," Lily said. "But someone might be there. The owner used to live upstairs. He might let me in. Just to get milk and eggs. And coffee." As Lily was pulling out of the drive, however, Marjorie Hockett pulled in behind her and beeped the horn. She leaned out the window while at the same time a dark-haired little boy piled out of the car door, and then another, and another, and another.

They seemed to be many versions of the same child, all of them with beautifully thick, short hair, almost exactly the color and sheen of a seal's coat.

"I didn't think you'd be here yet," Marjorie said loudly over the clamor all around her. "But don't worry! I come bearing gifts!" she said. "And friends!" she added as she, too, climbed out of the car, encumbered by a large basket. "I didn't know you'd arrived yet. I was just going to stop by and close the windows and leave you some supper," she said as she gave Lily a quick hug with her free arm and smiled a welcome to Agnes. "My niece is leaving in the morning, and this is the boys' favorite spot on the peninsula." She gestured at an attractive couple probably in their thirties who had emerged finally from the backseat and were shaking hands and introducing themselves.

"Aunt Marjorie talks about you all the time," Carolyn Hupper said to Lily. "But we didn't mean to intrude. . . . Dora said they weren't expecting you until this evening, so we thought the boys could get one more look. . . . I mean, we've been so looking forward to meeting you, but we wouldn't have descended like this." Meanwhile, it seemed to the stunned travelers that children of every size swarmed around Carolyn Hupper's skirt and her husband John's long legs.

"The Huppers — and all the little Hups — stay for a few weeks every summer," Marjorie said breezily, while handing a bag of groceries to one or another of those boys who then carried it into the house. "You knew my brother died a few years ago?" she asked Lily, more seriously, and Lily nodded. "I'm always hoping Regina — his wife?" —

and again Lily signified that she remembered — "I'm always hoping she'll visit as well," Marjorie continued, "but I think it's hard for her to travel so far. And she's probably afraid of all these little rascals," she said to her great-nephews, all of whom seemed to take it as an inordinate compliment. "They're wild as marsh hens," she said, but fondly, "as soon as they get out of the city. Only a mother — or a great-aunt — could love them when they're awake. And, oh," she said, looking around to find her, "this is my friend Dorothy Admunson."

"Oh, Marjorie. Please! I'm 'Dora' to everyone," she said. She was a tall, trim, tanned woman with a slight foreign accent of some kind, who looked to be about Agnes's age.

"Do you remember Mrs. Rupert's lemon meringue pie, Lily?" Marjorie asked. "Do you remember? We thought it was the height of culinary achievement. . . . Well, Dora wouldn't stoop so low!" she said. "The things she bakes. . . . You'll see for yourself. We've brought dinner for everyone and supplies for the kitchen. For breakfast, at least. Probably enough to get you through tomorrow. I thought you'd all be tired, but you look wonderful. Fresh as daisies! And these must be your granddaughters. Warren's granddaughters. I know you wrote me, Lily, but it really is uncanny. You can't miss the resemblance! I'm so glad to see you!" she said to Amelia Anne and Mary Alcorn. Dora and the Hupper parents murmured and nodded in agreement. The four boys had put the groceries on the kitchen table and headed straight through the meadow toward the water, and Carolyn held the fifth little boy, who was just a toddler, in her arms, although he was struggling to get down. Lily was gazing at her speculatively, and Carolyn said, "The third two are twins."

Lily was startled at being caught out in wondering why in the world anyone would have so many children. "Oh! No, I was just thinking . . . Well, I was just thinking that they're beautiful children," she said to Carolyn. "And they're exactly the opposite of these two. Both Amelia Anne and Mary Alcorn have dark eyes and light hair," she went on, with her hands on Amelia Anne's shoulders as she slumped back against her grandmother. "Your boys have such blue eyes . . . such dark hair . . ."

"Probably some Irish in there somewhere," Marjorie said.

"Now that's a coincidence!" John Hupper said to Agnes, but Agnes looked blank. "The little girls? They're twins, too, aren't they?" he asked.

"Aunt Marjorie!" his wife said, speaking simultaneously. "I know you love to bait me! You know all the Huppers are Scots. On both sides of John's family!"

Lily and Agnes carried a few of their suitcases and bags upstairs and helped Amelia Anne and Mary Alcorn choose the bedroom each wanted. Agnes tried to convince them that they should take a bath and rest before joining the others, but they were fragilely stubborn, their elation transparent over their deep exhaustion, and Agnes decided they wouldn't rest whether they stayed upstairs or not.

Marjorie had thrown a quilt over the old picnic table and also spread blankets under the trees, and Dora had set out a feast. Food far more exotic than any Sam had yet prepared, Lily and Agnes agreed, explaining all about Sam's weekly dinners in a way that also complimented Dora's efforts. Amelia Anne and Mary Alcorn didn't venture beyond the mown backyard; they were euphoric and giddy, but they had seen at once that all those little boys were entirely acquainted with the landscape, which was still a foreign country to them.

They sat together on one of the blankets, with Bobbin cowed and huddled between them; Flotsam and Jetsam had made themselves scarce inside the house as soon as they were released. Lily brought the girls each a plate of various treats she thought they might enjoy, or at least be tempted by, since she knew it was unlikely they would eat much at all with this unexpected excitement. The clutch of little boys eventually straggled back for sustenance, lagging about the table familiarly, leaning into some adult's lap, only casting an occasional glance toward the girls on their blanket, and finally Marjorie left the table and ushered all the children around the side of the house to the barn, where two bicycles, a croquet game, a badminton set, and a host of other amusements were stored.

"Jamie," she said to the tallest of the boys, "these girls have never been to Maine before. I know you'll all be friends! They're going to be here for at least two weeks. Amelia Anne and Mary Alcorn are exactly your age, and, Daniel, you're just a year younger. Why don't you find something in the barn and play a game? Or the bicycles are over there.... But they may need oil...." She was slipping away as she directed them, hoping they would entertain each other so the adults could say more than two sentences to each other without being interrupted.

At the table John and Carolyn Hupper were regaling Agnes and Lily with what seemed to be a comparative tale of traveling with their children. "I'll gladly swap," Carolyn was saying, "because nothing could settle him down, and the captain threatened to make him walk the plank. The thing is, Jamie believed him. . . . We couldn't find him anywhere. John says they're like wine. That they don't travel well. Oh, the crew had the dory in the water and were about to cast off. . . . I wasn't so calm myself. Finally he turned up. . . ."

In no more than twenty minutes, the children's angry voices reached them from the front yard. Lily and Agnes got up. "I'll go," Agnes said to the company at large. "I know the girls are tired . . ." But Lily and John Hupper trailed along as well, while the other three stayed behind and began making a halfhearted attempt to put things in order. Jamie and his younger brother Daniel had commandeered the bicycles for themselves and were flying over the drive and the lane that ran in front of the house, and Agnes thought that must the trouble. But then she realized that Mary Alcorn and Amelia Anne were faced off toward each other in a caricature of children arguing. They had their hands on their hips and stood far enough apart that each girl leaned toward the other, like enraged parentheses.

"You do too have two names! You do, too. And there isn't anything silly about my name," Amelia Anne was shouting furiously at Mary Alcorn.

"I don't! That's just stupid! 'Alcorn' is my last name! I don't have two names. Besides, it was Jamie who said —" By then the boys had gathered to see what was going on.

"I didn't say 'silly'!" Jamie protested. "I just said it was too much trouble —"

"I think it's silly," one of the smaller boys said, but Carolyn had come around the corner, swooped in, and was herding her children into a flock, circling and shushing them, so that as a group they moved in increments across the grass in the direction of Marjorie's car.

"Your last name is '*Scofield,*'" Amelia Anne said, her eyes full and puffy with restrained tears, and Mary Alcorn faced her straight on with an expression of shocked outrage.

"It's not either! It's not! My father died! You can ask my mother! Mary Alcorn isn't two names like Amelia Anne. . . ."

Lily caught Agnes's eye above the fray. "Let's get these two apart," she said in a regular tone of voice, which no one except Agnes heard. "I'm putting Amelia Anne in the tub," she said in Agnes's direction, and Agnes nodded and took Mary Alcorn's arm and, guiding her a little distance away, then crouched to the little girl's height so she could talk to her.

"You and Amelia Anne shouldn't argue," she said calmly, as though she hoped her tone would be catching. "Here, you come along with me," she said, "and we'll go get a treat for everyone."

"But Jamie's the one who said our names were silly because we have two names. I don't have two names. . . ." Her voice was whiny with heat and petulance, and Agnes led her along to Lily's green Buick, put her in the front seat, and backed out right over the lawn in order to skirt Marjorie's car.

"Put your window all the way down," she told Mary Alcorn, "and you'll feel better right away." They made the twenty-mile drive to Dorman's Dairy Dream, which Agnes had first visited with Warren over thirty years ago. She was relieved to find it open and also to find an empty parking space under the trees. She and Mary Alcorn stood in line, waiting for their turn. When they were back in the car once more, each with an ice-cream cone and two pints of Dorman's Dairy Dream's famous ginger ice cream packed in a sturdy bag with crushed ice, Agnes was beset with exhaustion and melancholy. It was no one's fault, of course, that she had traveled so far but hadn't managed to escape anything, after all. In fact, the images and ideas of Warren Scofield as he had been when he and Agnes were together at this very spot so long ago were urgently vivid once more, and Agnes was plagued with guilt and grief.

Mary Alcorn began to regain her composure. She and Agnes sat in the car and watched through the front window while a man on a ladder labored to refurbish the Dorman's Dairy Dream billboard, bit by bit, adding one panel of the picture after another, pasting the puzzle pieces of paper to the backboard with the sweep of a long-handled brush.

Mary Alcorn had a double-scoop vanilla cone, which she had initially attacked from the top down, but now, Agnes noticed with dismay, she had bitten off the bottom of the pointed cone and was holding it above her head, letting the ice cream melt drop by drop into her open mouth. Agnes leaned against the door frame and tilted her head back against the window, still watching the workman slowly fashioning a picture of what was shaping up to be a banana split. But the billboard was so big. Briefly it seemed to Agnes that he would never finish, that his was a hopeless task. She had the dreary feeling that all the time in the universe waited implacably for him, and for her, and even for Mary Alcorn, right outside in the dusky twilight of the Dorman's Dairy Dream parking lot.

Their fatigue was so great that the first few days in the rambling, creaky farmhouse moved along with a sort of laxity, one day falling into another in unstructured domesticity. Of course Lily and Agnes looked after Mary Alcorn and Amelia — who refused to answer to the familiar "Amelia Anne" forever after. But the little girls required very little other than food and baths. No one took charge, and since Marjorie Hockett had hired two women from Port Clyde to get the house in order before Agnes and Lily had even arrived, there was very little that needed to be seen to. Lily had a telephone installed, and she had a wide swath mown through the meadow all the way to the ocean, where there was a rather rickety set of stairs leading down the cliff to the rocks, and they all settled there for hours. Lily and Agnes read and watched the waves come in with the high tide; the girls crouched over the tidal pools among the enormous, smooth boulders, collecting shells and starfish and beautiful bits of colored glass that had been tumbled into jewel-like shapes by the abrasion of the waves over who knew what length of time.

"For all you know," Lily said, "Christopher Columbus may have dropped a bottle of cherry soda over the side of his ship," Lily told them, and that produced a hail of corrections and laughter. Lily promised to have bracelets made up of the girls' glass gems.

The Huppers and all their little boys had departed for the summer, and Lily and Agnes were often joined by Marjorie and Dora, who, it turned out, spent her vacations from her job as dietician at Bowdoin College at Marjorie's big house in Port Clyde, which had been built and lived in by Hocketts for over a hundred years. In return, Marjorie had a room in Dora's little cottage on the Bowdoin College campus during the academic year, where she was an instructor in the biology department.

Agnes hadn't given herself over with such abandon to reading since she was in school, and if she wasn't careful, she felt guilty. She had pulled Christina Stead's *The Man Who Loved Children* off the shelves in the house, and she found a nook in the rocks that was warm and remarkably comfortable. She could recline with a pillow beneath her head and another across her lap, where she rested her book, and she was entirely absorbed in the hair-raising world of Henny and Sam Pollit. Marjorie and Dora brought books, too, as well as often appearing with a wonderful lunch for everyone.

The few days it rained they played cards or Scrabble. Lily usually built a fire. By the middle of their second week, none of them even pretended that they were visiting Maine in order to get things in shape; they drifted through the days without any order, doing what they liked whenever they wanted to do it, and for Mary Alcorn and Amelia, when impressions of that first trip to Maine came back to them over the years, each remembered it as dreamlike; it had been so gentle and easy that the days they spent there seemed outside the ordinary chronology of their lives.

"Listen, Agnes," Lily said one night after the girls had gone upstairs to bed and she and Agnes were settled reading. "I honestly don't think I can stand that trip home. That drive! Why don't we go by train? Bobbin and the cats could travel in the baggage car. If we have crates, I think they could. I bet Marjorie'll know where we can find crates."

Agnes didn't respond for a moment. "It seems so soon," Agnes said. "It doesn't feel like I've been away much time at all. What about the car?"

"I've been thinking about that. None of us is ever going to want to drive this distance again, and we're always going to need a car here, anyway. I thought I'd ask Marjorie where we could store it. There's room in the barn, but I think we're supposed to take off the tires or something. I'm not sure it's a good idea to make a trip that long in a car that's over ten years old, anyway. Oh, you know, if we didn't have the animals, we could fly home. From Boston or New York."

Dora and Marjorie showed up the next day with a picnic hamper, and the whole group wandered disorganizedly toward their accustomed place on the rocks. It was the first day that the weather wasn't pleasant. The rain hadn't bothered any of them, but this Thursday before they departed was heavy with humidity, and instead of sitting in the sun, they clustered under the trees. Marjorie was knitting, but in a moment of uncharacteristic frustration she tossed the whole bundle into her knitting bag. "My hands are sticky in this air. And in that wool. I think I'd better go home and cool off."

They were all ready to retreat to the relative cool of the indoors, and Lily and Agnes also started to gather their belongings and the little girls' discarded sandals and sweaters. In the middle of all that, though, they were interrupted by a man's voice "helloing" down the meadow and calling Lily's name. They stopped in the middle of shaking out blankets and replacing items in the hamper in order to peer up the rise to see who it was, but Mary Alcorn and Amelia were the first to realize it was Sam Holloway. They rushed up the hill, and he caught them up and came the rest of the way down the path, carrying both of them, one in each arm, and complaining that he could hardly stand up, what had they been eating. It was the perfect tonic, Sam's company, and after Marjorie and Dora were introduced, the whole group settled back down again, and everyone offered Sam something to eat.

"Did you know you can get here by boat?" he said, then he laughed. "Well, nothing like stating the obvious. I've never been to Maine, though, and I thought that since you all were here . . . And I liked the thought of taking a break. When I found out I could take the mail boat from Boston, I thought, Why not? I had to be in Framingham. At Cardinal Homes' headquarters," he explained. "I think I finally straightened out the problem that was holding up our shipment. You'd be amazed at how much has been done," he said to Lily and Agnes. "The construction site is finished. It looks pretty good."

That evening Sam listened to the tale of Lily and

Agnes, Mary Alcorn, and Amelia's endless odyssey to reach Maine, and he got on the phone right after dinner. In no time he had arranged for Lily and Agnes and the girls to fly home — he would see them off himself — and he offered to crate the pets and have them moved by rail or perhaps by air cargo. He knew a man who raised pure-bred horses and was familiar with shipping live animals. The prospect of traveling home in an airplane overcame any qualms Amelia or Mary Alcorn might have had about leaving Bobbin and the cats behind. In one fell swoop, Sam had made them thrilled to be going home again, and the next day, they stayed occupied packing for and planning their Saturday departure.

But Agnes wasn't ready yet to go home, and she and Lily talked it over. "If you don't mind being in charge of the little girls," Agnes said, "I'll stay on for a little while longer and then travel on the same train with Bobbin and the cats. I'll get Sam to tell me who to get in touch with. . . . I don't know what it is," she said, "but I really would like to stay on a little longer, if you don't mind." Lily had no objection at all; in fact, she was gratified. She had hoped Agnes would enjoy getting away, and when Sam heard about it, he thought it was a good idea.

"Agnes, your house is the headquarters for making the sesquicentennial queen's float. It's pretty much a mad-house," he said. "I'm staying on a few days, too, at the Ocean House in Port Clyde."

"Why?" Lily asked. "Why wouldn't you just stay on here? . . . Oh, Sam! For goodness sake! I don't think you have to worry about proprieties!" And Agnes was startled by the idea that Sam even considered observing such formal decorum when it hadn't even crossed her mind; she thought of Sam Holloway as family. On Saturday morning Lily and the girls, with Sam escorting them, were off to Boston. It was the first time Agnes had been in the big house all by herself, and she trailed through the rooms absorbing the atmosphere.

At Scofields she had been unable to stop dwelling on the ways in which she had disappointed her children, especially in light, just recently, of poor Betts. No letters for anyone had come from Betts or Will, who were on their honeymoon, after all, and Agnes chose to see that as a good sign. If Betts wasn't writing *anyone* . . . If Will hadn't been in touch with Sam . . . And, too, Agnes discovered that she was suddenly feeling grieved — almost bitter — at the ways in which her children had disappointed her: that she knew they struggled between irritable dislike and great fondness toward her, the fact that she had glimpses of the possibility that one or another of them wasn't happy in his or her job or marriage or circumstances.

It seemed to Agnes very cruel that her own children wouldn't spare her the pain of that knowledge, when they also wouldn't ever act on her advice. On the other hand, she often suspected that they kept most of what they felt secret from her. How could all this time of her life have passed and still she hadn't straightened out or pinned down the way to spend whatever was left? When she was younger, she would never have guessed a fifty-year-old woman could be so at sea.

Agnes had never admitted to anyone the thing she deemed the greatest failure of her life. She had realized that there had only been a little time — perhaps nine years per child, seventeen years altogether — when she had thought she was essential to the lives of the children who grew up in her house. Seventeen years should be enough, she thought. Seventeen years is great good luck. But somehow or other, as she had been forced to re-evaluate her own life in light of her grown children's presence, she had come to understand quite clearly that there were so many ways she had failed them as far as playing any sort of heroic role in their lives.

It might be that you could only occupy a hero's role if you died as early in your children's lives as Warren had. And, certainly, he was the hero of their lives. She had never revealed to anyone, though, how profoundly she had failed Warren, or how he had failed her. Even given the black moods he endured, he wouldn't have died if not for her terrible judgment. Well, her pettiness. But, in Warren's case, Agnes couldn't forgive him or herself for an act so entirely removed from her idea of heroism. The whole thing, however, was so fraught with self-pity, melodrama, and humiliating pathos, that, for the most part, she put it out of her head and plodded on as best she could.

The third day she spent in Maine without the distraction of Lily or the girls or even a book, Sam returned from somewhere or other late in the afternoon, and the two of them settled in the same spot Agnes and Lily had staked out on the rocks. And gradually she realized that she was, in fact, telling the whole dreary tale to Sam Holloway. It surprised her even as she found herself talking about Warren, but she didn't worry about Sam's judgment of her or of Warren; she felt no need to protect anyone from Sam's consideration, because he seemed able to accommodate and be interested in villains and heroes alike, as well as everyone in between. She told him that she was certain Warren had committed suicide, and for a moment Sam looked across the pink-flecked rock on which they sat, and then he shook his head.

"Oh, I don't think so. I doubt that," he said, but not argumentively, just as a matter of fact.

"I'm certain of it, Sam. I've seen it over and over again in my head, just exactly like it happened. You see, Uncle Leo hadn't gotten over Audra's death. He was as blue as I'd ever known him to be. And Warren was in terrible shape. But I had all the children. . . . I was so tired. I should never have let them go. But sometimes . . . sometimes Warren was just mean. I always knew when he got like that it was his own demons. . . . Well, I'm not sure I did know that then, in fact. I would remind myself. But I'm not sure I knew it when he would say something hurtful," she mused.

"I did know he would apologize. And, oh, I got so tired of that. The morning before he left for Arbor City, I just didn't want to hear it anymore. He tried to say he was sorry. He said he was just worthless. That he knew that. But it was too easy for him to say he was worthless! Warren could be really unkind, but he wasn't ever worthless. I was sick and tired of hearing him say it. I was sick of letting him off the hook! Because he would just . . . Well. I told him that morning that there were some things you can't apologize for. Some things can't be taken back. Oh, Sam, I was so mad at him."

Sam didn't say anything; he just nodded, and his expression was impassive.

"Do you know what I said to him? Oh, Lord. I don't think I'd ever lost my temper that way before. Not at Warren, anyway. But I said we should just figure it out finally. Sit down and decide what he did mean when he said the things he said to me. I told him that I could see him starting to say the same sorts of things to Claytor — never to Dwight, though. Probably because nothing Dwight did could be accounted for by Warren's own nature. Oh, I don't know." She shook her head and paused for a moment.

"He agreed, though," she said finally. "He said he wanted to do that. That he thought he was going to have to get over even touching any alcohol. That he didn't want to turn out like his own father. But, you know what? I got so furious at him! I challenged him. I said, 'Well, I can't stay here if we don't sit down and settle this right now. I'll be gone if you leave this house before we work this out. I'll take the children to my father's house. We'll live in Washington.' But Warren said he had to go to Pennsylvania that day. That he couldn't put the trip off. He was the one trying to be the peacemaker. Not in that . . . oh, that pleading sort of way. But I had surprised myself, you see. I couldn't get over how good it felt to be mad at him. To say what I thought — to say more than I thought!"

She was silent for a few minutes, as though she were deciding something, and Sam didn't make any comment, only a sort of murmur of attention.

"I said to Warren, 'I'm so mad at you I could spit! Go on your trip! Just go! I don't care if you drive off a cliff!' That's what I said, Sam, and I don't know how I can stand it. I was so much in love with him." She put her chin down on her crossed arms, still peering out at the waves rolling in, crashing and breaking upwards in plumes of spray. "And I loved him, too. How could I have said such a thing? It wasn't just romance, or some silly sort of thing. . . . I mean, I was his wife and I loved him."

Sam just sat alongside her for a little while, thinking over what she had told him. "But Agnes, that's not the way a person's thinking before he kills himself. I don't think a state of mind like that could have come over him so fast. I don't think a man who is about to try to put things straight is going to kill himself on his way to Pennsylvania! But also, Agnes, everything I've ever heard about Warren Scofield has made me like him. Even though I can see now that he was just a human being. But I've never heard anything that would let me believe that Warren would do something that might put his uncle in danger. I don't think, either, that Warren would have made that choice for Leo Scofield. Just from what Lily and Robert say . . . Claytor and Dwight, too.

"It always sounds to me like Warren should have been Leo's son instead of John Scofield's. It always sounds to me that John Scofield worked hard to be the black sheep. But the idea that Warren drove off that road on purpose . . . I have to say it seems unlikely to me. It seems impossible, frankly. Warren wasn't a fool. A car wreck isn't a very smart way to kill yourself. You could just as well end up paralyzed." Sam had thought it over carefully all the while Agnes had been speaking; he wasn't trying to make her feel better or to persuade her that it couldn't be her fault Warren was dead; he was merely laying out for her what he thought was the most logical conclusion.

They sat on without speaking for a while, although Sam didn't take note of the pause; he was one of those rare people who felt no need to fill any silence that might fall during a conversation. Eventually Agnes turned her head his way and smiled at him. "Oh, Sam," she said, "I hope you're right."

For a little while they remained exactly as they were, but then Sam had to go meet a fellow who was interested in supplying granite for Cardinal Homes. Within no more than five days, Sam already had a network of good friends and many acquaintances in Port Clyde and Tenants Harbor.

Agnes stayed just where she was, gazing out at Matinicus and Brothers Island. She thought Brothers Island looked like the most desolate spot on earth, with only two spindly trees at one end and one stark house at the other. When she had first visited Maine with Warren, though, just after they were married, she hadn't noticed anything at all about the place, really. She had once said to him that she didn't like scenery. He had laughed. "That's pretty sweeping," he had said. "There must be some scenery someplace in the world that you'd like."

"Oh, well," she had said, "I don't mean that it's any particular place that I do or don't like," she explained.

"I've just always thought there was nothing more boring than having to admire scenery. Those long drives . . . And what can you say after a while about whatever it is? No matter how pretty it is, there's not that much to say about a nice view." She had only been interested in Warren, then, and in what Warren thought about her.

This evening as she sat on the rocks in Martinsville, Maine, however, at this moment in her life, Agnes found she had no desire to go inside, just now, as she studied the end of the day. She didn't look at the scenery, really: the lighthouse seeming toylike at the end of Mosquito Point, or the several islands scattered in the distance, the lobstermen puttering close to shore in a cloud of gulls, and one lone sailboat farther out, moving needle-like through the water, as opposed to the chunky, bouncing working motor boats. Agnes sat out on the rocks and merely inhabited her surroundings. She existed in the moment and at that particular place without self-consciousness, and without the sticky dailiness of the constant comparison of one thing with another. Winter or summer, morning versus evening, the shroud of fog or the alarming clarity of illumination, sunshine as opposed to rain. She had no need to form an opinion of the weather; all sorts of it would come and go.

She did understand that somehow or other she had fallen into a momentary state of grace; she suddenly found herself in an exquisite circumstance she had never yearned for or even imagined. She didn't take into particular account the tide coming in with unusual, rolling intensity, the curling bands of water pale green but harboring darker flecks of tiny fish or other debris, and crashing in enormous plumes of spray against the rocks. Just in the past few moments, she had reached a point where she no longer categorized and catalogued each individual element as she watched the evening close in. She simply basked in a state of inhabiting a landscape that was all of a piece and in which she was no more than part of the whole. This unexpected solace delighted her, and yet she hadn't known until now that it was a circumstance waiting to be happened upon — that out of the blue she might come across a smooth, clear, gleaming state of discrete serenity. She hadn't guessed sooner that there were lovely and sometimes astonishing aspects of existence that would continue to clarify themselves to her only as she passed year after year through the relatively small drama of living out the length of her own life.

❧

In February of 1930, Warren Scofield and his uncle Leo were on their way to Arbor City, Pennsylvania, to continue working out the details of the merger of Scofields & Company with Arthur Fitch and Sons. Warren was rounding an icy descending curve in the mountains of western Pennsylvania when a sudden burly flutter caught his eye, and, although he veered away from it, the thing seemed to rise toward the car. Warren instinctively turned the steering wheel hard to the left in order to avoid it. For a brief moment the creature was familiar, but Warren didn't live long enough to name it. The big car gathered momentum on the black ice and slid across the opposite lane and over the white furze of grass until coming to rest when the edge of the right bumper slammed into a lone maple tree. Not long after the big black Packard came to rest and the resonance of its crash no longer vibrated through the air, although its motor still hummed, the big turkey hen led her chicks across the road, her feathers still ruffled aggressively, and the birds disappeared into the scrub as it thickened farther down the hill.

ROBB FORMAN DEW is the author of the novels *Dale Loves Sophie to Death,* for which she received the National Book Award; *The Time of Her Life; Fortunate Lives;* and, most recently, *The Evidence Against Her;* as well as a memoir, *The Family Heart*. She lives in Williamstown, Massachusetts, with her husband, who is a professor of history at Williams College and the author of several books on Southern history.